A FRIEND OF THE FAMILY

A FRIEND OF THE FAMILY
BOOK 1

STUART FIELD

This book is for all the fantastic people who work tirelessly in the medial and care-giving world.
To those who care for the elderly and those who need the support of others, both physically and mentally.
To all the medical staff, and emergency services, that have given so much, especially these past few years.

This is for you.
Thank you all.

ACKNOWLEDGMENTS

I would like to thank
my Amazing Wife, Ani, and my family and friends for their
constant support.
To my fantastic daughter, who always makes me proud.
To Gail Williams and Tyler Colins who edited this book.
To Next Chapter books, my publisher.

CHAPTER ONE

Monday, the 22nd of April.
Village of Duckton, North Yorkshire, United Kingdom.

TWO GIRLS HAD BLESSED THE HOUSE OF JAKE AND ABBY Freeman. After years of trying to conceive, their prayers had been answered.

Twelve years later, the Freeman house was abuzz with excitement at the twin girls' coming birthday party.

Danni Freeman was outgoing, a friendly child who was made friends easily. She was a little charmer, a girl who relied on her charms and beauty to get what she wanted. Melanie Freeman, on the other hand, was quite different. Quiet and reserved, inquisitive and cunning. She was a loner who relied on nobody but herself – the other side of the coin.

When Melanie was younger, she was tested for behavioural problems. All the tests came back with one astonishing fact: little Melanie was a gifted child. She was also diagnosed with having an eidetic memory, and possibly hyperthymesia; more tests would have to be conducted when she was older.

The psychologist the Freeman's had been referred to, Professor Samuel Hicks, had told them that her behaviour could be put down to Melanie feeling different. Hicks had seen it with many talented children who were trying to find their place in what some would consider 'a normal world'.

This gift, or curse, meant she remembered everything.

This news came with both shock and fear as far as Abby Freeman was concerned.

Abby looked at Melanie with different eyes after that. It should have been Danni who was the gifted one, not Melanie. Danni had always been Abby's favourite, whereas Melanie had been Daddy's little girl.

As the years passed, Danni became more outgoing and became more and more charming. On the other hand, Melanie buried herself in books and kept herself to herself most of the time.

One day Jake bought the family a computer. He needed one for work anyway, so it made sense.

Danni had used it to boost her social media contacts. Something that Jake disproved of due to her only being twelve. But Abby encouraged it.

Melanie had been banned from the computer several times after men from the police had been over to question her regarding incidents of hacking. Now she was only allowed twenty minutes of supervised computer time.

Melanie was fascinated by this whole information network. While Danni was simply interested in who did what with who, and who ate what and where.

———

On Saturday the family had gone to Abby's sister's home for a small gathering. There had been food and drink, a chance to catch up. It was something the sisters liked to do once a month, a family ritual that had started years before. This time it was Ellen Newman's turn.

Ellen was the eldest of the sisters. She was tall like the others, with dark hair and a slim figure. Her eyes were dark and held a wide gaze. Like her sisters, Ellen was attractive without being beautiful.

She had married a member of Parliament, Colin Newman. He was Minister of Health. They had been married for four years but had no children as Ellen could not conceive. But this had the effect of making Ellen and Colin's relationship stronger – or at least that was what they told people.

The children had played hide-and-seek while the adults chatted. The women in one room while the men drank brandy and smoked cigars out in the garden.

The Newman residence was a two-story house built in the 1930s; it had a short driveway and bushes lined the front lawn. At the rear of the house was a sizeable garden with a large lawn and apple tree. A small patio sat between the home and the lawn. Between the terrace and the lush green of the grass were rows of rose bushes that bloomed in various colours.

It was Monday, the day of the girls' birthday, and the thought of the gathering still lingered in the Freeman family's minds. All had a fond memory of that night.

All except little Melanie.

That was when her nightmares started. When she began to mutter under her breath.

———

The birthday party had started, and all of Danni's friends were there, but Melanie stayed in her room and read. She had no friends, not those sorts of friends anyway. Sure, there were kids at school Melanie hung out with. But she had not invited them. Melanie did not need to start a war during her birthday, so she let Danni make the day all about her.

Melanie looked over to the wall above her bookshelf. She stared at the mask that hung there. It was a copy of an old Venetian ball mask. Both She and Danni had gotten one.

Melanie's mask was pale with dark eyes and red lips. There was a hint of red on the cheeks. It was haunting, but there was beauty about it. Danni's mask appeared to be the same, but it wore a curious grin, where Melanie's looked thoughtful.

Her father had told Melanie that it was called Adrasteia, and Danni's was called Laverna. Neither Melanie nor Danni thought any more about the names, and why should they? Both girls hung their masks in their rooms like trophies.

At nine o'clock, the party ended, and both girls were in bed while Abby and Jake tidied up the chaos left behind by ten twelve-year-old girls.

'Well, that went off without anything getting broken,' Jake laughed.

Abby shot him a sour look. 'They were six when that happened, and it was the Todd boy that broke the vase.'

A noise behind them caused Abby and Jake to turn to find Danni in the doorway. She was pale and shivering with fear. Abby rushed over to Danni and flung her arms around her and held her tight.

'What is it baby, what's wrong?' Abby asked.

'It's Melanie ...' Danni said. Tears began to flow down her cheeks.

'What ... what's wrong with your sister?' Jake asked, concerned, his gaze shooting over to the stairwell.

'She scares me,' Danni said, closing her eyes as if trying to wish something terrible away.

Abby raced upstairs with Jake not far behind, furious at the thought that Melanie had played a trick on her precious little girl.

When they entered Melanie's room, they found her sitting with her back to the door, sitting in her reading chair, and staring out of the window.

'Melanie, what the hell is going on? Have you been playing tricks on your sister?' Abby yelled.

Jake looked at Abby with surprise, as though she had suddenly gotten the sisters mixed up. Danni was the trickster, not Melanie.

'Melanie, sweety, what's up? Why are you out of bed? Come on. It's past your bedtime,' Jake said, stepping into the room.

Slowly Melanie turned around, the mask coving her face. 'They are going to die, and I'm going to take satisfaction in it,' Melanie said in a low voice.

CHAPTER TWO

Monday, the 29th of April.

It had been a week after the nightmares and the daymares.

Little Melanie Freeman saw Professor Hicks at his Leeds office several times for therapy. Then, after that week was up, he suggested it may be in Melanie's best interest for her to go to his clinic near Harrogate.

Abby Freeman had agreed readily; Jake Freeman wasn't so sure.

Little Melanie was taken to Larksford House Clinic to start her treatment. The drive over had been long and silent. Abby drove the Jaguar hard along the snaking country lanes. Her gaze was fixed in concentration at the road ahead.

Jake Freeman sat next to her on the passenger side. He was staring out of the window as if looking at Melanie would rip out his heart.

Melanie's gaze switched between the two adults. She still

didn't know what was going on apart from what she had been told.

'You're going to stay in a special place, darling, just until you are better,' Abby had said.

Melanie had not responded. She had just looked blankly at her parents. Then she had packed some items into her green rucksack, including her mask and a thick leatherbound Russian novel. The backpack had a single shoulder strap and was fastened with leather straps and brass buckles. Hanging from one of the straps was a pink teddy bear roughly two inches in length. It was tatty and dirty, but she had had it since she was a baby.

Abby pulled up to a massive iron gate stuck between two sides of a long, high wall. As they waited for someone to meet them, the Freemans could see a colossal white-stone building surrounded by gardens.

CHAPTER THREE

Saturday, the 22nd April.

NINE YEARS YEARS HAD PASSED, AND A LOT HAD CHANGED.
Seasons had come and gone, and natural processes had repeated. The time had passed everywhere else, except within the isolated walls of Larksford. The winters had been mild, the spring and summers had been dry, the autumns had been wet.
Old man Hicks was dead.
But Larksford House remained.
And so had Melanie ... but she was little no more.

Toby Washington had travelled by taxi from the hotel in Duckton to the clinic. He was to be a new nurse at Larksford House. A temporary situation in the fold to see how he did. Six-month probation. But Toby had no doubts that he would become a permanent resident there. In fact, he was counting on it.
The sky was grey with loitering clouds. From time-to-time,

the clouds shifted and changed and the sunlight. or a patch of blue. broke through. Despite the gloom from above, it was warm.

A perfect summer day, some would say.

Toby was in his early thirties, tall with a slim build – but not skinny. He'd flown in from LA a week ago. Naturally, he had done his homework on the establishment. And Toby knew they had done theirs on him.

Toby had remembered his friends and his family's – mostly his father's – displeasure, and also puzzlement, at his career choice.

'Why in God's name are you going there? It's in the back and beyond of fuckin' nowhere?' they'd said, and they had been correct.

North Yorkshire was no California.

But that was the point.

He was a man who was looking to make a career out of psychology, but not just that, he was a man who wanted to do something in a place where nobody knew him.

He would be outside his father's shadow and, more importantly, his influence.

Toby's father was a big shot of a surgeon back in the States, but Toby had different passions. Of course, dear old Dad disapproved, saying it wasn't real medicine he was going into – meaning there was no money to be made more than anything. Toby disagreed. In his eyes, what he was getting into was more important than what his father was doing.

After years of arguments and threats about being cut off, Toby's father finally conceded. Toby couldn't be sure, but he could have sworn his father's breaking point was when Toby's best friend ditched medical school and joined a Goth band.

Thousands of dollars for the best schools waisted in a blink of a black mascaraed eye.

Toby had been met at the main entrance of Larksford House by a huge man. The man's bulky frame looked odd in the tight uniform, which made him seem even bigger. His naturally dark skin was made more prominent by the light-coloured clothing. At first glance, Toby thought the guy was a bouncer or the muscle for the place. He had the form, as well as the height, of a player for the All Blacks rugby team.

The guy was *huge*.

The giant introduced himself as Eric Chapple and said Toby could call him Eric. Likewise, Toby told him his name, which he found with relief that Eric already knew.

Toby walked alongside Eric Chapple as they took the tour of the place. They had stopped at a staff room and found Toby's locker, where he stashed his backpack.

At first glance, Eric seemed a pleasant, friendly man, with a smile and a skip in his step. He had been there a long time and seen just about everything. Toby followed Eric through the dog-leg corridors and through fire doors and security doors, and up and down staircases.

Toby had known the hall's history, how it had once been a family estate – a grand hall. But he was overwhelmed by the actual size. During the Second World War, it had been used as one of the command centres because it was far from London and less likely to be bombed. Now it was a clinic for people with mental and psychological problems.

'We got an easy job here,' Eric said. They had just walked into the main building from the lobby.

The voice didn't match the man. Here was a mountain of a man, but his voice rang with a normal tone and not a booming, resonant baritone. This caused Toby to smile. Eric was the ultimate interpretation of a gentle giant.

'This is the quiet ward,' Eric said. Waving his hand about as if to show the rooms in front of them. 'This lot are depressed – or just don't know what friggin' day it is.'

Toby followed Eric down a long white corridor, their shoes squeaking from the non-slip flooring. The laminate tiles, dull grey, stood out from the bright white walls, making the hallway seem longer than it was. There was an armoured-glass half-wall every so often on the left or right, showing the room inside. The rooms looked like living rooms or anterooms in the large house. They had comfortable armchairs and large circular tables; there were no pictures with frames or glass on the walls. Toby watched as patients sat doing puzzles, others doing nothing, just staring into space.

As Toby wandered the hallways, he took note of the newness of the place. There had been a refurbishment around five years ago after the original dean and owner had passed away, and his son had taken it over. Toby had seen the pictures of what the place had looked like before. It had become a cold and uninviting place by the time Hicks Senior had died. Now, after the refurbishment, the building had less of a rundown feel about it. It was bright, modern – expensive.

'Most of the patients here just sit around and stare out of the window, others wander about the gardens,' Eric said. 'Most of 'em have had a breakdown, others just feel the world is too much to bear – poor fuckers.' Eric shook his head. The light from the strip-halogen bulb of the ceiling lamp reflected off his shaven, bulbous scalp.

He nodded to one room on the right, and they looked through the plated window at the room. It was around the size of a large dining room. Full of what Toby now considered standard seating, but not much else in the way of furniture.

At first, Toby thought the room looked quite bleak and unfriendly, but he noticed the patients. They simply sat, motionless most of them. Oblivious of the world others wanted them to see, but happy in their own little world.

'And others just need a break from it all,' Eric said, pointing to one of the windows on the left.

Toby could see out onto the front of the house. He witnessed some patients strolling about the gardens – like people walking in a park on a Sunday afternoon. He smiled to himself. He had expected this to be one of those 'take a handful of pills and don't bother me' places. But they were accomodating the patients.

As they moved across the main entrance, the two were stopped by a brash looking nurse. She was a heavily built woman who stood around five-seven in height. She had silver-grey hair with strands of the original red colour left. Her eyes were blue – at least from what Toby could make out from the tiny, angry slits that glared at him.

'You must be the new lad, I take it?' she inquired. Her gaze was deep, almost venomous. There was something about her that reminded Toby of his school nurse. An evil woman that didn't care much for snivelling wimps. Unless there was considerable blood flow or loss of a limb, you were deemed fit.

Toby shuddered at the sudden memory of her.

'Yes, ma'am, Toby Washington, pleased to meet you,' he said, stretching a hand.

The nurse just gave him a once over and snorted before walking off.

'Well, that was Nurse Hawthorn ... lovely lady, great bedside manner.' Eric laughed.

Toby stood motionless, shocked at the encounter.

'She's been here forever. In fact, she worked here when it first opened they say – as a hospital, not the hall that it was two-hundred years ago, but then you never know.' Eric laughed again and gave Toby a friendly punch to the shoulder. 'Right, now that excitement's over.'

Toby looked over to his left and saw a door that seemed to lead to another part of the building. The door was solid and without windows, almost as if someone were sending a message that the door should never be opened or there was a corridor which should never be entered.

Toby was intrigued. Like a child told he that he couldn't do something. Like that primal naughty feeling, everyone had in the back of their minds when they saw a sign saying: DO NOT WALK ON THE GRASS.

'What's in there?' he asked, nodding in the direction of the door.

'Nuffin for you to worry about matey ... alright,' Eric said with a low growl.

'Yeah – OK, no problem man. Jeez,' Toby replied, standing back. But the warning just made him even more curious about what was behind that door. They pressed on.

Next, Eric showed Toby the dispensary, then the TV room and, most importantly, the breakroom.

'Shit,' Eric said suddenly, looking down at his watch. 'He's gonna bloody kill me.' His voice was full of panic. 'Look, you stay here and make sure everyone is alright, I gotta ... never mind. I'll be back soon. Just – I dunno, watch V or somethin',' Eric mumbled, looking at his watch again.

'OK, no problem, man; you go ahead, do what ya gotta do,' Toby shrugged.

'Awesome,' Eric said, giving him a smile and a thumbs up.

Toby watched as he scampered across the lobby and headed towards the door. His eyes narrowed as he watched Eric unlock the door with a key from his pocket and swung it wide as he entered in haste. Toby smiled as he noticed the door closed slowly on the automatic shutter. Eric's mistake had given Toby a chance to feed his curiosity.

He launched forwards and headed towards the door, dodging patients as he went. Just as it was closing, his hand shot into the gap and stopped the heavy door from closing. He smiled and held the door open enough to allow himself to squeeze inside.

There was a long dimly lit corridor with windows on the right side and blank-white walls on the left. It felt cold and unwelcoming, unlike the rest of the clinic. At the end was a small room with a long window. As Toby grew near, he could see two people inside. Both sat at a U-shaped desk full of monitors.

Next to the room was another door, this one made from thick metal; it had re-enforced glass and a lock made for a key. From what he could determine, this led to another section of the building.

A secure wing?

As he headed towards the door, the two women looked up briefly at Toby, who nodded a greeting. They nodded back and got back to the television series they'd been watching on a small TV.

He looked at the door and groaned with irritation. He didn't have a key. Hell, he shouldn't be here in the first place.

He couldn't ask the two to open the door, that would be suspicious; besides, that would lead to the question of how did he get there in the first place? Toby went to turn around and leave. He had no plan on what to do next. The thought of losing his job before he had even started suddenly became a scary reality.

There was a click and the door in front opened. A nurse struggled to make it through the door, her arms stacked full of blankets. Toby rushed forwards and held the door open and smiled as she thanked him. As he watched her walk away, he slipped inside the next corridor, then turned quickly as he heard the bolt click shut behind. 'Shit,' he cursed softly, seeing there was no handle and it was key-access only.

'Oh, fucking great.' He swore at his stupidity. In his haste to get in he hadn't checked that he could get out. Cursing himself once again, he turned to face this new part of the building.

The new corridor was shorter than the last, with a turn to the left at the end. The lighting was bad – none of the overhead lights being on in the daylight – but some murky light came through the windows.

Cautiously, Toby made his way down the corridor. He moved slowly. Not so much that if someone came around the corner, he would draw attention to himself, but enough to not rush into God knew what at that darkened corner.

Near the end of the corridor, Toby stopped. He took a deep breath and walked casually around the corner, working on the old idea, *if you look like you are meant to be there, people will think you are meant to be there.*

The adjoining corridor was just as dimly lit, but had more windows. These were arched, the old wooden frames exchanged for hard plastic, the glass thick and shatterproof. The three windows looked out on the rear of the house and the other gardens. Also in view were the orchards, the vegetable patch – the massive stone wall.

At one of the windows stood a young woman in casual nightwear: grey shorts and t-shirt. She had her back to him, still and silent like a statue or store mannequin.

'Hi, are you OK there?' Toby asked in an almost whisper, fearing that Eric – or worse, one of the doctors – would catch him there.

The strange woman didn't move. She said nothing, just continued to stare out the window.

'You shouldn't be here, you know,' Toby said, afraid she had become lost and had somehow gotten herself locked in this strange wing, just like he had.

But the difference being, he had done it on purpose.

'I shouldn't? Strange ... where should I be then?' Her voice was like silk.

Toby went to walk towards her but stopped on his heels as she turned to look at him. He froze with horror as all he could see was the mask. A pale white Venetian masquerade mask, with red lips and long painted lashes.

He felt her eyes upon him. They were warm and caring, not fitting with her demeanour. He had expected cold lifeless eyes or even ones that held a psychotic blood lust – but not these. He felt himself staring into those large blue pools of emotion – lost in her ocular grasp, like she were a silent siren from Greek mythology. Instead of a haunting song, she enchanted him with a captivating stare. His mouth fell open but he didn't know what to say. Hello probably, but he was lost, transfixed by those blue orbs.

A large hand slapped his shoulder, making him yelp in panic. The woman with the mask giggled like a little girl, then shot back into her room on the left.

'Bye, strange man, glad to have met you,' she said before closing the door.

Toby turned to see Eric. He wasn't angry. No, something else gripped him: shock.

'Sorry, Eric, I know I'm in shit, but I can explain,' Toby started.

Eric shook his head and looked down at him. His face was still filled with bewilderment. 'Man, you have no idea how much shit you're in,' he said. Then he smiled broadly and pulled the small American towards him in a shoulder hug and laughed. 'Yep, you have no friggin' idea. You poor bastard.'

CHAPTER FOUR

PROFESSOR ALBERT HICKS SAT IN HIS OFFICE AND SIPPED brandy from a crystal snifter.

He was a short heavy-built man with a straight back which pushed out his broad shoulders, even as he sat. His mousey hair was styled with a side parting and had signs of once being blonde, but age had taken a bitter toll. A handsome man in an aged sort of way, but he didn't dwell on it, or use it.

He had money that could do the same job as good looks, without the extra effort.

The room was dark except for the light from the computer monitor. The room was bathed in a flickering blue light. A headache had forced him to take an aspirin and block out the menacing natural illumination by closing the long velvet drapes.

Nurse Hawthorn sat in a chesterfield armchair opposite him. Even with her bathed in shadow, with only her outline visible, her bulky frame and bun made for an unmistakable silhouette.

'The new lad, Toby Washington, what do you make of

him?' Hicks asked, sitting back in his chair, causing it to creak with age. His voice was stern and rang with authority. He had been brought up to show he was better than anyone else. That others were beneath him, he was the lord and master. His tone oozed with arrogance and self-worth.

They had both watched the footage from the corridor camera – and had seen that the patient had conversed with the new man.

'He's an outsider,' she replied. Her words were cold and hard.

'True, maybe that is what makes him different. But that doesn't answer my question: what do you think of him?' Hicks asked again. He leaned forward, the light from the monitor illuminating his face, showing his features more clearly.

'I don't care much for him. Personally, he's too—,'

'American?' Hicks laughed.

'I was going to say too good-looking; he'll be a distraction,' Nurse Hawthorn growled, crossing her arms across her chest the best she could. Her short thick arms struggled to meet past the ample cleavage.

'A distraction for whom? You or the other nurses?' Hicks said with an evil grin.

'The other nurses, of course. Half of them are fresh out of medical school, young things like that, well ... you know?' she huffed.

'I think he can be trusted, but if not – well, things do happen out in the country. It can be a dangerous place.' Hicks sat back and rocked in his chair. 'Tell Eric to brief him. However, I want Eric to film Melanie and Toby together. I want to know how they interact.'

Nurse Hawthorn stood up and brushed her uniform back into place. 'And as for the other matter ... they're asking questions.' Nurse Hawthorn's voice was low and gravelly.

'Don't worry, it's all in hand,' Hicks said.

She nodded before turning and heading for the door. Leaving Hicks to ponder his next move.

Toby waited in a small room at the end of the corridor. From what he could make out, it was a staff room for those allowed access to that area. It was long, around ten-by-twelve feet. The breakroom had little in the way of furnishings. There was an old metal desk which faced the door, a heavy-looking thing with a grey melamine top, and metal draws for storage. The computer chair was old, the blue fabric worn and one of the arms missing. A phone and a computer sat on the desk. Both were old, but only by a few years. The computer, of course, had one crucial feature: internet access.

In the back right-hand corner of the room was a fridge, which was next to a small sink. This was for the staff to store their meals for the day or the night shift. Next to the refrigerator was a long table which held a coffee machine, a kettle, a selection of mugs and a microwave. On the wall opposite the sofa was a small flatscreen television. It too was old, but functional.

All the comforts of home.

Along the right-hand wall was a sofa which seemed long enough for a person of six-foot to stretch out on comfortably. The blue fabric was worn and held together in places by heavy visible stitches. Large cushions lay at both corners, ready to be used as pillows at a moment's notice.

Eric had told Toby to wait in the room and not to leave – on that, Eric was most insistent. Toby wandered about the room like a scolded child waiting for the headmaster to dish out punishment. He spent some time sitting, then wandered about in circles. Then he sat again, his hands rubbing his thighs until his palms hurt. Then, he would repeat the process – each time looking at the coffee machine.

Toby was thirsty. His panicked state had left his mouth dry, but he wasn't sure whether this would bring him more trouble. After all, this wasn't his ward. A long debate with himself led to the conclusion that he was already screwed, so Toby helped himself to a coffee.

'Fuck it,' he thought, taking the largest cup he could find and filling it.

Toby returned to the sofa, sipping his coffee as he went. It was surprisingly good coffee. He took a seat on the firm cushion and continued his defiant drinking while he awaited his fate. As he sat in the soft-cushioned seat, Toby couldn't help but wonder who the young woman was and why she was there.

The door opened and Toby turned to face whoever had just entered. Eric's vast bulk filled the doorway.

'Right then, ya fukka, come with me,' he said with a curious look on his face.

'Where are we going?' Toby asked sheepishly.

'It looks like your little stunt in the corridor got you into the club,' Eric laughed.

'What club's that?' Toby asked nervously.

'The special ward club, so special it don't exist, so keep ya gob shut about it, got it?' Eric said angrily and suddenly, glaring at Toby.

'Yeah, yeah, sure ... it don't exist, got it,' Toby said, backing off. He felt his heart racing in his chest. What the hell had he gotten into here?

He followed Eric back to the girl's room, both silent the whole time, Toby out of fear and suspicion, Eric because he simply had nothing to say. They stopped and Eric stood opposite the door Toby had seen the woman go into. Toby leaned against the white wall and felt the cold of the brick through his blue scrubs. Causing him to shiver slightly.

Or was it the feeling of unease because he had no idea why they had come back to her room ... or what the professor had conjured up for him in way of punishment?

Eric slumped against the wall opposite the woman's door.

'This one is Melanie. She's been here a long time. To be honest, she isn't officially here – a pet project of the professor's or summat, dunno, I don't ask,' Eric said. His tone was cold, as if trying to sound unattached. But Toby knew he was just covering his backside. 'We have to hide her away when there is an inspection, but they don't know about this wing anyways.' He laughed as though they had won one over the system. 'Bloody nosey buggers at the health department. Shit, if they knew she was here and how long she'd bin wiv us, none of us would be getting out of nick.'

Toby stood, shocked at the revelation. But what could he do? He was now apart of it.

Why the hell did he have to be so fuckin' inquisitive? Asshole, Toby thought, but kept his thoughts and emotions to himself.

Now he was the one under observation. Seeming unaffected by what Eric had said, Toby looked at the girl through the small window in her door.

The room was a sterile white with a blue-grey laminate floor. There was a bed, a side table, and a dresser. Directly in front of the door was a large window which allowed a stream of sunlight into the room. Toby couldn't see that much out of the window from where he stood, just a big blue blur due to the bright afternoon sun. But he guessed she had a view of the front grounds and driveway.

A thickly padded red-velvet armchair faced the window, next to which was a square table, a simple three-foot square thing, found mostly in school dining rooms. On the cream-coloured melamine top was a bottle of water and a stack of books. There were more books on the small bookshelf, which seemed to overflow with reading material. Beside that were more stacked books due to a lack of space on the shelving. Then Toby's gaze fell onto the bed. It looked all the other beds there – except for the padded board which covered the bottom gap. Making it impossible for anyone to go underneath.

Toby figured one of the patients had disappeared under the bed once and attacked one of the orderlies when they checked on the patient. At med school, Toby's teacher had told the class that people in institutions weren't crazy; they had a different level of intelligence and insight into the world. The teacher soon changed that theory after one of the misunderstood people tried to strangle him with his bare hands. All because he thought the professor was a green man from planet Vultex. However, some of what the teacher had said made sense for most of the patients, or the misunderstood anyway. They were in their worlds and had their level of intelligence.

'Why is she here?' Toby asked inquisitively, his eyes trans-fixed on this strange young woman in her grey pyjamas and pink slippers.

She had long blonde hair, but her face was obscured by the haunting mask. It was a full-faced Venetian Volto mask, the kind they used in the old days at masked balls. The face was a ghostly white with ruby red lips. The eyes were dark painted sockets with long painted lashes beneath extended, painted eyebrows, and the high cheekbones had tints of pale red and purple.

'Self-harm issues?' Toby asked.

Eric shook that massive head. 'You ain't ever seen anything like this bollocks ... I can tell you.' He pulled Toby away from the door, as if he was worried the woman would hear. 'She was brought in when she was twelve years old. She kept on telling everyone she was going to kill the family and she was going to enjoy it. So, naturally, the dad picks up the poor little thing and brings her here. But I tell you, back in them days, this place wasn't like this; the patients just wandered around ... not like today.'

'So, was she was raped?' Toby queried as if he understood. Then he looked up at the big man who was shaking his head, fear screaming through his eyes.

'Apparently, one guy tried ... she made sure he never did it again,' Eric said, his eyes wide with horror.

'OK, so she stabbed the guy. I probably would have done the same, I guess,' Toby surmised.

'Nah, the guy pulled out his thing and stuck it into her mouth,' Eric winced. A cold shiver evidently ran down his spine at the thought of the story.

Toby just stood open-mouthed, a look of disbelief on his face. 'How old was she when it happened?' Toby finally asked, his gaze fixed on the innocent-looking woman.

'Ten. Nasty little bitch bit that thing off and spat it back at him. Danced around after, laughing and saying what she always says,' Eric explained.

'And what's that ... what does she always say?' Toby switched his gaze back to Eric.

'They are going to die, and I'm going to take pleasure in it,' came the voice of an angel from the room.

'Jesus,' both men yelped and jumped back to see the masked girl staring back at them through the small window in the door.

Melanie turned and walked back to the chair that faced the window and sat. As Toby listened, he could hear her hum a tune. One he'd never heard before – or, at least didn't recognise.

'You OK?' Eric asked. Standing up straight as though she hadn't shocked him.

'Yeah, fine. May need some new shorts though,' Toby laughed, making Eric smile.

'Come on, I'll show you the rest of the place.' Eric gave Toby a friendly punch to the shoulder.

As the two men left, Melanie stopped humming and stared at the door. 'Nearly time now, nearly time to make them pay,' Melanie said, rocking in her chair.

CHAPTER FIVE

IT WAS ALL OVER THE TEN O'CLOCK EVENING NEWS. THE family killer had struck again.

The police had no witnesses; forensics had come up empty as well. Whoever was doing this had done their homework. The only prints found at the scene were the victims' and their friends'. They had discovered latex residue in the other cases, meaning the killer wore gloves.

Mrs Evelyn Baxter, a widow from the house next door, had discovered bodies.

She'd let her pet dog out to play with the family's kids like she did every day. It had never trailed mud or anything back to her home before. However, this time when it returned, the dog had walked in with what she had thought to be red paint all over the kitchen floor.

Of course, Mrs Baxter had gone around to complain. At 8:32 p.m., she was found screaming in the street by passers-by. At 8:34, the school kids had called the police, or at least one of them had. The others stood on the small front lawn, throwing up. At 8:50, the police arrived in force – three squad cars, the DI and his DS and a couple of ambulances for the shocked victims. The local doctor was en route, and so was the pathologist. By 9:00, it was a media circus.

Paparazzi stood with their big heavy cameras equipped with telephoto lenses that were perched on tripods. The TV film crews, with their media trucks and cameras, were getting set up, while the news reporters used makeup to hide their bad complexions from the world.

The circus had officially arrived.

The ten o'clock evening news reported on the latest victims of Britain's deadliest serial killer. The killer always chose a family – more specifically, one with a wife and one daughter. The males of the family were unimportant, or so it seemed. It was always the wife and the daughter that were the killer's primary targets. The victims were always of the same age range.

This time, it was the Thomas family on a small housing estate in the town of Farnbrook. Farnbrook was a small town just off the A1(M) near Hopperton. Farnbrook had supermarkets, a town hall, a small industrial estate, a church with an alarmingly large graveyard – most of which was due to two World Wars and the Black Death. It had a local pub and off-licence, a post office and a cinema.

And a large police station was in charge of most of the area of North Yorkshire.

The killer's latest victims had been forty-two-year-old Christina Thomas. She had been the mother of Tibbey Thomas, the eighteen-year-old daughter. Both women had had short blonde hair, blue eyes, and an athletic build. The father, Ray Thomas, had been forty-four with brown hair and hazelnut eyes, their son Andy had been the spitting image of Ray.

But the killer didn't care about the males.

Never did.

The killer's type had had always been the same: a mother and daughter, blonde hair, blue eyes, athletic build. The mothers were always in their the early forties and the daughter around eighteen years old. The killer had taken his time with the women. They had died slowly and painfully. Tortured, raped and butchered. The men had simply been killed and tossed into a corner.

But the press didn't get that information. All they knew was another family had been murdered while they slept. Which was also another lie for the media to mislead copycats.

The victims had been very much awake.

Detective Inspector Richard Platt was a tall, stocky man, with black greying hair that looked as if it had never seen a hairdresser or a comb. His skin was pale and clammy, as though he had never spent much time in the sun. Platt was in his midforties, a career copper for sure. He had sailed through the ranks to the disgust of other higher-ranking officers, who'd had friends nudged to the wayside because of him. But the powers that be loved him. Some said he had a sixth sense when it came to crime. Platt closed cases, and that made him – for a time – bulletproof.

But that had changed. Platt used to be smartly dressed; he used to have a presence about him. But now he was a broken man, and there were whispers that this would be his last case.

Platt had become an embracement to the force. His poster boy image was gone – and so too was his career. Platt was a troubled man. The last couple of years had not been kind, but the job – this case – was all that he had.

Detective Sergeant David Elford, on the other hand, was

the opposite. He was younger by at least ten years with a tall, athletic frame. He had a natural tan and a healthy look about him. His suit was brown with a cheap look to it, meaning he was used to doing all the heavy lifting while his boss did all the thinking. But Elford didn't mind. Platt was an excellent detective. They had both been assigned to the task force, picking up where others had failed. Unusually, Platt and Elford had been on the previous task force as hands-on-deck detectives. But the old team leader quit after an incident involving the team.

And Platt, being the only DI available, was thrown in to take up the slack.

The Thomas house had been cordoned off, cutting off access to the road near the scene. Platt wasn't bothered whether it was an inconvenience to the locals or nosey passers-by. It was a crime scene, not a damned attraction at some theme park. The press was set up behind one of the barriers. Camera flashes flickered like a New Year's Eve firework display. The news reports announced the latest tragedy to the world. Platt stood outside with Elford while they waited for CSI to do their tests.

Usually, the team would have been straight up there, but Platt wanted this scene fresh.

Pristine.

A mistake his predecessor had often made, that Platt himself had pointed out, and had been told to be quiet.

As far as Platt was concerned, the last person inside was the killer, and he didn't want to risk any cross-contamination from the police. So anyone not wearing the correct gear stayed outside until CSI was finished.

Even him.

Platt pulled on his black woollen trench coat over his blue

pinstriped suit. The wind had begun to pick up, and he feared it might rain. Platt stroked a large rough-skinned palm over his jaw. The several days worth of stubble had started to give him an unkept look rather than a manly one. His eyes were red from lack of sleep and caffeine.

'Nobody in until CSI has finished. Then, only the doc can go in. Her gurney boys can wait out here,' Platt said, taking a look at his watch.

'She's not going to like that guv,' Elford said, cracking a smile.

'Bollocks to her. The people are dead, nothin' more we can do for them apart from catching the bastard. The last thing we need is anyone inside bumbling around, destroying our crime scene.' Platt's voice was rough, like someone who had just gargled a bottle of whiskey, which suited his East London accent.

The sudden appearance of a golden-brown Range Rover made both men look over at the street.

Platt smiled as he took the lid off the metal flask, placed it on the bonnet of the unmarked police Jaguar, and poured himself a coffee in the cover, which doubled up as a cup.

'You want to talk to her, guv?' Elford asked, almost hoping Platt would say yes.

'Why? She's your girlfriend.' Platt laughed and closed up the flask before placing it next to the lid.

A woman got out of the car and looked around at the circus before shaking her head. She was in her late thirties but looked slightly older because of the sombre blue trouser suit, which also made her appear tall and slender. This was Doctor Owen, the medical examiner.

Doctor Owen reached inside the boot of her car and pulled out her bag and a paper forensics suit, then headed over to the waiting policemen. The only smile she wore was in greeting to them both, seeing no sense in giving the press the wrong idea about medical examiners or crime scene techs.

'Evening, gents,' Doctor Owen greeted them with a warming smile. Her voice was soft, her tone warm; it rang with sadness but was also alluring.

'Evening Doctor Owen,' Platt responded, shaking her hand.

'I take it you're outside because CSIs are upstairs?' Sarah Owen asked, shaking her head. 'You know they could contaminate the bodies? That's worse,' she said, looking at Platt.

'Ah, don't worry, the guv took care of that,' Elford said, trying to sound reassuring.

'Why, what did you have them do? Wrap them in plastic cling-film?' Sarah asked with a raised eyebrow. Her hands tugged at her long blonde hair as she fought to tie it up into a bun.

'Nah, bin bags,' Platt said with a straight face, causing Sarah's mouth to fall open. 'Put your knickers back on, Doc,' Platt smiled. 'I told CSI to dust everywhere except for the room until you were done and even then you are the only one allowed in. Plus one other to take your notes or whatever.' Platt smiled as if taking pleasure in her brief heartache.

'I'll go up when my assistant gets here.' She set down her bag and rechecked the contents.

'I'm afraid it's all you, Doc. She called ahead; she can't make it, so you're on your own,' Platt shrugged.

'What do you mean, *she can't make it?*' Sarah asked, almost in a panic.

'Something about appendicitis ... she sends her apologies. Oh, and more good news, the pathologist is also sick, but they're looking for a new one. Should be there tomorrow, ready to do the autopsy,' Platt said with a smile. 'But don't worry, Dave loves taking notes, don't you, Dave?' Platt nudged Elford forwards and walked back to his car.

'Right Dave, suit up.' She smiled and broke the seal on the package holding the suit.

CHAPTER SIX

THE LOCAL PUB AT DUCKTON WAS BUSY BECAUSE Saturday was always darts night at the Lion's Head.

Duckton was a small village not far from Harrogate. It was mostly comprised of farmers, a vet, a small post office which was also the local shop. The church dated back to William the Conqueror, as did most of the farms. But it was too small for a large police station. They had a local police officer stationed in an old police station, which was also his home. The local doctor, Sarah Owen, worked mainly out of her farmhouse located just outside of the village. But most of her time was spent doing house calls and helping the police as an on-call medical examiner.

The village green hosted cricket matches, summer fetes, and the bonfire on Guy Folks. The Lion's Head local pub was the only entertainment for miles, even though a bus took people into Harrogate, which suited the younger generation.

It was a small but happy village.

. . .

A man sat in the Lion's Head pub and finished his meal. The inside was full of heavy oak tables, benches, stools. The bar was made of the same oak, and it angled around to accommodate the maximum amount of customers. There were brass beer taps and a footrail, and behind the bar was a large mirror so the staff could keep an eye on the punters. One of the corners had a snug with an old brick fireplace and a copper chimney cover. The floor had no carpet, just polished boards which made cleaning easier. It was what a person, locals and visitors alike, would expect from a normal village pub.

The man sat silently amid the laughter and shouting of the drunk locals. He'd found himself a place in a corner and sipped his pint of local ale while he read the paper from that morning. He hadn't bought it. Someone had left it sitting on a table of his corner stall. The man took a sip and placed the glass down on the polished wood table, next to an empty plate that had once contained a steak-and-ale pie, served with a generous portion of chips and peas and plenty of thick gravy. Now, the cheap white crockery only held a gravy-stained stainless-steel knife and fork, which lay together side by side.

He looked up at the TV placed high in the corner. The noise of drunken punters drowned out the report, but the footage spoke for itself. The female reporter was a pretty woman in her thirties, possibly of Indian descent. Her long black hair was unstyled but somehow didn't need to be, hanging flawlessly down to the shoulders of her beige overcoat. The man looked over the crease in the paper at the report, his curiosity gripped by the story, so much so he failed to see the clean-up boy take the empty plate from the table.

The killer strikes again, they were saying; *police have still no clue* said the report. The man shook his head and sipped his beer. Hehad recognised the two policemen from other news reports about the killer through the years. They had been sent up north with a task force to help catch the killer. Scotland Yard had sent them, or that was what the news had said on the television and in the papers.

A new guy in charge, a fresh perspective? Time would tell.

———

This family killer had been at large for many years, constantly evading the police.

Never setting a pattern.

They were smart, that was for sure.

The man lost interest in the news story and grew fixed on his paper and the sports page. Liverpool football team had won again – to his disappointment.

The deaths, though tragic, were getting to be old news for some. For others, it filled them with fear after each report. These were primarily people with families with daughters of a similar age to the victims.

The killings had started six years ago. Six years and six attacks, but with no pattern.

They had been indiscriminate. There had been one murder in the first month, then two the next. The fourth month had only seen one murder. The last month,which had been number five, had had only one death. The Thomas family had made six, and the police hoped it stayed at one for that year.

The police tried looking for a pattern, anything that linked them all except the age and hair colour. But apart from the usual Modus Operandi – or MO as the cops would call it – the police had nothing. Each one was done in a different part of the country, so there was no central point.

Most serial killers killed close to home, somewhere safe, where they could retreat and hide. But this killer liked to travel. Breaking all the usual rules of tracking a serial killer.

The police had originally thought the killer lived on the road. A tramp or hitchhiker, picking up jobs here and there. This, of course, was quickly dismissed and put at the bottom of the list but not ruled out. The police profiler ascertained the killer was in his thirties, possibly a family man with a high-paying job. The randomness of the killings could be put down to a spur-of-the-moment thing. He had probably been nearby on business and spied the mother and daughter together ... and the fixation with the mother and daughter was perhaps due to some childhood trauma or abuse.

Finishing his drink, the man folded the paper and left it on the table for the next person. He sighed as he stood up, allowing the perfect creases in his black trousers to drop and stand out like razor edges. Then, reaching over, and took his black suit jacket from the seat and pushed his arms through the tailored sleaves. Next, he grabbed a brown fedora from the bench and placed it onto his styled dark-brown hair.

He was medium height with a medium build, and a fifty-two-year-old man. Nothing out of the ordinary except an aura he gave off. An aura that came in useful for his line of work.

After all, nobody would let you in their house if they didn't trust you.

His skin was slightly tanned from driving in the summer sun. But there were some lighter patches around his eyes, where his sunglasses had blocked the rays. His brown eyes sparkled with self-confidence but were glazed and bloodshot from the long travel.

The man manoeuvred his way to the door, ensuring to avoid the drunken men at the bar. It was late, and he was tired. It had been a long day.

He walked back to his hotel room. A crisp westerly wind blew discarded paper cups and bits of paper along the wet asphalt. It had rained earlier. Not a heavy shower, just a brief downpour, enough to drench everything and anyone in its wake. Luckily, the man had finished his business appointment before the heavens had opened.

The air was thick with a metallic smell of electricity. There was another storm approaching. Just as well, the country needed more rain. The summer had been ferocious that year. High thirties, close to forties. The weather girl had predicted nothing but rain for the rest of the night.

The man smiled as he saw television sets flicker as people watched TV in their front rooms. He was was amazed that folks never closed their curtains in the evening, letting the world see their routines. Most were watching the same thing, a police drama he suspected. The man smiled to himself at the thought of the dramas and films ... how the good guy always caught the bad guy. But people liked those happy ends.

Justice had been done, the hero prevailed.

However, in the real world, things were less tidy, more complicated. More often than not, the killer got away. The smart ones stopped, moved away. But for others, it was a compulsion, an itch that needed scratching.

The man stopped in front of the hotel, a grand old building with 1930s charm. Polished wood floors met with 'Lilac Everlasting' gold-coloured wallpaper. Brass lamps and imitation antique oak furniture littered the main entrance. There was a door to his left that led to the bar and sitting area. To the right was a reception desk and a set of carpeted winding stairs that led to the upper floors.

He greeted the young receptionist before heading for the stairs. His room was located on the first floor but on the far side of the building. Far enough away from the bar. The man was a light sleeper and the noise from drunken guests would keep him awake. *Thank God for sleeping pills and earplugs,* he'd often thought.

He entered the room using his keycard and placed it back into his pocket. There was a slot for the card which switched on the power. Still, he'd asked for a second card. That way, there was constant power to the room and uninterrupted power to his laptop.

In his business, he needed to have continuous power and online feed. He needed to know what was going on at every minute of every hour of every day.

The man sat on the bed in his hotel room. The room was small but comfortable – just a simple place to store clothes, wash and put down your head. It was far from the Ritz, but it had everything he needed, including tea and coffee facilities.

Grabbing the remote from the bedside cabinet, he turned on the small TV and sat on a small desk opposite the bed. The news was on but on a different channel from the pub.

The BBC broadcaster was a tall, thin man with styled black hair and a dark blue suit. The matching tie colour was brought out by the plain white shirt. He had a northern accent instead of the usual posh London one most had. Possibly a local boy that had made it big.

The man opened his briefcase and checked the file on the next person on his list. He smiled when he saw the address; it wasn't too far away from his own home.

Home.

The thought of his family made him smile. He looked at the picture that was in a silver frame next to the bed. There he stood with his blonde short-haired wife and daughter.

The thought of a killer on the loose should have made him nervous, but he knew they would be fine. Everything would be fine. He turned his attention back to the TV and the reporter, who was not as appealing as the woman had been; she'd had something about her. He just looked like a stockbroker with a microphone.

The man looked at his watch and sighed. It was nearly eleven o'clock. He was tired, and the effects of the strong beer were getting to him. He stood and pulled off his clothes, ensuring to hang them up so they wouldn't crease. Then he put on his blue silk pyjamas and climbed between the starched cotton sheets. Tomorrow he would have one more stop-off, and then he would be home. The thought made him smile as he opened a bottle of sleeping tablets, took one out, and swallowed it dry.

As he switched off the light and slipped into a well-deserved sleep, he couldn't help but think about the families that had been murdered. Then he thought about his own family, and a tear rolled down his face and onto the pillow.

CHAPTER SEVEN

TOBY HAD NEVER DONE A GRAVEYARD SHIFT BEFORE. Especially in a place like this. His thoughts drifted back to the young woman in the mask. Eric never explained why she had a mask on.

Nor did he ask.

Toby could see that Eric was scared of the woman – they all were. The poor girl had been in care most of her life. Her family had never been to see her once in ten years. A problem that was better forgotten about than pondered, Toby thought. His gaze flicked from one monitor to the next. Having a perfect view of the hallways while he sipped his coffee.

It was a quarter to midnight. Eric sat only a few feet from him, arms crossed, feet up on a desk, eyes closed. The sound of the local radio station was taking the edge off the silence. It wasn't loud, but enough for Toby's brain to have something to absorb and work on.

Toby's eyes flitted across the images until he got to Melanie's corridor. Suddenly, his gaze froze as he saw the young woman walk out of her room. Her *locked* room.

His eyes were transfixed. She looked so ... helpless, fragile even. He had heard the stories about her and put them down to just that: stories. For all Toby knew, it could be a hazing trick. After all, he was the new guy, and he had expected a prank to be sprung.

Toby's gaze remained transfixed on her. Nothing sexual – even though there was something sensual about her. No, the interest was more of a scientific nature. But, nevertheless, he was beginning to appreciate Hicks' interest in her.

But how could this meek-looking creature have everyone jumping out of their skins?

That was until she looked up at the camera and waved.

Toby's mouth fell open. Spine-tingling fear crept through him, almost as if she knew he was watching. 'You gotta be shitin' me,' Toby said in surprise and yelled, 'Hey man, wake up, the girl ... she's out of her room!'

'Hey, what ... who?' Eric asked, disorientated after being woken from his slumber. He rubbed his eyes as if to readjust them to the light. Instead, he looked over at the panicked Toby, who was pointing frantically at the monitors. Eric's gaze fell on each picture in turn, until he got to the one with Melanie.

He stared at the screen for a moment, then slapped Toby on the shoulder as if to say, *come on!* The two men rushed down the corridor towards Melanie. Winding through the dimly lit dog-leg passages.

'She waved at me. I swear she waved at me,' Toby said in a low but frantic voice.

'Yeah, that's the other thing about her ... she's psychic,' Eric delivered with a straight face.

'Seriously? Fuck!' A cold chill ran down Toby's spine.

'Nah, ya daft wanka; she's just waving at the camera,' Eric laughed. 'Asshole before me never told me she did that either. Man, the first time she did it, I almost shit my pants.'

'You mean, like you forgot to tell me?' Toby asked with a suspicious look.

'Forgot ... yeah. Let's go with that, shall we?' Eric laughed.

Toby smiled and shook his head, having the feeling he'd just been hazed. 'Man, your such an asshole.' He laughed.

'I know. It keeps things interesting, though, don't it,' Eric bellowed with laughter.

'Anything else I should know about her?' Toby frowned.

'Well, she doesn't talk. To us, anyway. Oh, and she is a bit of an escape artist, as you've probably noticed, though, she's never left the grounds,' Eric said, his voice suggesting puzzlement, as if he never quite understood why. 'Mostly, she likes to spend time at the pond and the fountain at the front of the estate. Fuckin weird kid,' Eric explained as they headed down the darkened corridor.

Even though the lights were on, their route was dimly lit. The ceiling lamp above the corner where Toby had met Melanie was broken. The only light illuminating the corridor was the blue glare from outside security lights. Bathing everything with eerie shadows.

They found Melanie standing by one of the corridor windows, looking at the full moon, transfixed by the colossal hunter's moon and the blood-red glow it was emitting. The rain had stopped some time ago. The clouds had departed, leaving a clear, haunting sky.

'Hey, Melanie, what you doing out of bed? It's late,' Eric said, his voice gentle and calming.

But Melanie said nothing, nor did she move. She just stared out of the window. As if oblivious to their presence – or unconcerned by it.

'Come on, Melanie, you'll need your rest,' Toby said. Hoping to coerce the woman back into her room.

Melanie turned and faced the new intern. Her blue eyes

stared back at him, cold and without emotion. It was almost like staring into the eyes of the dolls his grandmother used to have.

'My rest. Yes, I'll need my rest,' Melanie replied and went to head back to her room. Again, she stopped and looked at Toby. But this time, her eyes were warm and friendly. She said nothing, simply looked deeply into his eyes before turning and walking into her room. Leaving Eric opened-mouthed and stunned.

CHAPTER EIGHT

Sunday, the 23rd April.

THE FOLLOWING DAY, THE MAN ROSE AT SIX O'CLOCK. HE didn't need an alarm clock. He had done it for so long, it was muscle memory. He showered and changed into his suit, taking care to roll the trousers gently off the hanger instead of disturbing the razor-like creases.

He then went downstairs to the breakfast room, where he found several other guests. Saying his good mornings, he sat at a table at the back of the room. Even though there was room by the window, he preferred not to be on display. The man sat and combed his long fingers through his brown hair and sighed. The sleeping tablet had done its job, and he'd had a good night of sleep, but he still felt tired.

Another day, another breakfast room in a cheap hotel.

Paying little attention to the others in the breakfast room, he took out his mobile telephone and checked his messages. There had been nothing remarkable, a couple of business reminders and junk mail. Nothing of consequence.

The tapping of heels made him look up as a waitress came over. She was a sweet thing, around eighteen years old, with short blonde hair and blue eyes.

Suddenly, his interest was awoken.

She pulled out a notepad and smiled. Her rosy red lips parted to reveal a pearly white set of teeth. 'Would you like to order?' asked the young woman.

The man sat there for a moment, transfixed.

'Sir, can I get you anything?' the woman replied in a slightly louder voice, which broke his concentration.

'What ... oh, sorry, do forgive me. I was miles away, thinking about work and things I have to take care of later,' he said with a smile. 'I'd love a cup of English breakfast tea if you have it.' Then, he offered an apologetic smile.

The girl smiled back as if she understood his moment of absence.

As she walked away, he watched her leave from the corner of his eye as he unfolded the morning's paper.

Killer strikes again. Police still clueless. Read the front page. The reporter had done a great job of making the police look bad, stating facts that were either wrong, made up, or plain hearsay. Luckily, this was the local rag that most people never bothered with since the internet gave them world news. He felt sorry for those in the small media business. Like everything else, the internet was making it obsolete. Now it was all blogs and media news 24/7.

He paid very little interest in the morning paper and had little hope there would be anything new in the tabloids to grasp his attention.

He was awaiting his much-needed beverage and the return of the girl. Suddenly, he looked up and raised an eyebrow. Instead of the girl, another woman approached. She, too, had short blonde hair and blue eyes. The man had to look again as she was the daughter's spitting image, but with added years ... and those years had been more than kind.

'I'm terribly sorry for staring, but are you the other girl's twin sister?' he asked, almost blushing with embarrassment.

The woman laughed and slapped the man's shoulder gently. 'Oh, you are terrible,' she giggled. 'Cindy is my daughter, but sweet of you to say.' She smiled and placed down the cup of tea. 'The breakfast buffet is through those doors,' she explained, pointing to a set of sliding doors just to his left.

The man thanked her and glared as the mother walked towards the dining room entrance. His eyebrow was still raised, his thoughts a million miles away, daydreaming. Sipping tea, he returned to the paper, specifically the front page and the main story. Again, risking quick, furtive gazes at the mother and the daughter as they took turns serving the Elfords.

But the man knew he couldn't stay. He had work.

His thoughts went back to the document and the trip back home. A smile lifted the side of his mouth. He took another sip of tea before standing and heading for the breakfast buffet. He was hungry. The work he had done the day before had drained his reserves. Even the meal last night hadn't satisfied his hunger. He piled the full English breakfast onto the breakfast plate provided. A big meal, but then he had a long drive ahead.

He sat and splashed on tomato ketchup and added salt and pepper. The man licked his lips before tucking into the feast. Everything was cooked to perfection, or to his standards anyway. At home, he never had a breakfast like this; it was primarily cereals and toast. The trips away offered a diet of other sorts, most of which he knew would send his cholesterol level through the roof.

But it was a small price to pay. After all, he only got to travel once a month.

CHAPTER NINE

'Is there a problem, Professor?' Toby asked nervously as he stood in front of the clinic's director, Professor Albert Hicks.

Hicks was a stout built man in his late fifties. His mousey-coloured hair had streaks of grey on the sides and was greased back across a large bulbous head. He wore a brown tweed suit with a cream-coloured shirt from one of the tailor shops in London.

Hicks sat back in his brown leather office chair and made an arch with his fingers, placing the tips together as if measuring what to say next. The office smelled of beeswax, leather, and old books, mixed with a heavy tobacco scent from where Hicks had been smoking his pipe earlier. The office was a great looking place with wood panel walls, oak bookcases, and antique furniture. The floor had a thick, red pile carpet with gold-coloured patterns embedded in the weave.

'No, no problem. In fact, you could say you have created somewhat of a medical breakthrough as far as the young woman is concerned. One we hope you will continue to help us with,' Hicks said with an almost sinister purr in his voice.

The man came from money. His father had owned the clinic before him and made a fortune from it. A feat Hicks hoped to do just as well – if not better. Toby suspected this breakthrough was more of a monetary benefit than helping the poor woman and guessed that once their gift horse stopped giving, she would be carted somewhere else.

However, the parents were paying a fortune for her care. And while they were still paying the bill, she would be allowed to stay. Or so Eric had divulged during a brief conversation after the incident with Melanie.

'What do you mean, sir? I didn't do anything. I just spoke to her.' Toby endeavoured to further himself from any harm to the woman.

'You made contact with her,' Hicks said. His eyes were wide with admiration. 'Melanie responded to you ... that means you can communicate with her, if that's indeed possible,' he murmured. His expression changed as he looked at something on his desk. A photograph or something in a frame that sat on the corner of his desk. 'Perhaps, in time, others could benefit once we understand what is required to make that connection possible,' Hicks said. Tapping his fingers together.

'What do you want me to do, sir?' Toby asked reluctantly, seeing no other option. If he refused, they would possibly do the woman harm. But, at least if he stayed, he could, in fact, help her.

'Just talk to her ... be there for her.'

'You mean, to be her friend?' Toby asked bluntly.

Hicks' eyes narrowed, making them into slits as he grinned. 'Exactly.' His grin turned into a false, compassionate smile. 'Be her ... *friend.*'

Toby nodded. He had understood exactly what the old man meant. But as he went to leave, Hicks spoke.

His voice had lost its pleasantness. 'However,' his voice boomed across the room, forcing Toby to stop in his tracks. 'If you could be so kind as to share any important information, that would be perfect,' Hicks said, with a sinister grin etched across his face.

'Important information?' Toby was suddenly confused by the request. What relevant information could this woman have?

'I'm sorry, I misspoke.' Hicks drew in a short breath and exhaled before speaking. 'I meant to say, any information she may have about her past that could have warranted her ...' He paused, as if trying to find diplomatic words to end his request, 'Stay with us.' Hicks' eyes grew full and humble, like a puppy that had done something wrong.

'You mean, what had she seen or heard to make her ga-ga?' Toby's words were hard and harsh, the tone directed towards Hicks.

Hicks sighed, squeezed his eyes together, and shook his head with displeasure at the uncouth tone Toby had displayed. 'Crude ... but accurate. What had happened all those years ago? What has she remembered of that time?' Hicks nodded, feeling his elegant words had been trampled on.

'Sure, if it helps her,' Toby replied, his voice unfeeling, cold.

Hicks nodded again, in response, and waved at Toby to leave.

The interview was over. The order had been given.

As Toby left the office, an uneasy feeling hung over him like a dark cloud. 'What the hell did she see?' he thought.

CHAPTER TEN

It was getting close to the tenth anniversary of Melanie's coming to the hospital. But her parents wouldn't be there. After all, how did someone celebrate incarcerating their child for all those years? They were feeling guilty or, more likely, too afraid she would finally do what she had been promising all those years. One psychologist wasn't sure that Melanie meant it was them who were in danger, but he was quickly told to dismiss the idea by the powers that be.

Of course, if he had convinced the family that Melanie wasn't a threat, they would take her out, and the clinic would lose a valuable client. When Melanie first arrived, Professor Hicks Senior had insisted it would be best if they never visited her. Believing that such an encounter could cause Melanie to relapse and hurt herself – or others.

Melanie's mother had readily agreed, thinking it was for the best despite her husband's reluctance to see it that way. Ten years had not changed her decision to stay away. If anything, she felt more comfortable not seeing Melanie after all that time.

However, Melanie's father was still haunted by the decision. Besides, what would they say after all that time? 'Hi, Melanie, we're your parents; sorry for locking you up.' As far as they knew, Melanie didn't even know they existed. She was in a world of her own – a better place for her.

And them.

Melanie's parents were good people. Jason Freeman was a local college teacher and Abby Freeman was a scientist at York University. They lived comfortably due to an inheritance Jason's parents had left to him after their passing years before. Jason was an only child whereas Abby had a twin sister called Ann, who lived not too far away from them in the next town.

Ann was more outgoing and fun-loving than her sister. But despite the distance, they often kept in touch. A weekly phone call to catch up on things.

Ann had moved away, primarily because of her marriage to a businessman named William. He already had a house and a good job. Ann and William were those 'happy you're not there often' kind of people. They loved each other and enjoyed each others' company, but they also enjoyed their own space. It had become routine that he worked so hard and she was left alone, but she liked that. Besides, their daughter Debs kept her company.

William, or Bill as he liked to be called, was a good and kind man, but his work forced him to make trips around the country once a month. Ann had grown accustomed to the tours to the point of even looking forward to them.

For Melanie, every day seemed to be the same. There were no clocks in the facility that patients could look at. For all the patients knew, they had been in there a week or even a year. Christmas wasn't celebrated or even acknowledged, nor was Easter, Halloween, or any other festival. The reason was because, some years ago, the festivities got out of control and people died.

The powers that be felt the lack of time differential made it easier to control the patients, despite the doctors wearing gold Rolex watches that everyone could see; they made a point of showing them off.

Melanie didn't care about the year, month, or hour – she had her own clock in her head. She would know when it was time. She'd had everything planned.

For her, the only significant time was the night. That was when it all started, and that would be when it ended. That was when the bad dreams came to her.

When Melanie closed her eyes, sometimes she could see another life through her own eyes. A man and a woman she knew, but didn't know from where. They'd had pictures of her all over the house, from when she was little all the way up to holiday photos. But this was all a dream – a place she had made up in her imagination. A safe and happy place.

She didn't know school and friends, a boy she liked but was afraid of talking to. A whole different life bottled up in her imagination – a life that only existed in a dream.

Melanie sat on her bed and read a book she had been reading for a while now. She liked to read. She loved to be lost in the stories, feel the paper between her fingers, the smell of the pages. And this novel was no different. It was a detective story written by some British author nobody had heard of before.

It was set in New York with a female cop and a British detective. She had read most of the other books in the series. For her, the bad guy who kept showing up in the series was the only fascinating character, even though the kick-ass female detective was fantastic.

She felt her stomach rumble, which meant it was breakfast time. A glass of milk, four pieces of toast with Marmite, strawberry yoghurt and four eggs scrambled, and an apple was what she'd had for years. It was all she knew, so the cooks were happy because she had no special dietary requirements, just plenty of carbs and proteins as per instructions. It was a two-choice menu: eat it or leave it.

But in her dreams, she'd had other options – things she had never seen before. The dreams had been so vivid that she had gotten the taste for the food without ever tasting it. For her, these dreams were the best.

At six o'clock, there was a tap on the door to signal the nurse was bringing breakfast. Melanie sat up straight on her bed and waited for Eric to enter. He'd say good morning.

She'd say nothing, just gave a simple nod.

Then he'd lay the tray on the bed in front of her and, like every morning, he would do his usual dance of going about the room. As if he were searching for something.

The door opened and her heart skipped a beat. It was the new guy who had brought her meal.

Underneath the mask, she smiled to herself. It wasn't a callous, wicked smile. It was a warm, affectionate one.

Toby placed the tray in front of her, then turned around the armchair that faced the window to meet her gaze. He sat quietly, hoping she would start the conversation. But Melanie just sat there and ate her toast, pulling up the mask enough so she could take a bite.

The mask had been her idea. 'Sheltering herself from the world,' one shrink had said. Another had said it was to stop her from self-harming, but that made no sense as she could take it off at any time.

Nobody really knew. But then, no one had asked her, only assumed. After all, everyone believed she was ready to commit murder.

'Hi, I'm Toby,' he said with a cheery smile.

Melanie said nothing, just tore off a corner piece of toast before pulling the mask back down.

'Nice view,' he said, looking back at the window. 'Bet it looks fantastic in winter?' He got nothing but a stare from those pale blue eyes. He crossed his left leg over his right knee and tapped his ankle bone with his fingers. Even though he had just started, he felt he was running out of things to talk about.

Melanie ate slowly in silence. Her eating motion was slower than usual. As if she knew that once she had finished, he would be leaving the room. She was savouring his company as much as she was the meal.

'Do you have any hobbies?' he asked, hoping for a reaction.

Melanie said nothing, but she froze for a moment as if the question confused her.

'You know, things you like to do?' Toby explained with a smile, knowing he had struck a nerve.

Melanie put down her piece of toast and leapt off the bed, and grabbed for him.

Eric, waiting outside, saw her lunge for the young man and burst in, ready to act if she harmed Toby. She gave Eric an evil look and let go before heading back to the bed, but Toby had already raised a hand at his partner as if to say he was OK.

As Eric backed out the door, Toby looked around the room and saw the books. Piles and piles of books. More than he had seen from the small window in the door.

'Your books ... you wanted to show me your books?' Toby reminded her calmly.

Melanie nodded quickly, as if excited at his understanding.

He held out his hand and waited for her to climb off the

bed and pull him once more to the bookcase which was full of books.

There was everything from science to maths and geometry, human biology to crime novels. Even ones on plants and animals, astrology and survival tips from some guy who had been in the SAS. She read everything and anything, even a book on electronics. One of the doctors had been a bit dubious about her reading, thinking she would use it to escape, but then he realised she could do it anyway, without the books.

'Do you have a favourite book?' Toby asked as he looked through the array of different literature.

Melanie inched forward and pulled out a large thick book by a Russian author he'd never heard of before. The novel had a leatherbound cover and had an old feel to it, and a hefty weight.

Toby looked at the first page and closed it shut. Just reading the prologue made his head hurt. This young woman was brilliant by most people's standards. To the people who worked there, she was trouble waiting to happen. Toby was an educated guy, but the things she was reading put him to shame. But then, he'd known people who had books of such calibre and they had never opened the covers. It was all for show. Perhaps that was her game. Keep everyone on their toes. But as he examined the books, he noticed they had all been read and handled with the care that books deserve.

Toby sat back in the chair and watched Melanie finish her breakfast. She bit the toast without slow chewing or overly small bites. Almost as if she knew Toby wasn't going anywhere once the meal had gone. He was as intrigued by her as she was him.

. . .

Hicks had Eric film the goings-on so he could observe Melanie and Toby together. He wanted to see how she reacted around the new boy.

Hicks sat impatiently in his office. He couldn't wait for the footage. At last, a breakthrough, not just for the woman, but for him and the hospital. He could see the money rolling in, funding from the government for research. However, how could he reveal such a thing, considering the two subjects weren't meant to exist?

He took a sip from freshly made tea in a Wedgwood china cup. It was a Chinese herb tea for medicinal purposes. The scent was strong and tasted like crap, but he swore it made him feel better.

A breeze found its way through an open window and brushed gently across his wrinkled skin. It felt refreshing on his warm flesh. Hicks sighed before taking another sip. Life was excellent and soon it would be getting even better. But he still had much work to do, several friends to visit. The work with Melanie would have to wait. His other business took priority. Besides, he had Eric document everything that Melanie and Toby did together.

Hicks put down the teacup and saucer and picked up a brown file that lay on the wooden desk's bare surface. He scanned through it, leering over the photographs and a complete outline of the family inside. They were perfect for his research.

Hicks stood up and headed for the door. 'So much to do, but I must bide my time. Everything should be done correctly, just as I have done before,' he muttered to himself, as if trying to calm himself from his excitement. With a turn of the brass handle, he opened the door and stepped into the hallway. The noise hit him like a strong gust of wind and he closed his eyes as screams and laughter filled his ears.

'I *will* cure them and take great pleasure in it,' he said before exhaling lungs full of air and made his way to the main entrance.

CHAPTER ELEVEN

THE KILLER HAD A FRONT PAGE SPREAD – OR AT LEAST HIS work had. But, unfortunately, DI Richard Platt and DS David Elford were no closer to catching the killer than before.

Platt was still open to suggestions that a woman liked to maim and demean other women. Tests had shown there was vaginal scaring on all the women and girls, and spermicide present, meaning the killer had worn a condom. However, the killer was intelligent. A simple misdirection like that could make everyone assume they were looking for a man. The lack of skin cells or hair fibres would indicate no physical contact, but there were also traces of cleaning fluid on the bodies.

The killer had cleaned up. He had also brutalised the groin area, possibly to cover the fact intercourse had taken place, but traces had still been picked up.

A mistake by the killer – or another misdirection?

Platt and Elford were set up at the local police station in a spare room the local nick had made available as an incident room. Several whiteboards, maps with pins, computers and, more importantly, a kettle and brew kit. The murders had gone on over six years, but Platt suspected that the killer had done this before.

Possibly more than once.

The killings were too meticulous, too detailed, and the cleanup was too thorough to be that of a first-timer. From Platt's experience, the first killing from a serial killer was messy, sloppy, uncontrolled. Later, as the killer developed, so did their art. And to some, it was an art in its purest form.

Elford was in the same clothes as he had worn the day before. He had spent all night looking through the police database to find any similar MOs but had come up empty. Almost as if this killer had appeared from nowhere.

However, Platt remained unconvinced. This killer had practice in what they were doing.

Unfortunately, it wasn't like the killer was good with a knife, so that could rule out surgeons. On the other hand, he – or she – had proven to be a cruel bastard and made people suffer before they died. Also, the use of duct tape on their mouths indicated that they had suffered in silence.

The killer wanted them to feel the pain and witness what was being done to the others.

These weren't murders of passion – these were done out of pure, unadulterated hate.

'You look like shit, Dave. You been here all night?' Platt asked, tossing a wrapped-up bacon sandwich to his partner.

Elford caught the package in mid-stretch. 'Pretty much, I wanted to check to back files, see if this guy had done it before, like you thought,' Elford said, unwrapping the sandwich and taking a bite. His eyes rolled back, as if it was the best thing he'd ever tasted.

'And, did you find anything?'

'Nah, bugger all. If this whack job had done it before, he ...'
Elford paused as Platt went to butt in.

'... or she,' Elford said. Correcting himself.

Platt gave him an appreciative nod before tucking into his
own sandwich.

'This is a different MO. This one doesn't fit anything we
have on record,' Elford said before taking another bite.

'Did you check with Interpol? See if they have anything?'
Platt lifted the kettle to surmise the water level. Happy that he
could get at least three cups of coffee out of it, Platt placed it
back on the stand and switched it on.

'We asked them months ago with the Skammel murders,'
Elford started, but Platt shot him one of those looks. 'Fine, I'll
ask them again, but don't be surprised if they tell us to fuck off,'
he laughed.

'This time, ask them if there were any cases where the
people were held somewhere else first, not a home invasion,'
Platt suggested, a thought suddenly popping into his head.

'You're thinking he ... or she ... have escalated from kidnap-
ping the victims to home invasions? Wow, ballsy,' Elford said
with a smile of admiration.

'They all start somewhere, some with the neighbour pet,
others with the girl next door. The thing is, they all have a first,
and that is always messy, unplanned. We find that and we may
have a chance of catching the bastard and going home,' Platt
said with a hint of loathing.

Elford said nothing. He merely nodded and bit his bottom
lip. He knew that this case had taken a lot from Platt personally
as well as emotionally.

Platt's family had followed him up north where he'd put in
for a post months before. The posting was for a small community copper in Yorkshire, where his wife was from. The plan
was to see out his twenty in the country, a village copper. The

family killings had taken their toll on Platt and burnt him out. All he wanted now was settle somewhere quiet.

The strain on Platt's family had started to show. Firstly with the arguments, then hateful words – the threats of leaving. The nightmares, coupled with the drinking, had forced him to sleep in a spare room. Platt had never felt so alone in his own house.

He couldn't discuss the case; it was ongoing. Plus, he didn't want to fill his wife's head with nightmarish thoughts. He knew then it was time for a change – for all of them.

The family killer had struck in a town near Leeds. The team had been dispatched to the scene to set up the investigation there. For Platt, it wasn't too bad. His family would be just half an hour away. Before, they had been bounced around the country. However, the murders seemed to be more localised to the Midlands and the north of England. This had proven some comfort to Platt's wife. At least he wouldn't be gone for weeks on end. He would be closer to home.

But Platt had been sent south, following a lead the team had found. Platt had exploded at the lead DCI for sending him on such a menial task, so far away from his family. But this had strengthened the man's resolve in sending Platt away.

That night there had been a break-in at Platt's home. The intruder had left Platt's wife and daughter alive. They had been found bound and gagged. The intruder had brutalised them both, espcially Platt's daughter, as if it was a personal attack on Platt rather than his family.

His wife and daughter had ended up in a local clinic on the promise they could help. That everything would be fine – they would be fine.

The intruder had been found at the scene of another break-in. Luckily, the police got to the scene before the guy could do anything and gave chase, but the intruder had died in a car accident while fleeing.

Elford knew that Platt wouldn't rest until this family killer was captured and brought to justice. However, Elford understood that he was using this killer as some form of substitute for justice. He had never caught the man who had hurt his family, the car accident had taken that from him, so he never got to make him pay. But Platt would stop this killer for all of them.

'The pathologist's report came in, saying the same thing as always,' Elford said, 'the killer wore a condom – as always. Nothing special about the damn thing, though. Which means it could have been bought at a petrol station, chemist, or vending machine at a nightclub.' Elford pointed to a stack of files on Platt's desk.

'Also, the same tape was used for gagging the victims. The killer still isn't leaving any trace evidence, and the smart bastard is even emptying the Hoover bags and taking them with him. This sick individual is watching too much TV or reading too many damned books,' Elford said, standing up and grabbing milk from the refrigerator.

'There is another option – the killer is one of us.' Platt leaned forward, onto his elbows.

'Just don't go there,' Elford said, waving a finger in defiance.

'I must admit, after the third one, I was having doubts about my theory because nothing fitted. It was more a hunch … gut feeling than anything. Every crime scene we went to, something seemed off. They were too clean. As cops, we don't get trained that highly in forensics, not to the grade of our killer or …' Platt looked back out amongst the local police officers.

'Please don't tell me you think it's a CSI tech?' Elford's mouth fell open in surprise.

'No, but we can't rule anything out at this point, I guess,' Platt said, handing over a fresh cup of tea.

Elford took the brew and thought for a moment, then shrugged in agreement before taking a sip of the hot drink. 'Bastards definitely did their homework.'

'There's no sign of forced entry or signs of a struggle, and the neighbours never reported anything unusual,' Platt said, taking his seat. He paused for a moment as if contemplating his next words. 'Our killer has made friends or is someone everyone is comfortable with.'

Elford was hearing what his boss was saying, and it made sense. He didn't like it. The thought the killer wasn't just targeting them but gaining their trust made him nauseous.

'You're saying the killer could be a copper!' Elford asked with a lowered voice so the others couldn't hear them.

'Not exactly. I said the victims felt comfortable with whoever they let it ... hell it could be the friggin' postman for all I know. So, I'm just saying we need to look into who these people knew more closely, and more importantly, who was the one person they all knew,' Platt explained.

Elford gave a quick smile and went back to his computer.

Platt could feel the young DS's frustration. He, too, was at the end of his tether with the case. It had gone on too long, with no signs of the killer making any mistakes. Usually, a killer like this got bolder as they felt the rush of the kill and the chase, but this one was smart, consistent.

Platt sat at his desk and picked up the pathologist's report. It read as all the others had. As if he was reading the report from the first murder. He looked for anything that stood out, but everything was the same. He tossed the report back onto the table and cupped his face in his hands as he stifled a cry of frustration.

The family were drugged before being tied up, which

meant the killer was free to tie them up without any fear of them resisting. The report also said that cuts were expertly done but made to look sloppy. That meant someone who had a lot of practice with knives, not as they had first thought.

This was new information. That could mean they were looking for a doctor, nurse, or a damned butcher after all. There was nothing that the profiler could say for sure, apart from the person being brilliant and patient. This narrowed it down to most of Britain's population who had served in the military, police service, or gone to med school.

DS David Elford sat at his computer and flicked through the database. Next to him was a stack of files he had printed off that Platt had asked him to check: had there been any other cases similar to those they were investigating ... on the off chance this wasn't just a random spate of attacks.

By ten o'clock, Elford had been at it for hours – or so it seemed. He was on his fifth cup of coffee and sixth sandwich. As he looked through the archives from ten years ago, he bit into the sandwich. Brown sauce spewed from the sides and fell onto his trouser leg and the keyboard.

'Oh, bollocks,' he swore and stood up quickly, grabbing a paper napkin from the stack he had brought with him, on the off chance of such an event.

Elford wiped his trousers and keyboard, being careful not to hit the delete key, and screwed up the paper napkin and tossed it into the nearest wastepaper basket. The ball hit the wall and went in, causing him to raise his hands in celebration.

'Three points for that, I believe, sarge,' said a female PC who was sitting at a nearby desk.

'Ten more likely, it was a long shot.' Elford laughed as he walked past her desk to get a damp cloth for his trousers.

'Talking of long shots, I think I found something,' she said.

Platt stood and moved over to her desk. 'What you got, constable?' he asked before taking a sip of coffee.

He and Elford peered over her shoulder at the monitor. The report was of a killing taken place years before; the mother and daughter had been murdered. The police had suspected the husband at first, even though he hadn't been at the scene; then they found out there had been an abusive ex-husband.

The police never found the ex-husband; however, the husband's remains had been found days later. He had died in a roadside accident. His car had come off the road and landed in an embankment. The report said he had been driving too fast, lost control, and crashed. Unfortunately, his route wasn't used very often, and so he must have bled out slowly.

The killer had never been caught and was still at large. Platt leant over and clicked the print button, and studied the file further. The killing seemed to be an isolated incident, and no further murders had occurred since – until now. However, the MO was different. There had been no rape of either victim, both had dark hair, and the stabbing was less violent. The printer whirred to life and started to spout out the document.

Elford shook his head as he headed back to his desk. 'Not wrong about a long shot, probably *was* the husband. Killed himself after realising what he'd done,' he said, shrugging off the theory it could have anything to do with their case. He folded over the paper the sandwich was wrapped in and took another bite.

The case had no similarities, but somehow it made the hairs stand up on the back of Platt's neck. He hovered over the printer as the last page spat out of the machine, Then rushed over to his own desk to check the last page for an address. He wrote it down and looked over to Elford, and smiled. 'Get your-self to this address, talk to the neighbours, anything. Find out more about the people and what happened. Whoever filed this report left massive gaps, almost as if he'd come to the same conclusion as you ... the husband did it,' Platt said as he handed a scrap of paper to Elford.

Elford rolled his eyes as he grabbed it with the sandwich gripped in his jaws. His eyes widened as he saw the address. 'Mm-mm,' Elford burbled, forgetting the food was still in his mouth. He shook his head and ripped the sandwich from his maw. 'This place is in fuckin' Nottingham. It'll take me friggin' ages to get there. So why not send her? She found the friggin' thing?' Elford growled at the order.

Platt smiled. He knew the road trip away would do Elford good – different scenery. Besides, as Elford had said: a long shot.

Probably nothing. But then it could be everything.

'It might be nothing, but it could be what we are looking for. Besides Dave, it looks like you need a break. Take your time. Stay overnight if you have to,' Platt nodded to Elford.

Elford wobbled his head like an indecisive child. 'Fine, but you know it's a waste of time,' he grumbled and grabbed the file.

Platt finished his brew while searching for the car keys in his pockets.

'Off somewhere, guv?'

'I'm going back to the Thomas house, see if there is anything we've missed. Get someone to check the families for that familiar link,' Platt replied. He headed for the door and pointed an index finger at a young DC. 'Constable Kate Summers, isn't it?'

The woman nodded.

'You're with me,' he said, tossing her the keys, 'and you're driving.' He smiled at Elford, who just shook his head with a grin.

As they left, Elford stood, grabbed his jacket from the back of the chair, and checked his watch and phone. He had one message. Elford smiled and tucked the phone away.

'If the guv wants me, I've just popped out to freshen up,' he told one of the other DCs.

Summers smiled and nodded in response. Then, he took car keys from his pocket and headed for the exit.

CHAPTER TWELVE

Toby had stayed with Melanie until Eric tapped on the door to signal it was time to go back to work. He looked at his watch. He'd been there for over an hour.

Toby had done all of the talking while Melanie sat and stared at him with those large, pondering blue eyes. She was like a child who was experiencing something beautiful for the first time.

He'd talked in length about his family, his life back home. How he'd decided to move from the United States to Britain, what his plans were. Starting with a chance for a new life – a new career working at Larksford.

Melanie had simply listened. Her eyes did all of the smiling. But even though she was silent, Toby knew she was taking it all in. If anything, he had the feeling she was more attuned to her surroundings than people gave her credit for.

Toby got up to leave. As he did, she grabbed his hand. Their eyes met for a moment. Her lingering stare seemed to be full of pain more than anything. Suddenly, her eyes shot towards the door and she shook her head slightly.

He couldn't be sure what she was telling him: *don't go* or *watch your arse*. He smiled and kissed the back of her hand and patted it gently. 'Don't worry. I'll be back soon. I gotta go, I got some work to do – apparently.' Toby laughed. Hoping to see a smile in her eyes, but there were only sadness and something else – something he couldn't quite place.

The door opened and Eric's bulky shape filled the doorway.

'Let's go, we got rounds to do before the doc comes back,' Eric said, his order sounding more like what it was, an excuse.

As Toby left, he closed the door. She saw his face through the small window as he looked in, smiled, and walked away.

Her gaze was fixed on the window, hoping he would take another look, but instead all she saw was Eric. He wore a broad, unkind grin and had wide, maddening eyes. Waved and blew Melanie a kiss, giving her an uneasy feeling. She never knew how to take Eric; sometimes he was kind, watched over her like a big brother, other times he was mean. Not so much mean to her – never to her. She had observed Eric's treatment of the other staff through a large window that looked onto the building's front.

Her room's watch tower – or so someone had once called it.

––––––

The hidden cameras had caught it all – how the family moved about the house, who spent more time, paying particular attention to the daughter's and parent's bedrooms. The parents had gone out for the morning, leaving the teenager alone with her boyfriend. The camera above the bed had filmed everything, absolutely everything: how the blonde woman moved around her man's body, how they pleasured each other. Everything that was recorded for research – data for analysis. She was tall, blonde, around eighteen years old, smart and beautiful. Everything that Mr and Mrs Freeman could have ever wanted from a daughter.

———

By ten o'clock the man had reached the residence of the people in his file. He rechecked the address said #11 on the piece of paper.

He smiled coldly to himself.

Yes, this was the correct house.

The man parked the car in an available spot in front of the house. He breathed in then, exhaled slowly before getting out of the vehicle. Stamping his feet, he made sure the trouser legs fell correctly and the creases stood prominently like knife edges.

Opening the rear passenger door, the sun reflected off the window, causing him to squint suddenly. After waiting for his vision to return, he reached inside. Taking his jacket from the coathanger that was attached to the headrest of the driver's seat. Carefully he slid on the suit jacket and used the wing mirror to adjust his tie. He smiled at himself as if to give himself a boost of confidence.

Not that he needed it.

Taking out his brown leather briefcase, he closed the door and locked the Ford Mondeo using the electric key. A clicking sound was followed by the car's indicators flashing twice to signal the alarm activation. As he walked up the short path to the front entrance, he took note of the garage and the windows - any weak points someone might use an entry. He smiled. One of the windows was old and could be opened in seconds with the correct equipment.

The man stood in front of the door and worked the muscles

in his mouth. As if he were expecting to be doing a great deal of smiling.

He reached out a bear-sized paw and pressed the doorbell and waited around a minute before he heard the sound of voices – a woman's voice to be more precise. She was on the telephone with someone.

As she opened the door, he saw her for the first time.

The woman had short blonde hair, blue eyes, around thirty to thirty-five years old. She said her goodbyes to the person on the other end of the line and shot him a smile before apologising for keeping him. Her voice was soft and without an accent.

'It's quite alright madam. My name is Bill, Bill Brown. I'm with Simmon's Security,' he said with a smile and showed her his business identification.

'Oh, brilliant. My husband mentioned you'd be coming around. Please, do come in. Do excuse the mess. Our daughter is home from uni, and she's brought a ton of washing back with her,' the woman laughed.

Her laugh made the hair on the back of his neck tingle ... and he shivered with excitement.

'Not a problem, Mrs Jackson. I fully understand, I have a daughter myself. I know they can be a handful sometimes ... especially teenagers.' Bill smiled again.

They both laughed as he followed her into the living room. It was a large room with a thick beige shag carpet covering all twenty-by-twenty feet. A brown brushed suede leather couch sat against the back wall with a long double-glazed window to the left. Hung on the wall in front of the couch was a 60' ultra-high-definition TV. The furnishings were a mix of modern and antique. Expensive wallpaper dressed up the walls and long velvet curtains were ready to shut out the world.

As Bill looked around, he could definitely see why the

husband had chosen to go for a security firm to prevent any possible break-in problems. 'I understand your husband works away a lot, hence the reason for the call to us,' Bill said in a quiet but understanding voice. 'I too have had quite a bit installed at home; I work away a lot too, and I know I can sleep better at night knowing my family are safe.'

'He wants it done because of all these killings, but that monster is miles away from here. I told him not to worry, I can take care of myself,' she said with a laugh and a shrug.

'I'm sure you can, Mrs Jackson.' Raising an eyebrow and hiding a sinister smirk, Bill followed her into the open-plan kitchen.

She clicked on the kettle and pulled two mugs from a red-painted cup tree.

'Tea or coffee?' she asked with a smile that made him shiver.

'Tea, please, Mrs Jackson.'

'Please ... call me Lucy,' she replied.

Bill smiled and said her name inside his head over and over. *Lucy, Lucy, Lucy.*

'Tea, would be great, thank you ... Lucy,' Bill purred. 'Milk, no sugar,' he said, instinctively knowing what she was going to ask next.

Lucy laughed as though he'd pulled off some kind of magic trick by reading her mind.

He laughed too because he knew he had just installed himself in her life. She felt comfortable with him. That was stage one.

Stage two: the rest of the family.

After finishing his tea and more small talk, Bill went around the house, making notes of what should be installed and where.

The husband had already stated the budget for the improvements, which was substantial. As he went around, Bill took note of the family pictures that were hung or sat in frames, more importantly, the wife and daughter. The two women could have been twins, they were so alike.

Bill thought back to his family and suddenly missed them. It had seemed so long since he had seen them and the thought of going home brought a smile to his lips.

Home.

But he still had things to do here at the new customer's house.

Lucy, Lucy, Lucy.

There was a noise from another room. It was her – Lucy – she was singing along to the radio. Bill had to admit she had a good voice.

He smiled as he closed his eyes and imagined dark, sexual thoughts as the sound of her lovely voice made him tingle.

Lucy had left him to it. This in itself was a sign of trust. *Good*, he thought.

He smiled again, openly, knowing he was alone. Left with his thoughts.

Suddenly there was a noise from the hallway. Lucy was closer than before. Possibly carrying freshly folded washing to the bedrooms.

Bill got back to drawing quick diagrams and took measurements from place to place. His list included movement sensors for the downstairs and alarms for the windows. Motion sensors and lights for the outside as well as cameras. Hidden cameras for each of the downstairs rooms, which would be in fake fire detectors. The feed would be stored on a hard drive that would record for thirty days and then write over itself. There weren't any tapes or CDs to change.

Bill thought it curious that the husband was most insistent

on the recording devices on the homepage list of all the security equipment. Perhaps the husband thought his wife was having an affair and the security thing was a bluff to catch her out.

He could understand the man's motive if that were the case. After all, he was probably worth a lot of money, and a divorce would end badly for her if he could prove she was screwing around. However, he was there to do a job and not speculate about what may or may not be happening in clients' homes.

Bill was just finishing off the assessment as Lucy entered the sitting room. He placed the paperwork back into his brief-case and closed it. Fixing the brass latch into place. Standing up, he brushed the creases back into place.

'Well, all done for now. I have the specs I need and will send the list off to your husband for him to check over,' Bill explained.

As he went to shake Lucy's hand, the front door opened and Lucy's daughter walked in. Eighteen years old and the mirror image of the mother. The young woman wore a short jeans skirt, baggy white t-shirt, and white training shoes.

'Hi Mum, do you know there's ...' The girl stopped as she saw the stranger in the living room with her mother and glared at him with a hint of suspicion.

'Brooke, this is Bill; he's here to look at the security system your father wants installed,' Lucy explained.

Brooke raised an eyebrow as she gave him the once over.

'Pleased to meet you miss,' Bill said, extending a hand.

Brooke's handshake was as limp as a dead fish, but her eyes still held the glare. She stood in silence, the look on her face signalling she was unsure about this stranger in their home.

'So, you're here to make sure we're all safe and sound?' Brooke asked sarcastically as she felt the warm, clammy skin of his palm against hers. Forcing her to cut short the greeting and wipe her palm against her skirt. She took a step back and folded her arms. Putting up the psychological barrier.

'Oh, don't you worry miss, by the time I'm through, you'll never have to worry again,' he said reassuringly, wearing a warm smile.

Something about him made Brooke shiver. 'So, you putting cameras in our rooms?' she asked, almost as if she was testing him.

'No, absolutely not,' Bill replied with shocked look on his face. 'Here, look.' Sitting down and pulling the paperwork from his bag, he sorted through the papers until he got to the plan for the downstairs. His fingers darted across the project, pointing out windows and doors that required alarms. Showing where motion sensors would be put into rooms so that they covered the windows and doors. Ensuring that the moment an intruder stepped inside the area, opening a window or door would trigger the alarm.

'So, what if I want a snack in the middle of the night?' Brooke asked. 'Won't that set anything off?'

'No, I have accounted for that,' Bill smiled, his fingers moving slowly over the diagram. 'The angles of the sensors will only cover the doors and windows. If you're coming from upstairs, you won't trip anything. It just goes off when people try and get in from outside.'

'Cool.' Brooke nodded, as if giving approval. She sat back and smiled softly.

But all Bill could see out of the corner of his eye as he put the documents away were Brooke's long bare-skinned legs.

'How long will it take?' Lucy asked.

'Well first, your husband has to approve the plan, then it's a case of setting a date after that ... two weeks at the most. Possibly less, depending on what has to be done.' Bill explained with a smile and a shrug. 'But it wouldn't be until next month anyway. We have lots of other customers due to ... well ... never mind.' He suddenly had to think about what he was going to say.

'The murders you mean?' Brooke asked, seeming to take pleasure in his discomfort.

'Yes, quite.' He was abruptly taken aback by the girl. 'I'll contact your husband tonight and arrange a meeting with him. I'm sure he'll fill you in with the rest of the details.' Standing, he picked up his briefcase.

Lucy walked him to the door where they said their farewells, with Brooke in the background. Arms still folded and the suspicious look back on her face. As the door closed behind him, Bill muttered something under his breath as if in hushed anger.

'One day, you'll get yours you little bitch, and I'll take *great* pleasure in it.'

CHAPTER THIRTEEN

MELANIE SAT FACING THE WINDOW LIKE SOMEONE DOING yoga, with her long legs crossed underneath her. The book in her hand was a detective novel set in Britain. The story was about a local doctor who worked with the police as a crime scene medical examiner. She had just started the book and was drawn into the characters and situation. She had finished her other book sometime in the early morning.

The sun gave off a gentle warmth which felt soothing against her pale skin. Melanie looked out of the window, the sudden noise of people talking drawing her attention from the novel. The other patients had begun to wander about the grounds. Some oblivious to their situation, others relaxed under the warmth of the sun.

Melanie stared at them for a moment, feeling a twinge of jealousy at their freedom. She had always wanted to venture outside during the day. With their consent, of course. Unfortunately, Hicks had deemed her a flight risk, as well as a danger to others and herself – or so she had been told.

Which she thought odd, considering the numerous times

she had escaped at night and had never made it past the pond. Besides, where should she go? She didn't know anywhere but the hospital. Of course, the real reason was apparent to all except her. If something happened to her, the family would seek to send her somewhere else – that meant Hicks losing money, and lots of it.

Melanie looked up from her book and gazed across the green of the lawn. Past the flower beds, and the tree line, the high stone wall, and onto the horizon. She gazed dreamily at the fantastic patchwork of colour from the treeline and pale blue sky.

She smiled to herself. Why would she want to leave here, stupid people?

Melanie returned her attention back to the novel. She was already on chapter three. Her stomach rumbled, and her mouth was dry. She was hungry and thirsty, but more the latter. Taking the book with her, she walked to the door and pressed the intercom button that reached the staff working at the gate.

There was no reply.

She tried again – still nothing.

Melanie sighed and walked to the bed. Placing down the book, she searched underneath the mattress and retrieved two hairpins. With a wicked smile, she headed to the door.

In the monitoring booth that sat between the secure wing and the open community, the two orderlies sat with their feet up, watching the Formula One on a small TV. They had heard the buzz from Melanie's room and chosen to ignore it.

After all, they were far too busy. Too busy to pay heed to her request. Far too busy to notice that the door to Melanie's room had opened.

She had grown weary of waiting. She had known who was

on duty ... and that they wouldn't come either, no matter how much she rang.

So – she left.

Melanie headed for the staff room down the dimly lit corridor, her slippers giving a gentle tapping sound on the linoleum flooring. After a short while, she returned. Clutching a bottle of water and a cup of hot chocolate – as well as a cheese and onion sandwich she had found in the small fridge in the staff room. The security room orderlies yelled and screamed at the television as their favourite driver was lapped by some other driver. Their attention was latched onto the happenings in Barcelona and not on the corridor just down the way.

The first bite of the sandwich made her eyes roll back with pleasure. The mix of thick, soft white bread, the taste of cheddar, and the tang of the onion came together in an explosive culinary delight.

Heaven.

The sandwich hadn't been a random choice. It had belonged to Eric. Perhaps it was her way of payback – or simply because she knew he had good taste when it came to food. Either way, *he* wasn't getting lunch today.

Melanie had been smart enough to leave the container in the fridge. She didn't need the evidence leading back to her. Besides, all he had to do was check the camera tapes to see who was the last one in the room. And even if he did, all he would see was her with a cup of hot chocolate and a bottle of water. The food had been concealed under her book.

Melanie knew about the cameras, the tapes, and alarms. She was in there because she had made a threat once – or so people thought. But she was by no means stupid.

In fact, she considered many times, if people were to look at the books she was reading, they'd either be amazed at how brilliant she was or be utterly terrified. Melanie had learned ages ago that people's perception of a person was all that was required to be invisible.

She would often break out in the middle of the night and use the office computer – which had internet access – down the hall. She knew she would have peace for hours, depending on who was on shift of course. If it were the two who had the shift now, she would be good all night. Others were more difficult as they never stuck with a pattern. She had been there long enough to learn those work patterns: who did what and who did as little as possible. Her mentor had taught her to watch and learn.

More to discover, including how to use a computer.

Melanie loved to learn but was frustrated that she couldn't tell anyone. Not yet.

But soon they'd find out.

The minute hand of Professor Albert Hicks' watch slid effortlessly onto the six. It was half-past ten in the morning, and he was on his third cup of coffee. The folded newspaper in the café had been left by the person before. It had been read, digested, and was now of no more use. Hicks had started the crossword that the person had attempted and corrected the spelling to some of the words, or changed them entirely to the right answers. He took solace in the fact that he was more intelligent than most people. But that came at a price. Loneliness for one. Who could love someone who corrected people all the time?

However, people needed to be taught that they were wrong; how else would they learn?

Professor Hicks got up from his seat and prepared to start his day. He'd already paid for the breakfast. He didn't believe in waiting for staff that seemed to disappear when it was time to pay the bill. He was a methodical man who chose efficiency in all its forms and hated wasting time. But something just went against his schedule. He had people to see, things to discuss, and he didn't want to be kept waiting. He was off to see an old friend and his family, people he had known since they were kids. A band of friends that did pretty much everything together, even attended the same university.

As Hicks reached the tea room door, he stepped to the side, allowing a family to enter. A little red-haired girl thanked him, causing him to smile.

The bright sun made Hicks shield his eyes as he stepped into the street. The smell of exhaust fumes suddenly filled his nostrils as an old VW van clattered past. Black smoke billowing from the tail-pipe like an old locomotive.

Hicks coughed and covered his mouth and nose with a handkerchief. The clean air of the town suddenly spoilt by the relic's oily breath. It had been a long time since he had been back in Harrogate. The bustling town was full of tourists who had come to take in the old buildings and the shopping: Bugattis, Porsches, and Aston Martins lined the streets. The town had money, that was for sure, culture and cash. Two things Hicks loved the most, but cash most of all.

The town where his friends lived wasn't far away, but Hicks used the journey as an excuse to see old haunts again. He smiled as he looked back across the street at the tea room. Its dark wood exterior with brass lettering and pillars with gold caps. Hanging baskets hung from the overhang, displaying a collage of colourful blooms. But he didn't have time to linger.

He had made his purchase at the tea house. Which had consisted of some special blended teas and coffees as well as a few niceties for afters. He had arranged to meet with them early that morning, a date that was set days before. Hicks didn't want to be late.

He couldn't wait to see them again. Especially her. The one that had slipped away from him so many years before.

She who he had loved from afar – she who had been seduced by the other man's charms. But that was all in the past.

Forgotten.

Hicks walked to his car and got in. He sighed gently, a sign of a hearty breakfast and the thought of what he was off to do next. He started the engine of his Mercedes-Benz GLE Coupe and waited. His hands, gripping the leather of the steering wheel until it creaked under pressure.

They had much to discuss.

This was a business.

The past was the past.

He was happy with what he was doing. After all, he didn't need them – not like that anyway. They had other uses; their money for one. Hicks straightened, and a false smile crossed his face. The fake gesture was more for himself than anything.

Things to do, people to see, he said to himself.

He put the automatic shift into drive and pulled onto the road.

This visit wasn't personal.

This was *all* business.

At ten-thirty, Toby came to visit Melanie. He brought a plastic mug with milk and cake. As he entered, he noticed the pile of books on the floor stacked next to her bed and freshly arranged. He figured they were new as he hadn't seen them on the last visit. *Books to read perhaps,* he thought. He paid no attention. The covers seemed old, possibly from the 1960s, maybe older.

Melanie sat in her chair, facing the window. She had seen him come in, using the reflection in the window as a mirror.

She didn't move but continued to read, as if she were oblivious to him standing there.

'Hi,' Toby said with a smile and placed the offering onto the table in front of the window.

Melanie said nothing, simply looked up at him and stared into his blue eyes.

He saw something in those pale blue pools of hers, a sadness of some kind. 'What's wrong?' His voice was filled with genuine concern. He went to hold her hand, but she pulled away. That look of distrust had returned.

Melanie stood and walked to the far corner of the room. Away from the door's window. Toby smiled, knowing she had figured out the professor was using Eric to film her. She sat in the corner and he joined her on the cold laminated floor.

'What you afraid of?' Toby asked, his voice soft and caring.

'Someone watching me, a scary person.' Her voice was gentle, like a whisper on a breeze.

'What person?' he asked, trying not to look at the door. He felt the woman's fear, and it wasn't due to a big black guy with a camera.

'Not here, in my dreams, but I'm awake, as if I'm looking through someone else's eyes, but it's me,' she tried to explain.

He smiled sympathetically and touched her shoulder. 'It's OK, nobody can get you here; you are safe.'

'But it's not me I'm afraid for,' she said.

'Oh, who then?'

'The family that is about to die.'

Toby stared into those blue eyes of hers and shivered. The look was cold and unfeeling, and he edged backwards slightly. So many questions buzzed through his mind. First of which was how did she know who was going to die and when?

Melanie laughed and slapped his leg before jumping up and running back to her chair.

'Jesus, you scared the shit out of me.' He held his chest and released the breath he had been holding. He picked himself off the floor and moved back to the table.

Melanie had started devouring the sponge cake. White sugar powder covered her mouth, and somehow the forehead of the mask.

'So, you cheeky little rat,' Toby said, looking out at the beautiful sunshine. He could feel the warmth it was giving from just being in the room. He smiled happily, gazing at Melanie.

She too was staring out across the lawns, at the pond and the fountain.

'How'd you like to take a walk around the gardens?' Toby whispered as if he were doing something terrible.

Melanie smiled with her eyes and nodded excitedly, unaware the professor had suggested it to Toby and had briefed the rest of the staff.

Soon she would be able to breathe in clean air, feel the sun on her skin and not through thick glass pains. She would smell the freshly mowed grass and the flowers.

But most of all she would see the pond.

And the fountain.

CHAPTER FOURTEEN

BILL BROWN ENTERED THE TEA HOUSE IN HARROGATE. HE had just placed his coat and hat down at a table that a man had just gotten up from. Knowing that he had to give his order to the counter.

The man Bill had seen had worn an expensive-looking suit of brown tweed. He had observed the man as he'd held the door open for a family to enter. The man had smiled when a little red-haired girl had thanked him. Bill's thoughts wandered to another place while he waited – the man and the women at the house he'd just been to.

Home.

His trail of thought was interrupted by a young man behind a glass-fronted display counter telling him it wasn't waiter service and to order. Bill left his hat and jacket to mark it as *this spot is taken*, his eyes transfixed on the mouthwatering goodies that lay on display. The fellow behind the counter was in his late teens, possibly early twenties. His black hair was styled with a side parting and the thin frame sported black trousers, waistcoat, and white shirt uniform.

'What can I get you, sir?' His tone was polite and friendly.

Bill wondered if the man was sick of false platitudes by the end of the day, or was he truly always that happy to see people? Bill knew all too well the difference between a sale and having the door slammed in one's face; it was indeed all about how you came across to people.

Bill tapped his lips with pressed together index fingers as he waited for his stomach to make up its mind. 'I'll have a cup of your special brew coffee and a slice of that.' He pointed to a three-inch-thick gateau that sat in the middle of other amazing looking cakes. He knew it was early, but it looked too good to pass up. Besides, he would soon be home and eating salads.

He paid and was informed his order would be brought over to him. Bill smiled and thanked the man, then returned to his seat, his thoughts now a million miles away.

The new job wouldn't take long. Once the fitters had been in, it was his job to go back and make sure everything worked and the customers were happy. He preferred the customer-service role. After all, he was a people person, a friendly sort which helped in so many ways.

Bill opened his briefcase and flicked through files. Two jobs had been finished recently, one not too far from his home; the other was twelve miles away. He looked at the pictures he had taken – most of all, the sneak shot of the mother and daughter together, both with short blonde hair, ages of around forty and eighteen.

The house nearby also had a mother and daughter, but they had strawberry-blonde hair, and there was also a son but his hair was dark, possibly like his father's. He knew he would have to make a call to see both families at some point to make sure that everything was working OK.

A small petite girl came over with his order. Her tiny voice brought him back to reality with an 'Excuse me, sir.'

He smiled and made room on the table for her to place the items.

The aroma of strong black coffee filled his nostrils and his mouth began to water at the sight of the cake. For a brief moment, all thought was put on hold as he dug the pudding fork into its soft structure and placed the piece into his hungry maw. His eyes closed and he let out a small whimper of pleasure; he was in heaven.

Bill devoured the gateau, savouring each delicious bite when he finally noticed the folded paper the man before must have left. The article on the front page caught his eye. An update on the killing was all over the papers and social media. His smile was subtle.

Someone was making a name for themselves, he decided, but his dark thoughts turned elsewhere. He could see blood or death – profit. Sales had already boosted since last month.

People were afraid, and that was good for business.

His other colleagues thought he was sick to suggest such a thing, but Bill was a realist. After twenty minutes, he stood, fed and watered and ready to hit the road. He looked at the briefcase and smiled; he didn't need to go straight home, not yet.

He walked to his Ford Mondeo and used the electronic key to open the door, took off his suit jacket and placed it on the seat hanger at the back. Getting in, he took out the one couple's file and typed the address into his satnav. It quickly calculated the distance: twelve miles.

He smiled and buckled up. One last stop off before he headed home.

Home.

'When can we go?' Melanie asked, her voice fluttering with excitement.

'Later, I have to do my rounds first. When I'm done, I'll come back and get you,' Toby answered with a reassuring smile. As he stared into her hypnotic blue eyes, he could swear he was looking at someone else. He stepped back, but her gaze was fixed as though she were frozen. 'Are you OK?'

Melanie shook her head and looked at him. Her eyes large, so very blue and playful.

'Yes, why?' she asked, as if oblivious to what had happened.

Toby shook his head and smiled. 'Nothing, you just zoned out for a second, that's all.'

'Did I? Strange ... I didn't feel any different. So, when are we going?' she asked, as though the last conversation had never taken place.

'Uhm – after my rounds. I'll come and get you. I told you like a second ago.' He was completely confused – and a little scared. Was this why she had been sent away? Was she schizophrenic? Had she multiple personalities? Suddenly, he didn't want to know. All he wanted to do was leave and never come back. But he had made contact, established a rapport. He was her only friend ... and that scared him the most.

What was *her* idea of friendship?

Toby left the room in silence. Melanie had gone back to her book. As the door clicked shut, he slammed his back against the sterile white walls and exhaled slowly. His eyes looked up at the ceiling as if seeking answers.

'You know you got to carry on with this or the prof is going to make your life hell,' Eric said sternly.

Toby looked at Eric, his face filled with mixed emotions. On one side, he felt sorry for the girl. On the other, he was bloody terrified by her. 'The prof can go fuck himself. There's no way I'm doing this, for her sake and my soul,' he growled.

'Sorry mate, you gave up your soul when you started working in this fuckin' dump,' Eric laughed, then shrugged, but somehow Toby knew the big man wasn't joking.

Hicks – like his father before him – was a control freak. Those sorts always got what they wanted, no matter who it hurt, or the consequences.

Toby looked back into the room at the helpless looking young woman. She was a little girl trapped in a woman's body, or so she would have people believe. That was her camouflage, but Toby didn't buy it. There was more too her, possibly a scary, even dangerous side, but curiosity was beginning to change his mind.

'Screw it, I'm gonna carry on trying to help her,' Toby declared, his gaze locked onto Melanie as she sat and read. He turned towards Eric, his face twisted with rage.

'See, knew you'd see it my way,' Eric grinned as he leant against the wall of the corridor.

'I'm not doing it for him, you, even me. I'm doing it for *her*,' Toby growled.

'Hey, whatever mate, don't really give a shit what you do as long as it gets the professors off our arses,' Eric laughed, tucking away the camera. 'Come on, we got shit to do.'

He slapped a giant arm around Toby's shoulders as the two walked back to the gate.

As the men walked away, Melanie's masked face was pressed up against the glass of the small window of the door. Her breath started to fog up the cold double-paned glass. She had heard everything. She had already suspected something was wrong.

Didn't matter. Soon she would be out.

Inhaling fresh air. Feeling the sun on her skin.

Re-checking the way out of the grounds.

CHAPTER FIFTEEN

PC SUMMERS DROVE THE JAGUAR XF LIKE A RALLY DRIVER down the country roads. Platt sat trying to look calm as she handled the police vehicle like a pro.

Summers was a tall woman, around six feet, with a slender build and long black hair tied up into a regulation bob at the back. At twenty-five, and after seven years of service, she had seen a lot – but nothing like what had come to her part of the country.

'So, you put in for CID last year?' Platt asked before she took a corner sharply.

'Yes, guv,' she replied with a concentrated look on her face.

'What took you so long?'

'Personal problems guv.'

'Your parents you mean? I believe they were the second family to ...'

'Yeah, the second family to make those bastards' headlines,' she growled before realising her outburst. 'Sorry, guv,' she said with a nervous smile.

'No need to apologise, I quite understand. The press had a

field day, possibly because you're a police officer.' Platt nodded, then looked out the window. 'Is that why you dyed your hair and grew it long?'

'Something like that, but I'd done it years before.'

'You think your decision to be independent, to not look like your sister and mother, saved your life?' Platt asked, intrigued.

'May have done, but I was in London when it happened. I was on a course with the Met.'

Platt nodded again as he stared at the countryside as it whizzed past. Suddenly, a thought came to him, something in the report of her family's murder. He opened up a leather-bound organiser that held the case files. He shuffled through them until he found the one on her parents. 'In all of the cases, the doors had been left opened when the response teams went in, apart from yours; they had said your door was locked, and they had to force it open,' Platt said, puzzled.

'Yeah, I used to lock it ... keep my sister out,' she replied with a broken smile and she suddenly missed telling her sister off for stealing her stuff.

'But how did the killer know you weren't there? I mean, if he had no idea you were gone, he would have kicked down the door himself, wouldn't he?'

'You mean ... the bastard has been watching us?' A look of horror crossed her face.

'It makes sense,' Platt said. 'I think our killer knew everything about all the victims because he was observing them.' He looked over at Summers as a terrifying thought entered his mind, but he didn't have the heart to share it, not while she was driving anyway.

What if the killer had chosen that night to kill her parents because she hadn't been there ... because she looked different meant he couldn't kill her? What would have happened if she had stayed? Would the killer have chosen someone else? Would her family still be alive?

'So, what's our first move, guv?' She held back the need to cry.

'We tear the latest victims' house apart. I want to know if there are any cameras in there,' Platt said, his face filled with rage. Angry that he hadn't thought of it months ago, but then this was the first indication that the killer had made a mistake. Also, he hadn't been in charge before.

Just the mishap he was waiting for.

As they drove up to the Thomas' house, Summers found a spot and parked the black unmarked vehicle near the driveway. The big yellow X-shaped police tape was still stuck to the front door, meant to deter people from entering.

They walked up and stopped. There was a breeze blowing from the north. A crisp, biting wind caused both of them to shiver.

'You OK with this?' Platt asked.

'You wouldn't have brought me if you didn't think I was ... would you, guv?' she replied. Causing Platt to smile, confirming his assessment of her.

He had followed her career ever since her application had been submitted. He wanted to know everything about each candidate. This was her hour to shine or crumble.

Platt unlocked the door using the key he had gotten from CSI. Inside was still a mess. Furniture had been overturned in either a struggle or because the killer was enraged.

'We going upstairs, sir?' Summers asked as she began to mount the staircase.

'Why Constable Summers, that's a little forward!' he

declared with an almost straight face. He could see she was uncomfortable, so he risked the joke, which seemed to work.

'Guv, really?'

'Yeah, I know,' he laughed and shrugged. 'No, first I want to look around the ground floor. It's the first time I've had a chance to look at this place without thousands of people everywhere,' he admitted. 'I can get a better feel for the place like this.'

He walked around slowly, with Summers close behind. She gave him space to do whatever it was he was doing. he moved about with his hands stretched out as though he were touching the walls from afar. For him, every piece of overturned furniture, every smashed plate and cup, everything that wasn't in place, told a story.

'What do you see, guv?'

Platt stopped, turned and smiled. 'The question is, what do *you* see?'

Summers nodded and began to move around.

'Stop, just look ... you don't need to move, it's all there.'

She nodded again and stood still, surveying the chaos before her.

'Everything has a pattern, a sign of movement if you will,' he started to explain.

Summers looked at him, puzzled.

'OK, take that vase over there. We know it wasn't thrown straight on because of the displacement patterns. The furniture was overturned—'

'In a clockwise manner, judging by the way everything is facing towards the centre of the room,' Summers noted aloud. Then she looked back at the staircase that ran up the side of the wall near the main entrance. 'The killer had done this after, possibly out of frustration or anger.' She looked back at Platt, who seemed to be smiling. 'What's wrong?'

'The killer made a mistake,' Platt stated.

'What do you mean?'

'He's never done this before, something went wrong ... he lost control.' He peered around for more evidence of this theory.

'Which means he isn't as cold and calculating as what we thought,' Summers said with a cunning grin.

'It also means we have a chance to catch the bastard.'

CHAPTER SIXTEEN

'THEY ARE GOING TO DIE, AND I'M GOING TO TAKE pleasure in it,' Melanie said again. Suddenly, she woke from the nightmare. A terrible dream she'd had for years. One that had gotten her locked up in the first place.

They had all misunderstood. Thinking that the words Melanie uttered were her own.

But it was the dream – no, the voice in the dream – the memory?

She sat up in the chair and took off the mask to rubbed her bloodshot eyes. She had no idea how long she had been sleeping, all she knew was that it was a lot later, judging by the sun's position in the sky. It had moved from one side of the window to the other ... around two hours then, give or take. Melanie glanced at the door. She felt sad and alone.

He hadn't come back, and she didn't know why. Perhaps he had come back while she was sleeping and hadn't wanted to disturb her?

She looked at the table and found the plate and plastic mug gone.

She smiled. He had come for her, but she had slept through it. Melanie wrapped her arms around herself and squeezed, giving herself a reassuring cuddle.

She gazed at the window and the gardens, the trees, the grass. She had missed her chance. He was probably busy with his rounds or taking a break. Hopefully, her chance would come again tomorrow.

There was a click as the door was unlocked and then opened. Melanie turned to see Toby standing there with a smile on his face.

'I was hoping you'd be awake. Still want to go?' He didn't need to ask a second time, as Melanie was already up on her feet and scampering across the floor.

She wrapped her arms around him and squeezed, and as she did so, she inhaled his scent. She had never smelt someone who smelled so good, not here anyway. Most wore too much perfume or deodorant – or worse, none.

But he smelt nice. No! Exciting.

She had no real idea because she'd never experienced a pleasant smell, well not since she was little anyway. All she knew was body odour, cleaning fluids, cheap perfume and, from time to time, a smell of something burnt – a cigar, a familiar scent that she had known from her childhood. But the aroma she was getting from Toby was different; she couldn't put a finger on it, just that it made her feel funny.

Most of the books and novels had called it *arousal*. But Melanie had no concept of the thing; how could she?

Not until now, anyway.

'Everything OK?' Toby asked, concerned that she was going to have another episode.

'Yeah. Just excited, I guess,' she lied. She was thankful for the mask; underneath it, she could have any expression she wanted. As far as Toby knew, she was smiling.

In reality, she was unsure – unsure about a great many things, one of which was this stranger she had built an attachment to. Why was it that she felt safe with him?

She trusted him implicitly, for a reason she couldn't explain. She felt drawn to him like a long-lost love she had known in a previous life.

'Come on then. Let's go,' he said with a smile and held out his hand.

Nervously, Melanie took it and let him lead her through bright corridors and to the gate at the security room. There was a buzzing noise and the gate opened as they approached. Toby waved at the two men who sat inside the security room. They waved back as the two passed through. Melanie had never been this way before, not for a long time anyway. Her normal exit was through the staff bathroom and the vent in the wall.

Or so they had thought.

In fact, she had stumbled onto the plans for the building one day on the internet. They had been blueprints of the place when it was a grand mansion, revealing all the floors and secret passages. The hall had been built in the Elizabethan era. Melanie had read about that period of British history; it had been when priests had been persecuted. When architects had placed priest holes and escape tunnels into most large estates, which had been owned by the Catholic priests or those sympathetic to them. The new owners cared little for the history of the place. This, fortunately for Melanie, meant that a passage in the staff office at the end of the corridor had remained undiscovered.

Until she came along, that is.

Melanie had gotten out many times. At least once a month, always at night for obvious reasons. But she always ended up at the pond and the fountain. Nobody had an idea why she still went there; it wasn't as if there was anything spectacular about them.

As they stepped outside, Toby released her hand. Melanie tipped her head back, stretched out her arms and began to twirl. She began to giggle like a little girl and skip on the gravelly driveway in her bare feet. She felt the warmth of the sun on her skin, and it was glorious. Toby watched with a broad smile.

Melanie seemed so innocent and ecstatic. Almost as if an eight-year-old version of her were there, moving across the driveway towards the grass. She danced, skipped, and hopped. Finally, she dropped onto the ground and made grass angels, feeling the warm blades of short-cut grass on her skin. She wanted to stay there all day, all week ... forever.

Then she looked up at Toby with gratitude. And then she saw Eric, who stood not far behind him with that damned camera. The smile left her eyes, and she stood.

Toby turned to see Eric's massive frame behind him, video camera in hand. 'Really, can't you give her five minutes of peace?' He shook his head and ran after Melanie, who had stormed off towards the fountain.

'Hey, the prof said I have to film everything, even you two getting cosy, or her cutting your friggin' head off,' Eric laughed.

'Melanie, wait!' Toby called. But she continued on her course. 'Hey, hold up!' He caught up with her and grabbed her arm.

Melanie stopped and shot him a look that caused him to let go and step back. Her eyes were bloodshot and large black pupils stared back at him angrily.

As if he were the one who had betrayed her. 'It's not me; it's the professor. He told Eric to film everything, apparently for research. They think I have done something miraculous because you talk to me.' Toby shrugged lamely. 'The professor thinks to be with me can help you, and he wants to document it all, possibly get himself a Nobel prize or some shit like that.' Toby laughed.

But her frightening stare didn't waver.

Finally, Melanie's eyes took on a long-dead stare – the one she gave the rest of the staff.

The trust had gone. He was now dead to her.

As Toby watched, she reached the fountain and placed her hand into the murky water.

Melanie felt the cold water on her fingers as she moved in small figure eights.

She was silent, lost in the moment – a moment Toby didn't want to disturb. He had already urged Eric to hold his distance, allowing this strange, masked angel to have a moment in the sunlight – a moment of bliss.

Melanie gazed over to the pond that lay just over the way, her fingers still feeling the top of the water. Sometimes her fingers would dip a little deeper, but never so deep to get her palm wet.

Toby was almost hypnotised by this display. There was an innocence about the scene that he could not understand.

Suddenly, she stopped. As if something had disturbed her, broken her concentration – disturbed her time of bliss. Melanie wrenched her hand back and ambled quietly back to her room, Toby immediately behind.

Her eyes remained cold. Everything – everyone – was dead to her.

'Nice going, jackass,' Toby growled at Eric as they passed him.

'What the fuck did I do? Hey, you ain't blame me for this,' Eric yelped. The giant realised Hicks would have his arse in a sling for messing up.

Toby followed Melanie back to her room, remaining silent

all the way, even as she entered her room and headed to her chair. She sat with her knees drawn to her chest and her arms wrapped around them, making herself a ball of self-comfort. As the door closed, her gaze remained on the grass, as if treasuring the moment. But under the mask, Melanie wore an evil grin.

Everything was still there.

Just as she had left it.

CHAPTER SEVENTEEN

It was around eleven o'clock in the morning when Bill Brown pulled up to the next house's driveway on his list of visits. As he drove towards the house, he could hear the thump-thump-thump of his car's tyres hammering against the drive-way's stone-slab construction. The car swayed as a result of the uneven ground where the stones were no longer as flat as they once were.

The house was impressive. A red-brick Georgian construction, with bright white-framed windows that contrasted nicely with red bricks, and a large sandstone balcony acted as an over-hanging entrance. The front garden was full with miniature ferns, summer plants in Greek-style urns. To the side, but not fixed to the house, was a double garage made from the same style brick, and the electric shutter doors were white-painted aluminium. The house, though old, fitted in well with the neighbouring houses.

Each one smelled of cash.

As Bill pulled up, he saw the man from the tea house again. This time he was saying his goodbyes and getting into his brand new silver Mercedes GLE. The air between the man and the family seemed friendly, but also held an atmosphere of tension.

As the German-made sports car pulled away, Bill drove up slowly and parked where the Mercedes had been.

Slowly, Bill breathed in, then out. Letting the air pass through his teeth. He was unaware of how his presence there would be received.

He watched the family as they waved their farewells to the man who had driven off, and waited for a moment. As if contemplating what the correct time to exit the vehicle and announce himself was.

He breathed in and out. All the while, his longing gaze fell on the woman.

The one that got away.

He breathed in and out, even more slowly this time, and watched as the other family members went inside, leaving the husband outside.

Bill unclipped his seat belt, opened his door, and put on a welcoming smile. 'Morning, Mr Freeman, how are we today?'

'Bugger off Bill, you old sod, you can drop the salesman shit,' Jason said with a laugh as he embarrassed his brother-in-law. 'Come in, I've just made coffee.' Jason let Bill in to greet the rest of the family. As Jason closed the door, he looked back at the empty driveway entrance; his face held a solemn look, as though he'd just gotten disturbing thought.

'Hi, Uncle Bill,' shouted a young woman from the kitchen.

'Danni, get your arse out here and say hello properly,' Jason yelled and shook his head, laughing. 'Bloody kids.'

Bill smiled and shrugged as if he understood. Bill looked over at the kitchen door as it opened, and a young blonde woman walked out to greet him.

'Hi Uncle Bill, how's it going?' Danni asked, shaking his hand with a lack of enthusiasm.

'Hi, how're things?' Not really expecting an answer of more than a shrug or a grunt, he was welcomed with both before she headed back to the kitchen.

Jason rolled his eyes with disappointment and slapped Bill on the shoulder. 'Come on, let's get you that coffee.'

Bill smiled and followed them into the kitchen.

But Jason's thoughts elsewhere – they wrestled with the conversation he'd had with the last visitor, Professor Albert Hicks.

As they entered the kitchen, Bill noted the vast modern kitchen area, with its grey marble-work surface and cream-coloured draws. The floor was comprised of the original black and white tiling. The walls were white with lots of stained wood shelving and brass ornaments. It was a pleasant medley of colour, a mix of old and new.

Bill's gaze was locked on the woman who stood next to the sink. She was blonde and tall. Behind her was a long window, which allowed the morning sun to pour in, shrouding the woman in a brilliant haze. She looked like an angel.

An angel that should have been his.

'So, how's my darling sister? Haven't heard from her for a while,' Abby Freeman said, combing her fingers through her short hair.

'Oh, she's fine. Mad at me as usual for being away, but it pays the bills,' Bill laughed.

Everyone took a seat at the breakfast bar while Jason set up coffee cups. They chatted mostly about family and what had been going on since their last get-together. The air was full of small talk and plans for future family gatherings.

None of which would ever happen.

'The reason I'm here is to check that everything is running OK with the security system they just installed,' Bill said with an apologetic smile and shrug.

'Sure, no probs,' Abby said, standing up to accompany him to the central server box that transmitted all the information to the security firm.

'Any problems?' Bill asked, knowing full well there wouldn't be.

'No, everything is great. I think we all sleep a lot better knowing it's there,' Abby admitted.

Bill smiled and nodded in appreciation for the review. 'Well, you can never be too careful, especially now.'

'What, with all the killings you mean?' Abby's smile began to fade as she shot a look over at Danni, her expression full of concern, as if she hoped Danni hadn't heard the conversation.

Danni just sat on the stool while she texted a friend. 'I'm sorry – what?' Her gaze shifted from person to person, as though she had missed something important.

'Nothing Danni, go back to your phone,' Bill laughed.

'I was referring to a spate of burglaries in the area,' Bill lied, knowing full well there had been only two in the last two weeks and they had been miles apart.

Abby smiled and nodded as if to confirm what he was saying.

The server was no bigger than a games console, which lived in a cupboard under the stairs. Danni had named it Harry, which Jason thought was weird but Abby found adorable.

'This may take a while, so there's no need to stick around if you don't need to,' Bill said, hoping his sister-in-law would leave him to it.

'Great, I have to pop to the shops anyway with Jason,' Abby said with relief that her plans for the day wouldn't be ruined. 'Danni will be here, probably in her room chatting online with her mates.' Abby grabbed her coat and handbag from behind the wall hangers behind him.

'No, probs, shouldn't be long. I'll probably be gone when

you get back though ... gotta get back home before your sister divorces me,' Bill laughed.

The two hugged and said their farewells, making plans to call, which probably would never happen. Bill got back to work as Abby left, taking his laptop from his briefcase and plugging it into the server. It took a moment while the PC found the server and opened a screen. Bill went into the access program and the hard drive. Several small windows opened, revealing the feed from the hidden cameras. Two of which were in the bedrooms. Bill smiled as he began to make copies of the feeds, paying particular interest to the bedrooms of his sister-in-law and niece.

As he waited for the download to finish, his gaze turned to Danni's room and the live feed. Saliva began to collect at the side of his mouth, his lecherous gaze transfixed as he watched Danni take off her clothes and get into training shorts and top, ready for her daily workout at the gym. It took everything in his willpower to keep him from sliding his hand down his trousers, touching himself as this sweet young thing paraded around half-naked.

Suddenly the peep show was interrupted by a large screen popping up to tell him that the download was complete. Bill wiped his mouth on his sleeve and packed away the equipment. His hands still shaking. As he closed the door to the closet, his back fell against the door, and he closed his eyes, as though trying to burn the image of his niece's supple body into his brain.

Bill pushed himself off the door and headed for the stair-well. 'I'm off then,.'

There was no reply.

'Danni, I'm off,' he shouted again, but louder. He looked up the slim staircase and started up. Taking each step slowly, all the while his imagination sending vivid images into his mind.

As he reached the door, he went to knock, but it opened. And there stood Danni in nothing but a towel barely wrapped around her.

'I'm off then,' Bill said nervously.

'Really, you could stay. My parent's aren't home; in fact, they'll be gone for ages,' Danni said, grabbing his tie and pulling him into the room. He followed like an obedient dog on a leash. Danni pushed him onto the bed and stood before him.

'Danni, I really should ...' His words were cut short as the towel fell, revealing that athletic body and those firm pert breasts.

Danni straddled him and kissed him hard. Bill wrapped his arms around her, but she pulled them off and forced them down onto the bed. She smiled and inched her way down his body, her fingers gently digging into the flesh under his clothes. As she reached his trousers, he closed his eyes, waiting to feel her mouth, her lips around him.

A loud shriek erupted as a black-and-white cat forced itself past Bill as he stood on the stairwell. The cat, unimpressed by the visitor disturbing its slumber, had shocked him back to reality.

'You OK Uncle Bill? Damn cat is always sleeping where it shouldn't,' Danni said, rushing out of her room to see what the noise was about.

'I'm fine, really. I called up, but I guess you were busy,' Bill said, eyeing the headphones and laptop in her hand.

'Yeah, sorry, just chatting with the girls,' she laughed.

'OK, well I'm off, so I'll catch you sometime soon,' Bill said with a quick wave.

'Bye then. Give my love to Aunty Ann and Debs.'

'Will do.' He started back down the stairs.

He was glad she hadn't seen him.

CHAPTER EIGHTEEN

IT WAS JUST AFTER LUNCHTIME WHEN HICKS RETURNED to the hospital. Melanie knew this because the staff had begun to herd the patients back inside, something she had noticed as she peered over the top of the book she was reading.

It was a book on medical procedures that she'd taken from the staff room library. Melanie didn't think anyone would mind – or probably notice.

She watched with amusement as the staff manoeuvred patients back inside like they were lost sheep.

Hicks drove the Mercedes onto the parking space and got out. As he moved towards the entrance, he locked the car using the electronic key without glancing back and hurried inside. Melanie observed the goings-on but paid the events little attention; nothing was out of the ordinary.

A daily occurrence, in fact.

Melanie had to admit she had never met the man in the car. She didn't even know who he was. She had only seen him from afar, coming and going. Usually, she could make out the same time of day without using a timepiece. Usually, just after or during breakfast, he would be back before lunch, but Melanie didn't care who he was.

Why should she?

To Hicks, however, Melanie was all part of the package. She came with the furniture, a problem he had inherited. Of course, this problem offered a handsome paycheque at the end of each month. She was money for nothing because she didn't cause him problems; she wasn't a bother to the staff. But, most of all, she didn't technically exist.

Melanie was given some leeway, especially with her breaking out every so often because they knew she wouldn't leave the grounds. She would just go for her midnight stroll.

To Hicks, she was *easy* money as long ... as she continued to behave.

Melanie lost interest in the performance outside and her attention returned to the book. Paying particular interest to the drugs and gases used during operations. She'd taken a book sleeve from one of her other books and wrapped it around this one, just in case there was an unexpected caller.

Melanie's eyes gazed up and across the lawns to the fountain and the lake. She smiled and went back to her reading. Digesting every word and technique. She had no idea when she would need this information, nor what had driven her to it in the first place; all she did know was that she had to be ready.

A long time had passed since her dreams had started, the other life full of love, laughter, family. But she had been told years ago that her family was dead. Murdered by the killer that now filled the newspapers and the internet.

Her mentor had spent years training her, teaching her about things and the world outside, preparing Melanie as best as possible for the day she left the clinic.

But Melanie – for all that she had learned – was still naive to the ways of the outside world. She was still unprepared for it, ... as much as it would be unprepared for her.

She had her own set of rules. All her right and wrong reasons came from novels, not taught by parents as they did other children. As far as Melanie was concerned, she had no parents; they had made that decision for her ten years ago.

She had read the news articles on the internet about the killer, making it her mission to find him – or her. She believed that the killer had something to do with her incarceration. There was something about how the killer picked the victims that seemed familiar, but she didn't know why.

Something in her dreams – or memories?

Melanie had also taken an interest in the two policemen who were in charge of the case: DI Richard Platt and DS David Elford.

They seemed capable, but there something was wrong. Why was it taking so long to catch the killer? She realised from reading crime novels, true crime and fiction, that the media didn't provide everything, mostly to prevent copycats.

So, what *weren't* they telling the press?

Of course, she realised that the whole dead-family explanation could possibly be to keep her there. Not that she felt the drive or need to try and get out and play Happy Families with them. Larksford had become her home.

Still, it was nearly time to leave. She had things to do.

She had someone to find.

Melanie's mentor had told her not to believe anything she heard in that place.

'Trust your instincts, trust your gut,' Melanie's mentor had told her. 'The world is full of bad people who will take everything from you, but there are also a few good ones. You will know which are which; you have a good take on people.'

Melanie turned the page and her eyes widened. There was a section on the correct drugs to stop someone from going into shock or cardiac arrest during a procedure. Her smile broadened as she studied the section at length.

A knock on the door made her look up and quickly close the book, just as it opened.

Toby stood at the entrance, looking sheepish and apologetic. Luckily, the mask hid her smile, making him unsure about her feelings at seeing him. Sure, she had been a bitch towards him, but she knew he'd come back, possibly feeling guilty.

'Sorry about that,' he apologised, his voice filled with sincerity.

Her smile changed to a cat-like a grin. She had him.

'I don't appreciate been taken advantage of,' she replied in a stern, but sultry tone. She knew there was no way they would stop filming even if she didn't want them to. She had to keep it together. 'I've no doubt asking for the filming to stop would have no effect?'

Her words puzzled Tony. She sounded more her age than the little girl persona.

She let out a laugh and jumped up and hugged him.

Toby grinned and shook his head. 'You know sometimes I don't know when you're making a joke, or you're being serious.' He strolled to the table.

Suddenly she shot between him and the table, grabbing his hand, and leading him in a waltz.

'All you people are too serious. You should laugh more,' Melanie said simply.

'You could be right.' Toby smiled, wondering about her. As he held her close, he could smell the strawberry-scented shampoo she used, and the warmth of her soft skin made him shudder. He pulled away and rubbed his hands together out of nervous frustration. The woman in the mask was hypnotic, like a siren from Greek tales.

'I thought we might try that walk again, this time without a chaperone,' Toby laughed.

Melanie stopped twirling as she danced with an invisible partner. 'Maybe, don't know yet, I'm still mad ...' She paused and looked around as if realising what she had just said and laughed. 'Mad at you I mean ... not mad mad.' She made a subtle gesture with her index finger twirling next to the side of her head. 'But then again, who knows?' She shrugged as she jumped onto her bed and sat crossed-legged. 'I'm sleepy. It's been a long day.'

Toby nodded and turned to walk away. 'I'll check on you later; maybe we could talk some more?'

'No, I'm good, I got a lot of reading to do ... maybe tomorrow,' Melanie replied blandly. Her mask was hiding her playful grin.

She was toying with him, seeing how far he would bend.

She knew the professor had sent him; after all, Toby had admitted as such. What she didn't know was why. Less for the cock-and-bull story he had come out with about the professor's interest in curing her. Why was *she* so unique?

She didn't need healing, and there was nothing wrong with her, less for being locked away with a bunch of lunatics – and they were the staff.

Toby waved goodbye and left. As the door closed, Melanie fell back onto the bed. She closed her eyes as she grinned with excitement. Then the grin faded and she looked over at the door. Her eyes became cold and unfeeling. The time was close, and she was almost ready. She couldn't let herself be distracted, especially by him.

There would be time for that later – or so she hoped, *when* it was all done.

When she was free ... and they all had gotten what they deserved.

CHAPTER NINETEEN

BILL HAD HEADED HOME. HE WAS TIRED AND WANTED nothing more than to be back with the family. Picking up his mobile telephone, he pressed the button that said *HOME* on display and let it ring for a while before the answering machine kicked in.

'Hi, honey, I'm on the way back now. I'll just pop into the shops first to pick up a few things on the way. Should be back in around an hour. Love you both ... speak to you later,' he said with a content smile.

After being away longer than he expected this time, he was finally going back home. Usually, his trips would only take a week at most, but this one required a little more time than expected.

But that was all in the past now.

Now, he could relax for a bit and put up his feet. He looked at his watch. It was nearly one o'clock. He could make a quick stop at the supermarket that was on the way and grab flowers and pizzas. Recently Ann hated to cook or go out for meals; they mostly ate what came out of a packet or could be delivered. But he didn't mind, even though she'd insisted on having a costly kitchen. Possibly to show off to her friends, but they didn't come around much any more – no one did. Even Debs stayed in. Both of them had no social life.

But that didn't matter, they were both home safe – away from the scum of the world.

He put on the stereo and chose one of the disks in the multi loader, smiling as the tune 'Take it Easy' came blaring over the speakers.

Bill was a happy man.

He was going home.

———

Bright honey-coloured shafts of sunlight shone through the double-pained windows of Hicks' office. The criss-cross effect of the leaded windows made long shadows on the polished wooden desk. Hicks sat with a large glass of whiskey in one hand and the computer's mouse in the other as he reviewed the recordings Eric had made.

Hicks watched intently, hoping for something ground-breaking, but there was nothing much to speak of. He'd almost given up watching when suddenly his eyes widened.

Melanie and Toby were outside. She'd lost her temper, but it was as though it wasn't her. Hicks smiled. Just the thing he was waiting for.

Had she multi-personality disorder? Hicks sat forward with interest. His appetite had been tantalised. Then, just as it was getting good, Melanie stormed off. Hicks sat back as he listened to Toby rip into Eric. He leant forwards and switched off the footage, unable to continue after such a blunder.

He had hoped that Toby would have taken after her, with the blundering Eric not far behind. But Toby had stayed in

place, allowing the girl some space. Maybe the lad was an innocent fool after all. Just by letting Melanie be alone, he had
shown her some decency. Hicks hoped *she* saw it that way.

Hicks rewound the footage and watched it several more
times. Her sudden mood change confused and excited him. She
had never displayed such behaviour before, so why now? What
had been the catalyst? Had it been the fresh air, the sunlight?

He took a sip and stood, and headed for the window that
overlooked the front of the building. He watched the patients
walking about freely. They seemed happy in their world. He
cracked a smile when he thought of what he had taken over.
Hicks' father had created a clinic to help mentally ill people.
Albert, on the other hand, he'd turned it into a business.

He didn't really care what happened to the patients as long
as the families kept paying. The nurses came from the bottom
of the barrel; they were cheap and did their jobs. There had
been no lawsuits, criminal proceedings, so he was happy.
Besides, he had enough problems with other things. This place
was just one more thing to worry about.

Hicks had never once spoken to Melanie. The other staff
members thought it odd, but he had his reasons. To Hicks, she
was a subject to be studied, and also a paycheck. He went to
the other window and looked out across the green. More
patients wandered about while some sat in chairs and stared
into whatever world they saw before them. Some lived in the
past and asked for old friends or loved ones, others danced on
another plane altogether. A few were experiencing depression
and needed a safe place to consider life. But there were no
Aldof Hitlers or Jesus Christs at the clinic, no one who thought
they were someone else.

Or maybe there was!

And she had been hiding in plain sight all those years.

Hicks regarded the people outside. Sure, this was a clinic,

but why did he feel like it was a prison ... and he was an inmate just like the rest of them?

———

Melanie sat up. Woken from her slumber by a nightmare. She looked around in a panic, as if she didn't recognise where she was. Rivers of sweat ran down her forehead and back. Her hands were gripping the sheets so tightly, her knuckles had turned white.

Melanie let out a piercing scream, then collapsed.

The door to her room swung open, and Toby and Eric rushed in.

'Melanie? Melanie, are you OK?' Toby asked trying to wake the girl. He felt her carotid artery for a pulse. 'I got a pulse, she's just unconscious.' Toby sighed with relief and turned to head for the door. 'Really? You're filming this?' Anger ripped through him as he spotted the camera in Eric's hand.

'The professor told me to film everything,' Eric explained with a shrug, remembering the scolding he had received from Hicks for messing up in the garden. 'We should wait until she wakes up.' He headed for the chair next to the window.

'We should leave and let her rest, screw your Goddamn movie,' Toby said, grabbing the big man's arm and leading him out.

As the door closed with a metallic thud, Melanie's eyes shot open. In her nightmares, she saw a man with no face ... no ... his face was distorted, as though she weren't paying attention or couldn't focus. The man she had seen before – a long time ago. A time before the nightmares – before the voices in her head.

But Melanie couldn't place where she had seen him. Was it in person, on TV, on the street far away? Everything was blurred. Her dreams were mixed with images from her imagination. Maybe none of it was real? Perhaps she was nuts after all? All she could say for sure was the man was wearing a suit.

Not much to go on.

But there was also a smell, a strange smell of something sweet, but it wasn't aftershave or deodorant.

No – something else.

Something she'd once known, but was now a lost memory. Melanie sat up slowly. Her muscles ached from her ordeal. As she placed a hand over her chest, she felt her heart pounding like an athlete after a marathon run. Melanie glanced at the table and the bottle of water.

Swinging her legs over the side of the bed, she forced herself off the bed. She licked her parched lips, her mouth was dry as a dessert. Pushing up, she headed for the bottled water. Her body screamed as her muscles started to work.

Melanie undid the screw top and pulled up her mask to take in the water. With a gasp, she emptied it. Never had she been so thirsty, but then she'd never had a nightmare like this one before. Melanie stretched her body and sat in the chair opposite the window, looked at the books piled up but didn't have the urge to start reading.

All she wanted to do was gaze out across the green lawn to the fountain and the pond.

'They are going to die, and I'm going to take pleasure in it,' she said, but it was more a recital than a statement. Those words had lost her ten years of her life, ten years of having no idea what they meant.

Who was going to die, and why should she take pleasure in it?

Was it her parents, her teachers? She had less of an idea now than then. But one thing she did know: it hadn't been her voice in her head that had initially spoken those words.

It had been someone else's.

Melanie stripped off her sweat-soaked clothes and wrapped a towel around her, then slipped on her bathrobe. There were no showers in the rooms, so she had to press the call button to get a nurse to take her to the washrooms. Melanie didn't mind; at least it got her out of the room for a while. She could hear the squeak of non-slip shoes on the laminate flooring. Melanie hoped it was anyone but Toby. She couldn't bear to face him – not yet. Not that she disliked his company. It was more the fact that having him around distracted her from her thoughts – and she needed to think.

Usually, for security reasons, it would be a woman. Or rather it was a case of covering arses if something misconstrued should take place. The last thing the clinic needed was a lawsuit because some nurse got handsy. Not that Melanie worried about that, not since the incident. Nothing quite said, 'I can handle myself,' like spitting a bloke's bitten-off cock back at him.

The door opened and a pretty blonde thing stood in the doorway. The nurse had long legs and an hour-glass figure. Her uniform looked as though it was two sizes too small. Melanie smiled behind her mask.

A new approach by the professor perhaps, Melanie wondered. She suspected Eric wouldn't be too far away with that damned camera, probably hoping for some girl-on-girl action. Melanie wondered what this professor's game was – first sending Toby to befriend her and now a woman who looked like she had fallen out of a men's magazine.

'I'm supposed to take you to the showers,' said the woman.

Melanie moved up close and stared the woman in the eyes.

Her eyes were kind, slightly clueless, but sweet.

She looked at the woman's name tag. *Liza* was written in thick black letters on a white name shield. The hospital's policy was first names only, to protect the staff if someone broke out and decided to hunt people down.

'Well, Liza, are you meant to guard me or watch me?' Melanie asked in a sultry voice. Her blue eyes were large and hypnotic.

'Uhm ... just to take you there ... uhm, that's all,' Liza answered, flustered by this young woman's charms.

Melanie pushed past her, ensuring their bodies made contact. As she started down the corridor, Liza held onto the doorframe, her knees close to buckling. Who the hell was this girl?

Melanie continued to smile under the mask. She had researched seduction techniques online, hoping they would help get her out of awkward situations. Now Melanie was just practising for fun and seeing if the instructors on the internet were correct, or just talking shit. So far, she thought she was doing quite well.

As they moved towards the shower stalls, Melanie could feel expectant eyes on her. Men were watching on their monitors in the small security room. Perverts who she had no time for, but they were a necessary evil for her final game.

Everything she had done, learnt and put up with, was all monumental in what she had to do.

But for now, she had to wait.

She had learnt so much, but Melanie still needed one more thing: the name of the person in her nightmares.

CHAPTER TWENTY

LIZA WATCHED AS MELANIE STRIPPED OFF HER BATHROBE and towel, revealing a perfect body. She stood with her back against the tiled wall as she observed the young woman with faltering breaths.

Melanie took the shower gel and lathered her young body, her movements slow and deliberate, ensuring she paid particular attention to her breasts and between her legs.

Liza could feel her legs buckle.

Melanie grinned with delight from behind her mask, which remained in place. She knew there were cameras in the washrooms; they would say it was for the security of staff and inmates, but Melanie knew that it was so these men could satisfy their perversions.

But she was enjoying making them all squirm in their seats. Everything she did was for the end game.

And that was all this was: a game.

'Can you pass me the shampoo, please?' Melanie asked in a tone fit for a siren.

Liza looked at the bottle that sat in the pocket of the

bathrobe, unsure whether Melanie had left it there on purpose. Whatever the reason, Liza felt compelled to retrieve it. She crept forward, the shampoo bottle extended in a straightened arm, ready to snatch it back at the first sign of trouble.

Melanie's movement was slow, almost serpentine. Their fingers and eyes met, and Liza felt herself move forward, drawn in by an invisible thread. Melanie took the bottle from the shivering woman and slinked back under the warm water that washed over her like a summer rain shower. All the while, Melanie's hands seductively moved over her body.

She had seen plenty of videos on the internet – adult films. Her mentor had suggested it would be a good way of learning about seduction. But it gave Melanie insight into what men wanted. Even though the acting was the worst she had ever seen, she knew it wasn't the real point of the movie. But they did teach her about sex.

Melanie's mentor had shown her the websites, told her that even though these things never happened in the real world, they were fantasy, and that's what seduction was: fantasy.

And seduction was misdirection.

All the while Melanie slid her hands over her body and writhed, she thought, 'If you want a show, I'll give you a show … pervs.'

Twenty-minutes later Melanie returned to her room and Liza hurried away. She wore a big smile under her mask. Sure, she'd had fun, but she had also set things in motion. Had Toby seen the feed? Had he stayed or told the others to stop watching? Then she wondered about the professor and his apparent fetish with her.

Melanie went to a small dresser that she'd had for what seemed forever and took out a matching grey t-shirt and shorts, and slipped them on. Her dirty clothes went into a linen laundry bag by the door.

She sighed deeply and somewhat contently, as if the last few hours had been part of a master plan and had gone well. She sat and picked up a book from the pile on the table: *The Idiot's Guide To Home Improvements*.

Her interest fell mainly on fitting and rewiring electrics. She took in the information like a sponge, her lust for knowledge married to her vault of a brain. Melanie could pick locks, hot-wire a car, work a computer, mix poisons and remedies. And she never forgot a fact, a face, a number, anything. Her mentor had diagnosed her with having an eidetic memory. Something, most people, claimed as photographic. Whatever it was, Melanie didn't forget anything.

She wasn't sure if it was that or something else that prompted her mentor's interest in her. But it didn't matter. Melanie had used the opportunity to learn from the woman.

The one thing she couldn't remember, however, was where she had first heard that voice, or who it had belonged too. Neither, did she know the date or the day, even the year. These facts were purposely hidden from her, or so the nurses and staff thought. But she didn't care about those things; they were trivial compared to what she needed to know.

Just like Sherlock Holmes failed to recognise that the Earth went around the sun, she too had little need to know the time in Larksford. It was useless information that took up vital space in her brain.

There was a metallic clunk as the door unlocked, and it opened. She was surprised at the sight of a thin man. Why was he there instead of Eric or Toby? The ghoulish-looking man walked in with a tray; on it rested a cup of milk and a sandwich. He placed it on the table and shot her a broad grin and winked.

'Good show you put on. Maybe we could have a go later?' asked the nurse. He was tall and spindly with black greased-back hair. His facial features had a Balkan or Romanian look.

Melanie leaned back in her chair and put down the book. Her long legs fell open slightly, as if inviting him in.

He wiped his hands down trousers and licked his lips, and his eyes widened as his grin broadened. Slowly, he moved forward.

She made hand movements he didn't understand, almost as if she were trying to send him away. Yet her body lanuague was saying something different, so he interpreted. The man lunged lustfully at her, grabbed her and pulled her close.

Melanie screamed and slapped him, but he seemed to enjoy it. She was glad he couldn't see under the mask.

Couldn't see her smile.

Almost as if she were expecting something to happen.

The door was flewopen, and Eric's massive frame rushed in. He pulled the nurse off Melanie as though he was made of paper.

'But she wants me ... she said so,' the man muttered, confused and angry. He rushed towards Melanie once more, but Eric's branch-like arm shot forwards and clothes-lined the man, knocking him unconscious.

Eric grabbed him and dragged him away by his feet, the bare flesh of the man's back creating a squeaking sound as it was pulled across the linoleum floor.

'Are you OK?' asked one of the other male nurses, his voice filled with genuine concern.

'I don't know what he wanted. Why would he do such a thing?' She sounded innocent.

'The showers ... he probably did it because of what happened in the shower room,' the man said, looking uncomfortable.

'Why, what happened in the shower room?' she asked.

'You know ... you and Liza, the nurse?'

'But I haven't had a shower today ... have I?' Melanie asked, then started to whimper. 'I don't know what's happening anymore.' Her voice was filled with anger and confusion.

The nurse went to place a sympathetic hand on her shoulder but drew back quickly. If she had schizophrenia, she might snap at any time and revert to the other-self.

He stepped toward the door and as he closed it behind him, he could hear Melanie crying – or at least, that's what he thought he was hearing.

———

Hicks sat in his office. He had seen the footage from the shower room. From what he'd viewed, he'd had no choice but to conclude that Melanie indeed had a multi-personality disorder. How many personalities were yet to be seen. So far, only two had come about – the innocent little girl and the brazen adult.

The thin nurse had to be let go. Hicks couldn't risk someone finding out. He looked back over the footage, something puzzling him. He found it odd that Melanie's face was always out of view, but how could she know where the cameras were?

Some years ago, Hicks had gotten a security firm to install the cameras. The feed went to the central server in the basement. It had been a local man, from one of the nearby towns, who had set up the contract. It made things more comfortable if there had been a problem. The work had been done during the refurbishment, making it easier to hide the fact covert cameras were being installed. Adding them after the refurbishment would have lead to too many questions, especially from staff.

Hicks turned to his computer and started to work on a paper he'd been preparing regarding Melanie's condition. He had considered that she was either a sociopath, lying, or a schiz-ophrenic. The idea of multiple personalities had also crossed his mind. He feared, however, that he would be pushing the boundaries without substantial evidence.

He had theorised that there would have to be more tests done to arrive at any conclusions. Eventually, he would send off the paper and get it published in a – or all – medical magazines. He set to work, noting the change from the passionate woman to the innocent child to the angry aggressive woman. There was no catalyst for a shift from one personality to the other from what he could detect.

For some, it was a stress factor, a smell, a taste, or even a word.

But for Melanie, it was different. She could come and go in the blink of an eye. But the only one that seemed to have some control over her was Toby.

Her attitude towards him was more that of a sibling than a sexual one. Almost as if they were related. But this of course was impossible. He was from the States and older than her.

Hicks rocked in his chair. Thoughts buzzed around in that brain of his like septic flies in a jar. He smiled smugly as he hatched a plan to see how she would react. However, the project would take some planning.

But he had time. She wasn't going anywhere.

CHAPTER TWENTY-ONE

In the Thomas house, Platt and Summers went to the upstairs bedroom where the bodies had been found. Summers held a hand over her nose and mouth to lessen the smell of lingering bodily fluids and the chemicals the CSIs had used to collect evidence.

The windows had been kept shut to stop insects from further contaminating the scene. There was a massive stain of blood on the parents' bed where both mother and daughter had been tied down and one at time, raped, tortured, and eventually killed. In the corner of the room was another blood pool, and the wall splattered with blood. Indicating where the father had been tossed after he'd been murdered. The marks indicated an arterial spray, which collaborated the pathologist's report, which stated the father had been shot in the top side of the head.

Summers fought the stench a little longer before running to the bathroom to puke. Platt smiled and shook his head. He remembered his first crime scene, but it was in Kosovo during the war. His squad had been sent to check out a village but found nothing but bodies. Women that had had their babies cut out of their bellies, children decapitated. All the men were gone; they were off fighting somewhere, leaving their homes undefended. He remembered walking into a school and quickly running out to throw up. The long summer had quickened decomposition, leaving a rank smell ... and wild dogs and rats had played their part in tearing at the bodies.

Platt was abruptly brought back to the present as his mobile telephone began to buzz, telling him he had a message. He took out the device and checked. It was the pathologist's office. It appeared that both the parents and the daughter had been moved since the time of death.

Platt sent an emoji of a thumbs up. And promptly got a smiley face in return.

'You done in there?' he shouted after Summers but got no reply. He left the bedroom and went in search of his temporary partner and found her not in the bathroom, but the room of the daughter.

'Find anything?' he asked, seeing that she seemed steadier.

'This is odd, guv,' Summers replied, looking at old photographs on the walls.

'What's odd?' Platt walked over to Summers, who was staring at one particular group of pictures.

'They recently changed their hairstyles; both mother and daughter used to be brunette with long hair up until these photographs.' She pointed to the set of holiday snaps.

'Well, I'll be ... find out when these photos were taken, get our techs to search any laptops, computers, social media, anything. Find out when they changed their hair colour.' Platt smiled, pleased. Finally, they might have something to work on!

As Summers went around collecting as many pictures as possible to refer to, Platt took out his phone and looked at his own family photos. They had been a happy family, Platt, his wife, and his twin eighteen-year-old son and daughter. While he and his son had dark hair, his wife and daughter had short blonde hair.

'I think I have enough, guv,' Summers said as she packed the last photograph into an evidence bag.

Platt didn't respond straight away; he was lost in his thoughts.

'Guv, you OK?' Summers' voice rang with concern.

'What? Yes, I'm fine, just looking at pictures of my family, sorry,' he apologised.

Being the inquisitive type, Summers bent her head to take a look.

'Beautiful, aren't they?' He showed a picture of them together in a park or someplace with a tree line and double-dish fountain with strange bronze creatures and a pond in the background.

'Great looking family, sir,' she smiled.

Platt nodded with a lost look on his face as he tucked the phone back into his pocket.

'Thanks.' He took a deep breath and exhaled slowly, as if composing himself. Then, he chuckled and said, 'Right, I think we're done here for now. Let's head back to see what trouble my DS has gotten himself into, shall we?'

Summers smiled broadly and nodded. As they left the house, she couldn't help but feel there had been something off about the photograph, but she couldn't put her finger on what.

Something didn't sit right about the killer's MO and this family.

CHAPTER TWENTY-TWO

Bill pulled up onto the driveway of his house. It was a modest size with concrete slabs down the centre and gravel at the sides for drainage. At the end of this was a single garage, which held his wife's car. The garage was built onto the house with an internal door for easy access. The dwelling was a post-war build, around 1950 or so, with red brick and white double-glazed windows. The front door was sheltered by a modest-sized overhang that held an old-style lamp with yellow dimpled glass.

Bill looked at the house and sighed. It felt like ages since he'd been home.

He turned off the engine and went to get out of the car. Suddenly, his mobile telephone began to ring with a tone from the phone's installed tunes. The electronic melody was annoying, but it forced him to answer or hang up.

'Yes, Bill here.' He seldom gave his last name, in case it was a telemarketer or someone fishing for personal details. 'Hi, glad you called ... oh, you're going for it. OK, right now.'

Bill glanced at his house. The new customers sounded

eager, and he needed another sale. Besides, he wasn't due home until that evening – what could it hurt?

'Right, no problem, give me ... uhm.' Bill glanced at his watch and worked out how long it would take to drive to the location. 'Say about an hour to get to your place ... what, yes, I have the address, don't worry. I have everything I need,' he said with a broad grin.

Bill knew his family would understand.

They always understood.

He would do the job and then be back – back to the safety of his home.

The job wasn't far – a nice residential place with a large garden at the back of the house and a spacious area at the front with a lawn and a gravel pathway, and a long asphalt driveway that ended at a double garage.

Bill had been waiting for the call all week. He'd spoken to the family before – a Sikh family named Singh – but they had never wanted to commit to a decision. Bill figured that the recent murders had made their minds up. Mr Singh was a businessman who owned a couple of restaurants and pubs in different countries. From what he had seen, the large family included four daughters and four sons. He knew this man was protective of his family and would pay through the nose to keep them safe.

However, Bill wasn't a crook; he would only sell what was necessary to the customers. This, and his friendly personality, was why people would ask for him. He wasn't just a salesman. He was like a friend of the family.

Bill pulled up onto the long driveway and parked behind Mr Singh's BMW SUV. He gazed at the house and automatically started making observations about possible entry points and blind spots. As an ex-policeman, he had learned a few things, especially working robbery cases. Unfortunately, a nervous breakdown had ushered him into early retirement.

But this wasn't so bad. His last case had been a Robbery-Homicide. A nasty one too.

Now, he worked nine-to-five and a couple of weekends, less for the one time in the month when he went round to clients' homes and did face-to-face assessments. Bill got out of his car and walked to the front door. The house was huge – five-bedrooms big he had calculated. The house was modern but held with the traditional aesthetics of the neighbourhood.

He rang the doorbell and waited several seconds before he heard the familiar sounds of family life: laughing, shouting, a dog barking, and then the ever welcoming, 'I'll get it.'

The door opened and a little girl opened the door; she must have been all of twelve-years-old with long, straight black hair and a broad smile. Her brown eyes were large and had a nice sparkle to them.

'Hello, are you the lady of the house?' Bill asked with a broad grin.

The little girl laughed. 'No.' Her voice sang with a high-pitched squeak. 'Mom, there's a strange bloke at the door,' she yelled with an unexpected bellow that startled him with the lung power of this little one. 'So, what you selling?' The innocent girl had turned into an obnoxious child.

'Security. Your parents are expecting me,' he said. His tone matching hers.

'Mom, he says he's a security guy—'

The child's holldering was cut off by a tall man in his forties.

'William, glad you could make it, please excuse my daughter. Mia has not learnt the art of announcing people, or anything, quietly,' Mr Singh laughed while he shook Bill's hand. 'Please, do come in,' the man said, hurrying his daughter out of the way.

Bill smiled as he entered.

The place was different; the family was different. Perhaps it was time to start with something new, he thought as the door closed behind them.

CHAPTER TWENTY-THREE

It was around six o'clock in the evening when Melanie's door opened again. She looked over with a sleepy gaze. Toby walked past the re-enforced door, holding a tray of food and a bottle of water, as well as the usual cup of milk. She sat up and stretched her muscles.

Melanie had no idea when she'd dropped off or how long she been asleep for. All she knew was she was hungry. She sniffed and caught the aroma of something new.

She looked at the strange-looking food, which had been cut into small bite-size pieces.

'What's that?' Her noise and stomach were inquisitive of this new food.

'What, you've never had pizza before?' His voice sounded puzzled and also rang with disappointment.

Had she had the *same* food for ten years?

'Well,' he pointed at the plate, 'this is called pizza. Its made from ... well, let's say thin bread.' He tried to think of a similar food source to explain what the food was made from. 'And on it, we have tomato sauce and salami, chilis and pepperoni and cheese.' As he peered into those large blue eyes, he could see she had no idea what he was talking about. She had no idea what any of the things were. Evidently, all she'd had was basic but nutritious food for ten years. The woman had no idea what salami or pepperoni was. It wouldn't surprise him if she didn't know what cheese was.

Toby smiled as a saying he'd once heard suddenly made sense: *how do you describe the colour blue to a blind man?*

Melanie jumped up and made her way to the table where Toby had placed the tray. He leant against the wall and watched as she sniffed the pizza. She backed away slightly, as if shocked. But then, slowly, she took one of the small pieces and turned around so Toby couldn't see her face.

Toby saw the mask lift slightly. He listened, hearing one noise after the other. Lots of mmms and yuks, and the sound of slapping, as though she were testing the food with her tongue first. Finally, Melanie turned and grabbed the plate, and leapt onto the bed to eat.

'I thought we could go for a walk later, I hear the moon will be full tonight,' Toby said, but she didn't respond.

She concentrated on the food as she looked out of the window. At first, he got the impression she was blanking him.

'Why?' Melanie asked simply. Her voice held the tone of a little girl.

'I thought you might want to, that was all. I hear you like to visit the grounds at night,' he replied, feeling the distance between them.

'You thought ... or the professor did?' The tone had changed to one more adult – and angry.

'I did; the professor doesn't even know I'm asking you,' Toby explained.

'Oh, well, in that case, I'd be delighted to walk with you,' Melanie said with a skip in her voice.

Toby smiled and watched as she finished her meal and slid the tray on the bed towards him.

'I suppose I better, get some sleep if we're going for a midnight stroll,' she said.

'Until later then.' Toby picked up the tray and headed for the door. 'Sweet dreams,' he said as he saw her eyelids close.

As the door shut behind him, her eyes shot open and stared coldly at the ceiling.

Hicks stared at the footage on his computer and the latest recording that Eric had made. This was average stuff compared with the last one.

He was disappointed that she had become shy once more. Had the trust between her and the new lad been broken because of the incident outside? Hicks looked over at another laptop. This one showed footage of a different kind – footage of another woman who had been brought in only a few months ago.

Her long blonde hair covered her face like a veil. She was thin and didn't move much. Her only distinguishing mark was a tattoo of a seahorse on her ankle. Hicks had been studying her as well. She was also suffering from the same memory loss symptoms as Melanie, but the woman wasn't as active. Melanie simply blanked out people, unlike the woman who blanked out *everything*. He knew something terrible had happened to her and her child because the child had taken her own life soon after being brought in.

So the report read.

Another reason he had cameras installed: the incident had nearly cost him the clinic. Luckily, the father had never pressed charges. There was an inquest and it was ruled suicide. The last thing Hicks needed was a rapist or, worse, a murderer loose in the place. The scandal would ruin him for sure.

The woman sat in her chair and looked out of the window.

The view was of the front gardens and the open lawns. But she didn't see any of the beauty. What she did see, no one could be sure.

Hicks turned his attention back to the recording of Melanie. She too sat in front of her window, but she was reading. He couldn't make out the cover or the title. For all he knew it was *Gulliver's Travels* or a book on plants and remedies. Hicks huffed loudly at the lack of progress and stood to get another drink from the cabinet. He figured if he could cure the girl, the woman would reveal her secrets, possibly remember what had happened. He had to be sure that she didn't suddenly come out of her state and start to talk, not without his control anyway.

Hicks poured himself a double whiskey and downed it in one gulp. He was feeling nervous and agitated.

Melanie's sudden lack of interest put things back slightly. He hoped the young nurse would get her to respond again. Come out of her state and give him something to work with. He moved back to the monitors and watched both footages. Neither Melanie nor the woman had moved, so he switched off the recordings and stood. He wanted to see what was happening, not rely on hours old footage.

What he needed was an actual camera *inside* Melanie's room. The only camera he currently had for Melanie's room was a side-angle shot from a security light. This gave a perfect view of her bed and the table through the small observation window in the door. But he'd never deemed Melanie important enough to warrant a camera before.

Hicks looked through old records to see who had installed the first cameras years ago. He found the number and dialled it. There was a long pause before a friendly male voice answered.

'Hi, this is Bill Brown, how can I help you today?'

CHAPTER TWENTY-FOUR

MELANIE WOKE AROUND NINE O'CLOCK AND BOLTED upright, disorientated and confused.

She had had one of those dreams again, but this time it was different. Melanie wasn't at home. She was in a park or wood, someplace with grass and trees. She had seen the stars and the full moon above; it was a beautiful clear night without a cloud in the sky.

Melanie felt the tickle of the grass on her skin. Wait – she was lying down!

But she wasn't alone. She was with someone – a man.

Melanie – no, the woman in her dreams, *she* was with that man again. The one that smelt so good.

Melanie felt the cool breeze against her bare skin and him deep inside her. But it hadn't been her – not the real her, only the one in her dreams.

She had often wondered what had sparked these dreams of the man and sex. Perhaps one of the books she had read? Maybe that and hidden feelings for Toby? Whatever it was, she was happy she had them. They were better than the other dreams.

The *nightmares.*

Melanie dragged herself out of bed and shuffled to the table where she had left her bottle of water. She cracked the top and went to drink.

Something from the corner of her eye stopped her.

Someone had pulled up to the driveway.

It was late. She knew that from the height and position of the moon. The man was driving a black car – a Jaguar XF series by the shape she figured. Melanie didn't know that much about cars, only how to break in and start the things.

Got to love the internet, she'd thought after finding several pages of what you could but shouldn't do.

The man was tall with a blue suit and dark hair. He stood straight, with his shoulders back. As she watched, another man approached the first man. He wore a brown suit and looked like one of those people from a documentary she'd seen about posh rich people, earls and such. They shook hands and seemed friendly enough, and spoke for a while. But then the man in the blue suit panicked about something. He tried to force his way in, but then Eric stepped in and held the man back. The man in the blue suit began waving a finger at them and then the building.

He was angry, to be sure.

He got back into his car and sped away, spitting gravel as he went towards the security gates. Melanie watched for a while longer before smiling and taking a mouthful of water. Even though she hadn't seen them fully, she knew the man in the brown suit must have been the professor people were talking about.

The other man she didn't know. But then again, she'd only seen them from afar.

Melanie took another mouthful, puzzled and intrigued at what she had seen.

Who was the man in the blue suit, and why was he angry with the man in the brown suit?

In any case, Toby would be here soon. She had a date at midnight.

Or so Toby thought.

CHAPTER TWENTY-FIVE

It was a little after nine when Bill arrived back home. He had bought Chinese takeaway on the way back and a bunch of flowers for Ann. He'd phoned ahead, warning her of the delay and that he was picking up something for dinner. It had been a long couple of days, but he had secured a couple of new customers and an old one. Ann sounded happy on the other end of the phone. He'd been worried she would be mad at him for being late, but everything was fine.

He pulled up the driveway and parked, took a deep breath and smiled, almost as if he were on a first date. The car door creaked as he opened it and a cold breeze blew into the vehicle, carrying the smell of food inside.

Bill's stomach growled in protest that he was taking his time. He patted his angry belly as if to calm the beast and pulled out the food and his briefcase. His suitcase could wait for now. No rush.

All he wanted to do was get inside, kiss his wife and daughter, and tuck into the feast. He slammed the car door shut with a hip and clicked the key fob to lock it. Luckily, the house key was on the same chain for simplicity of ease.

He could see lights on in the living room and his daughter's bedroom upstairs. Ann was probably watching her series, and Debs was more than likely on social media with her mates. Bill let himself in and shut the door behind him.

'I'm back, and I've got dinner,' he called out as the door closed behind him.

The neighbour over the road watched through her curtains at the display. Mrs Bellington had kept watch on the street for a long time. But then, at eighty-four, she had that luxury. She had often seen him leave throughout the daytime. He did all of the shopping as far as she could see. And once a month, around the same time each month, he would go on those business trips.

Some had been longer than others.

But if she hadn't seen the man's wife before she would swear he was single. She hadn't seen the wife or the daughter for some time now. With a shake of her head, she closed the curtains. Really, it was none of her concern what other people got up to, just as long as nobody bothered her or her fifteen cats.

At ten minutes past ten, Melanie broke out of her room. A simple thing to do considering cameras were watching the corridors.

A good thing they didn't care.

Melanie knew who was on shift. It was the lazy men again. So, she wasn't worried. They had already done their rounds, and there wouldn't be another until early morning before handover.

Melanie entered the staffroom and smiled as she walked to the small refrigerator in the corner. She peered inside to see what goodies were available, and what wouldn't be missed straight away. She found a row of small cartons containing strawberry milkshakes. Obviously, these had been brought for everyone – Melanie concluded that must also mean her. There were ten in total, more than enough in fact in Melanie's eyes.

She smiled and took one from the back, knowing if she took one from the front, it would be quickly noticed. Removing the straw from the side, she pierced the aluminium seal. There was a tiny sound as the vacuum seal was broken, followed by a strong scent of strawberry.

She had never had an actual strawberry. The only tastes she knew were what she had acquired from the refrigerator. She hadn't any food allergies because she had been tested when she first came to the clinic. Looking back, Melanie believed most of the tests the clinic staff had performed on her were mostly for their amusement rather than her benefit.

She hacked into the computer in the restroom and started a search on the good professor. He hadn't sparked her interest until now. Before, Hicks was merely a name she'd heard, a faceless entity that ran the place. But now he was looking into her life. So, in her eyes, it was only fair she did likewise.

The search engine spouted out details on the man's research and portfolio, family history and about the hospital. She had no idea why she had never thought to research the place or staff before. But then she had had another agenda.

For years, she had felt something was wrong with her; that's why her family wanted nothing to do with her anymore. She had memories of when she had been brought to the home, but couldn't remember why. Only those words that rang in her head. Like a song you heard once and it ingrained itself into the back of your mind.

Melanie had learned to conceal herself, make herself be what they wanted her to be. To camouflage her real intent.

She needed to find who had said those words and discover what terrible thing they had done all those years ago.

Words so terrifying she couldn't forget them, even in her nightmares.

She'd had ten years to learn all she could. Having an eidetic memory helped.

When she was ten, Melanie had a mentor, a woman who had been in the room next to Melanie's long before the other woman had arrived.

The mentor had taught Melanie many things: how to use a computer, how to pick locks. How to read and which books to concentrate on. She'd also taught Melanie about the power of misdirection. She had told Melanie it was necessary to exercise and dance. The mentor had shown Melanie a dance which she found strange at first, a mix of ballet and Tai-chi. Still, Little Melanie didn't know either so for her, it was just a dance – one she practised every morning and every night.

Melanie hadn't understood the importance of what she was being taught, but she had learned to enjoy them. Every morning, ten sit-ups and ten press-ups, which increased month by month.

The woman had taught Melanie about sex and using it to get what she wanted. The power of seduction and flirtation. She also taught her how to fight clean, and more importantly, *not clean*. The meaner and dirtier, the better her mentor had declared. People who fought clean were the first ones dead.

When Melanie was around fifteen, the woman had stopped

coming. She had been transferred to another clinic one nurse had said. For months after, Melanie had just sat and stared out the window. Hoping to catch a glimpse of her friend.

But she never came.

It had taken a letter to bring Melanie back from the depression. A letter the woman had written to Melanie and had left in one of her books. A simple note.

My Dearest Melanie,

Be strong, use your gifts, find your purpose in life. Train, train and train. Learn all that is learnable. Learn about the world outside as it is not a nice place. Learn how to defend yourself; you will need it. Be careful who you call friend, as people wear many faces. Trust no one because they will let you down. Use your body to distract, your brain as a weapon and your fists to defend. The mask you have is your best camouflage here as nobody can see your true feelings so never take it off. Look after yourself and get revenge on those who have wronged you. I am so proud of you little one, remember that. You have been loved, and I will always love you as the daughter I never had.

Love

M. xxx

Melanie had learned much from the woman. Including one important lesson. *You are the only person you can trust; only you can look after yourself.*

The mentor had told her to find a way to hide from the world, to be invisible. Melanie remembered the mask she had as a child. The perfect hiding place.

As she scrolled down, Melanie found a picture of Hicks and his father. She grabbed her head as a memory tried to force its way out, but her brain fought to keep it hidden. Melanie fell to the floor. She had seen flashes of faces. Some Melanie knew while others were alien. What the hell had she seen to make her mind want to forget?

Ten minutes had passed before Melanie woke. She had fallen unconscious from the strain. Too much information coming too quickly. She sat up and shook her head, listening to her tense muscles crack. As she stood, Melanie grabbed the side of the table; she felt weak from the episode but stable. Fit enough to finish what she was about to do, before her trip that was.

Melanie began to read up on Hicks.

He was a man obsessed with memory. How amnesia patients could get their memories back and how others blocked things out – mostly people so traumatised, they forgot everything. The research was more for military and government use than helping ordinary people, at least from what she could tell. If he could prove it was possible to control memories without drugs or side effects, it would be worth millions. The more she read, the more she was convinced that Hicks Junior was running the place for profit, unlike Senior who truly wanted to help people.

Hicks Junior had worked with hypnosis and methods which had proven successful. Still, they had a short-term impact, sooner or later the memory came back, mostly in flashbacks.

Melanie read on. But at the same time, keeping a close eye on the clock in the corner of the monitor. Toby would be back around twelve. So Melanie knew she'd have to be out of there and back in her room before then.

She read the last article, which was nothing more than a fluff piece on Hicks and his incredible work. She shut down the search engine and deleted the browser history.

She had ten minutes before she would have to be back in her room. Melanie had cut the time short, thinking she'd have enough time, given her room was just a few feet away.

Melanie left the staff room and headed back, her heart racing with excitement. A sudden noise made her stop dead in her tracks.

Melanie listened hard. What was that?

Then she heard it again – the squeak of approaching footsteps.

Was Toby early?

A chill ran through her veins.

The steps were heavy and rapid – as though the person was in a hurry. Melanie's heart began to pound in her chest – excitement? But why?

All she had to do was look out the window and fake it, like she'd done countless times.

But somehow this was different.

The footsteps were causing Melanie to panic. Nobody ever rushed down this corridor – ever. The last time had been when they'd found that girl hanging in her room.

Melanie darted back to her room and fumbled with the lock in a desperate effort to lock it before anyone arrived. The last thing she needed was for someone to find the door unlocked. But Melanie couldn't seem to get the damned door to lock. She'd done it a thousand times without a single problem; now, however, she was having a *big* problem.

Her fingers began to sweat and the metal strips began to dig into her palms as they slid back into her flesh. Melanie let out a tiny yelp of pain and shook off the small injury before starting again.

She could hear the person getting closer. The squeak-squeak-squeak of the rubber soles on the non-slip floor seemed to echo more intensely the closer the person got.

But the pace had slowed. They were no longer rushing – they were walking slowly, as if they enjoyed the fear the footsteps were causing.

Suddenly there was silence. The person was at the door.

Melanie froze. She didn't want to fumble around at the lock just in case whoever it was heard her.

Then, the sound of keys rattling. The person was getting ready to open the door.

But *whose* door?

Melanie felt fear washing over her and she didn't know why. Her back and forehead were drenched as sweat began to pour out of her.

Then came the sound of a key slipping into a lock and the other keys rattling against one another.

She forced her back against the door as if hoping to stop the person from entering. As she pressed herself against the cold metal, she heard the person breathing. It was heavy, as if the person might be out of breath or panting.

Melanie started to have flashes of images ... images of madmen hungry to cause obscenities on people.

The squeal of metal on unoiled metal as the key was turned.

Melanie felt her heart pounding in her chest as she closed her eyes, waiting for the inevitable shove of the door. If the person found her lockpicks, they would take them away, and she would be trapped – unable to get out and finish her mission.

She scampered the short distance back to her bed and hid the picks. If the nurse asked about the unlocked door, she'd just play dumb. Then came the creak of the hinges as the door was opened slowly – Melanie dove under the bed covers. She had no idea why – as though a sheet could prevent anything from happening?

'Hello, I'm Professor Hicks, I think its time we had a chat.' He moved slowly into the darkened room. A stream of moonlight illuminated the small space, making it as bright as the midday sun.

Melanie began to shake, her breathing sounding more like panting. The fear of the situation caused her muscles to tense, as if preparing for something terrible.

'I'm sorry it has taken me a long time to see you, my dear, but I'm here for you now,' Hicks crossed the room towards the bed. He wore a sickening grin and evil thoughts in his mind. As Hicks stood at the side of the bed, he noticed the bedcovers were pulled up over the Melanie's head. He smiled, feeling the fear, the cry for help. He reached down.

He would be gentle. After all, he was there to help.

Melanie held onto the covers as though her life depended on it – but apart from her feelings, it was a dumb idea. She should be out of bed, confronting the intruder, not cowering.

Hicks paused. He could see the sheet was moving slightly, as though the person was shaking. He smiled again and sighed deeply. 'Now, now my dear, there is nothing to be scared of ... I am a doctor, after all. I'm here to help,' His words hissed past his teeth like a viper.

Melanie gritted her teeth.

She wasn't going to be scared anymore. She'd had enough of hiding.

She threw back the covers, screaming, hoping it would scare the person shitless for a second – a second she could use to her advantage. She yanked the sheets around her and continued to scream, launching herself out of the other side of the bed.

She stood for a moment. Panting and bearing her teeth, ready to fight whoever it was.

Hicks stared at the wall next to the bed. The screaming

from Melanie amused him. He just wished he knew what had caused it. Slowly, he reached over and pulled back the bedsheets, revealing a thin beautiful woman.

Her eyes were vacant, lost in her own little world.

CHAPTER TWENTY-SIX

TOBY HAD PICKED UP MELANIE FROM HER ROOM AT midnight. She was still sweating and shaking from the incident. A close call to be sure, but now she wondered who was in the room next door.

Who had the person with the heavy footsteps visited at such an hour? The woman next door?

That was a question for later; for now, she just wondered what Toby was up to, taking her for a midnight stroll? As though this were some kind of date?

Melanie had an idea of what he had planned. Their falling out had probably made the professor angry, and poor Toby had to make amends. Regardless, she had her own agenda. Melanie wanted to be out to see if the full moon was too bright; she needed shadows to work with. If the moon was too bright, Melanie had to rethink her plan.

She had seen there would be similar weather conditions the week after. That was when she would bring her plan into action.

'Are you cold?' Toby asked as he watched Melanie wrap her arms around herself.

'No, I'm fine ... thank you,' she replied, but didn't look at Toby, her gaze fixed on the bushes, structures, trees. She was planning a route to the fountain and pond.

'I heard it's your anniversary soon?' Toby asked, grasping at things to talk about.

'Anniversary ... of what?' Melanie asked with surprise. Had she missed something?

'It's been ten years since you were brought here, so they were saying,' Toby stated, cursing silently that he had started this conversation. He had forgotten that residents had no concept of time in the clinic, and he had just broken down that wall.

Melanie stopped and looked back at the building. Images flashed before her eyes like old reruns of a home movie.

She began to remember being brought to the hospital. The old man that had greeted them and a younger man who had stood with them. Melanie began to remember her parents' faces. Sad-looking people, scared even – images of her outstretched hand as she screamed for her mother as they took her away. Her parents simply turned and walked away, and then her mother looked back at her with a strange look.

Had she been smiling? No. Tears had begun to cascade down Melanie's face. That had been the last time Melanie had cried.

'Don't worry, we will take care of you here; you'll get better and go home soon,' said the older man. His voice was deep. His face was round with red cheeks and a nose ruddy from too much drink. His white coat was pressed and starched with pens sticking from the outer breast pocket. Melanie remembered the smell of tobacco and strange aftershave.

But most of all, she remembered his eyes: they were dark and cruel, like a man with alternative motives.

Melanie reached out to nothing. The ghosts of her past had faded away and she slumped to the ground. The sudden mass of information had been too much. She had been looking for answers, and now she felt she was one step closer. However, she still had no idea why she had been brought to Larksford or whose voice she kept hearing.

———

'Melanie, what's wrong?' Toby said, rushing over to catch her.

'Why did you bring me out here? What do you people want from me?' she screamed.

Her voice was loud, a piercing shriek that immediately caused other nurses to come running. As they ran over to the fountain, they found a terrified Toby with an unconscious Melanie in his arms.

'What the hell happened?' Eric shouted angrily.

But Toby suspected Eric was angrier about not filming it than what had actually taken place. 'Fuck knows ... we were talking and then she went all weird, as if she had seen a ghost or something,' Toby explained as two nurses arrived with a stretcher.

'And then what?' Eric asked. His mood had changed from anger to interest.

'And then she just keeled over,' Toby said, shrugging. He had no idea what had happened or what he had said to cause Melanie's hysteria.

But one thing was for sure. Hicks would want a full report – and he would want it like yesterday.

———

It had been ten years since little eight-year-old Melanie had been brought to Larksford House clinic. Ten years of care. Ten years of being hidden from the truth.

Now, Melanie was older, and a hell of a lot smarter.

As she lay in bed, Melanie's thoughts raced through her head. Images that flashed before her eyes made no sense at all. It was as if her memories were trying to return ... like a cascade of memories washing over her. A torrent of the past crashing over her. Images came at the same time, but in no real order.

Her hands clenched the bedclothes, gripping them tightly as if using them as a braking system.

Suddenly, her eyes shot open. Her pupils were as large as saucers. Melanie reached up to touch her face. Sighing with relief as she felt the cold plastic of the mask against her fingertips.

Melanie had been afraid they had removed her shroud, but she suspected Eric had stopped them. Sure, he could be an arse, but the gentle giant had a soft spot for her. Melanie sat up and looked around. The room was brightly lit by the morning sun. *Damn,* she thought. *It's morning.*

She eased herself off the bed and staggered to the window to peer across the grounds. Melanie was glad she hadn't gotten the room over the way; this room had a view of the front of the building. But more importantly – a view of the pond and the fountain.

She picked up a new water bottle and cracked the top before taking a mouthful. Her mouth was dry from the night before, but she didn't know why. Hell, she had no idea what had happened the night before. She looked over at the sun, just breaking over the tree line. It was early.

She smiled to herself, glad she hadn't missed too much of the day.

A tap on the door signalled someone was about to enter. She knew it was either Eric or Toby – they were the only ones who ever knocked. The others would barge in without a care.

It was Toby who entered. He was wearing a broken smile of an apologetic man.

She smiled under her mask, glad it was him.

'Are you OK?' he asked, setting the tray that contained her breakfast on the table.

'I think so ... what happened?' She was still confused about what had actually taken place.

'You seemed to have gone into a trance or something. I don't know ... it was weird,' he shrugged.

Melanie said nothing. She just looked out across the lawn and tree line.

'Do you remember anything?' he asked, his voice full of concern.

'Yes ... I remember everything,' Melanie said, her voice a low growl, her eyes cruel and hard.

———

Jason Freeman sat at the kitchen table and drank a cup of hot chocolate before bed. It was around eleven o'clock and he was having trouble sleeping. Today had been his day off, and he was hoping to have enjoyed it. But, in reality, the visit from Hicks had got him thinking. His daughter had been locked up in that place for ten years. Ten years of her life had been missed, based on Hicks' and his father's advice.

Melanie was coming up to her twenty-first birthday. That was far too many birthdays that they had not celebrated together.

Hicks had been there the other day to tell Jason and Abby that Melanie's mental health had deteriorated. He had explained that she was now in a ward for the most dangerous people after she'd had an episode and nearly killed another patient and a nurse.

Jason still couldn't believe his daughter was not just insane but also psychotic – his little girl was a born killer.

The mug fell from his grip and smashed into a thousand pieces as it impacted the stone tiles. The chocolate drink started to seep into the joints, creating canals of brown liquid. Jason was unaware of anything; he was lost in his tears and screams of frustration as he buried his face into his hands. He didn't even notice Abby rush in to see what was wrong.

She flung her arms around him, and they both sobbed. Years of keeping a clear lid on things had suddenly blown off.

'I want to see our little girl, I have to stare her in the eyes and see what she has become,' Jason said, coughing back his emotions.

'Why?' Abby asked with a heavy sigh.

'Why?' Jason murmured with anger and pain in his eyes. 'Because I have to see for myself. We are told stories but never allowed to see her.'

'We agreed we wouldn't, the doctor said—'

'We?' Jason growled. 'You decided; *you* said that we wouldn't.'

'So, why didn't you say anything; you could have said no?' Abby barked back.

'Yeah, right, like I'm ever allowed to make a decision. You would have done it behind my back anyway – hell, you *did*. When we got there, she already had a room,' Jason said, shaking his head, tears streaming down his face.

'But not now,' Jason affirmed, straightening. 'We have abandoned her for the last time. I need to see her, see for myself.'

His voice was calm, but anger rattled within the words. 'I ... we need closure. I have to see her as the woman she has become and finally realise she will never be coming home.'

Then he climbed off the chair and started picking up the broken pieces of what used to be his favourite mug.

Abby knew deep down he was right. They needed closure like a person who'd lost a loved one had to say goodbye at the funeral. They would telephone Hicks and let him know. They wanted to say goodbye to their little girl.

It was late when Hicks received the phone call from the Freemans, which meant he couldn't sleep for the rest of the night. He would have to leave for Nottingham early the next day.

He had made plans, and those could not wait, not even to accommodate the stupid Freemans. This most untimely decision of theirs had put a dark cloud over his plans. They definitely couldn't see her as she was. They were expecting an animal, not some quiet, shy girl in a mask. Then, he thought. He smiled as a plan formed.

'Of course, that's brilliant. They haven't seen Melanie for ten years. Who's to say that the girl they see isn't little Melanie?' Hicks laughed out loud at his genius. Now all he had to do was find the right person to take her place. The mask she always wore would also help with the deception. As far as he was concerned, any mask would do; after all, she had started to wear it soon after her arrival.

As he sped down the motorway towards the south, he let his mind wander and plan. There was a way to go until he arrived at the old house. He just hoped the counter measures he had introduced had been enough to ward off any unwanted attention.

CHAPTER TWENTY-SEVEN

Monday, the 24th April.

DS DAVID ELFORD WOKE UP IN HIS CAR. HE HAD SLEPT the night in the parking area of a service station. Elford had travelled south towards Nottingham, but the late hour and lack of sleep the nights before had taken their toll. Elford screamed as he tried to contort his body back into its normal shape. The sound of his joints cracking, aggravated by the pins and needles in his right arm, proved he had slept awkwardly.

He wiped the condensation off the windscreen and checked that the roadside café was open. Then, with a grumble, he noticed the motel's sign behind the restaurant, which somehow he had missed.

Elford put it down to being completely knackered the night before. On the journey, he had fought to keep awake, hearing the whining sounds of the raised white lines on the side of the road. The annoying song activated when tyres met the side of the road.

A wonderfully irritating safety feature.

. . .

He was going south to Nottingham, to the scene of a cold case which had the makings of being from the same person they were hunting.

Or so Platt thought.

Elford was less optimistic and he'd said so – a long shot at best, or grasping at straws was more likely.

Elford was pissed because that young Summers had found the possible lead, so why the hell wasn't she going?

He was still tired and hungry and in desperate need of coffee.

'When the bloody hell is this caff opening?' he muttered. Stretching the rest of his muscles.

Despite his reluctance to chase down a false lead, he had to admit that even though the MO was different, there had been something familiar about it.

The murder had happened around ten years ago. A woman was found murdered in the same manner as the recent murders. The pathologist at the time had said, due to her wounds, she hadn't died quickly. In fact, the pathologist had suggested it might have taken a half-hour to an hour.

The husband had been top of the list, but then news of a not so happy ex-husband caught their attention; nobody, however, had been charged.

The victim's body had been found bound and her mouth sealed shut with ducktape, which happened to be the same MO as the present killer. Platt never liked the word coincidence, but they did happen, very rarely ... still, they did. But he didn't think so in this case. In fact, Platt considered every bit of information that could have a possible tie to the case.

At first, the investigators thought it was domestic violence. The husband had gone nuts or something. Then the husband had been found dead at the scene of an RTA. Not him, but his time of death, said that he had died before her.

Not him for sure. Being dead was a hell of an alibi.

Then they shifted to their theory to the ex-husband. After all, he'd smacked her around before – or so the police reports read. He had gone inside for it but had been released sometime before the murders.

He probably had no alibi for the time of the murder. Home alone, sleeping. In other words: possibly guilty as hell.

But the ex had disappeared before they could find him to question him.

Now, he was even more guilty as hell.

But how the hell did the killer get in the building?

The neighbours hadn't seen anything unusual. None of the neighbours remembered seeing anyone hanging around the house or even visiting the residence. After the murders, the place went on sale, unsuccessfully though.

Understandable, Elford had thought.

Who the hell would want to live in a place that had people murdered in it?

Elford thought more about the MO. If it was the same person, how did they go from dark-haired to blonde women? Elford understood there was usually a progression in the crime, but the type of victim typically stayed the same.

The house he was going to was still on the market, which was unsurprising. Nobody would want to have a house with that kind of history. The murdered woman was found in one of the bedrooms, stabbed several times and then raped.

Elford remembered Platt's face cringe with distaste as he read the report on the murder. 'Sick bastard,' Platt had said as he read through the story.

Elford had been too tired and too angry about being sent there to care at that point.

Now, it was a rundown place with boarded-up windows. Moss and mould had started to grow on the boards which covered the windows. The grass in the front was at least waist height. Ivy had completely shrouded one corner of the house. The guttering hung from the roof in places with substantial green pools of algae covering the paving slabs that circled the house.

The FOR SALE sign was so old the wood had rotted away; the pole that had once held it up lay on the ground with moss and grass hiding most of it.

But nobody wanted it. Who would? Even if the history didn't put them off, the cost of renovation would. The place was so rundown that even the homeless avoided it.

Some had said it was haunted – the ghost of the woman still walked the hallways.

Elford had seen the photos of the place as it now stood. And even the pictures gave him the willies.

He looked over at the roadside café as he felt his belly growl. It was time for breakfast and a big mug of coffee. He pulled himself out of his car and walked over to the restaurant, his files tucked under his left arm. His plan was to look them over while he ate. Hoping the coffee infusion would stimulate his brain.

Inside was clean. With white coloured walls and red laminate floor. The seats where stalls instead of square tables, possibly to maximise space. The tables where long and stretched the same length as the red PU leather seats of the booths. The usual sat on top of the tables: menus, metal basket holders for the ketchup, brown sauce, salt and pepper, and vinegar. Napkins were stacked in a polished aluminium holder. All stacked, nice and neat.

Topped up and arranged before the end of the shift the night before.

At this time, the restaurant was virtually deserted. Which suited Elford just fine.

Three men sat at three different tables around the spacious restaurant. Elford figured they were the drivers of the big rigs in the parking lot. He'd noted one of the licence plates was from Poland, the other two from the UK.

All three looked freshly washed and well slept; possibly all of them had taken rooms at the motel.

Elford looked like he felt – and possibly worse. He was unwashed, unshaven, and looked like he'd slept in his clothes, which obviously, he had.

He took a seat at a corner booth and waited for someone to take his order. He didn't need a menu. He'd already made his mind up at what he wanted: a full English with a bucket of coffee. Usually, he'd have tea, a nice cup of Yorkshire's finest. But after the drive and the time this morning – coffee, and lots of it.

A large perky woman with flaming red hair came to take his order. The name shield on her chest said *Berol.* Her round face sported rosy cheeks and a welcoming smile.

'Mornin' luv, what can I get ya?' Berol asked in a broad Midlands accent. She was a rotund woman, possibly in her mid-forties. Her red-and-white checkered uniform bulged with her large figure. But from what Elford could tell it was more genetic than an eating disorder. Her calf muscles could put a bodybuilder to shame and her arms were thicker than tree trunks, but firm. Elford had seen this many times, mostly from the farms. It wasn't fat, but camouflaged muscle.

'A full English and a mug of black coffee, please,' Elford answered with a broad grin and trying his best not to yawn.

'Smashin',' she said.

He watched as she lumbered back to the kitchen to place the order. She walked like a man on a building site, arms arched to the sides as if she were carrying carpets under each arm. Elford smiled.

He had known a PC who was built about the same. To look at her, you assumed you could outrun her. Many had made that assumption and were surprised at the unbridled speed of the woman. And once she caught you, that was when those big guns came in.

Elford surmised it wouldn't be long before the food arrived. The place was empty, less for the four people, and most chefs pre-cooked stuff anyway, in case of a rush. But he was in no hurry. In fact, the wait would give him time to read up on a few things.

The waitress brought his coffee almost immediately and placed it on the table. She raised an eyebrow as she noticed the police file on the killings ten years ago.

'Oh, nasty business that,' she said, giving an apologetic smile. Realising she shouldn't have been rubbernecking.

'No, wait,' Elford said gently, grabbing her arm. 'Please, tell me about it,' he urged, ushering her to take the seat opposite him.

Berol looked around as if she didn't want to be overheard. But the other customers were more interested in the newspapers they were reading, and the Polish guy was on his mobile phone watching a TV series. In fact, the men couldn't have been less interested, especially the guy from Poland.

'Well, it was ten years ago now. But I remember it like it was yesterday, all those coppers and reporters,' Berol said.

'You were there?' Elford asked, puzzled.

'Naw, I caught it on the news, bad business though,' Berol shrugged.

'So, why do you remember it so vividly; surely it was just another news report?'

'Well, the reason it sticks aut was I knew the people who lived in the ause,' she said almost proudly. Her strong Midlands accent clawed at him.

'People?' Elford asked, looking through his notes. 'I thought it was just a couple who lived there, a Mr—'

'Bill Morris ... his wife Cindy, ah,' Berol started to explain. A sudden metallic clang-clang-clang as the pick-up bell was hammered by the angry-looking cook. 'That will be your breaky, love. Won't be a sec,' she smiled.

As she left to get his food, Elford made some quick notes. So he didn't forget about the waitress.

CHAPTER TWENTY-EIGHT

A HOT SPRAY OF WATER WASHED OVER MELANIE'S BODY.
The water felt like small marbles massaging her aching flesh.

She stood alone. The nurse had waited outside at Melanie's request, which she gladly did without argument.

After ten years of trying to decipher dreams that she thought were part of her imagination, suddenly everything was starting to come together. In that split second at the fountain, things began to make sense.

Sure, there were gaps. Holes that needed filling, but she was sure she'd gotten the gist the story. She had been brought in on a lie.

Condemned to a life of solitude because of something someone else had done.

Her parents hadn't been killed like she had been told. They merely wished nothing to do with her – or, was that too, a lie? Had they been told she was dead, so far gone there wasn't anything left to fix?

But then Melanie remembered her mother's smile. It wasn't a warm, compassionate 'it will be alright' kind of smile. It was cold, cruel – loathing. Had her mother been glad she was at the clinic?

But her father? He had wept uncontrollably.

As far as she remembered, she had always been his favourite. He had been devastated by it all. So, was he part of the lie? Or a mere pawn in someone's twisted game?

Melanie had so many questions – far too many for her head to handle at that moment.

But she had to be smart. She was close to getting out. Close to finding out who had done this to her. Close to getting revenge.

However, the clinic was her alibi. She knew a way to get in and out without being noticed. After all, she had done it several times before. But where should she go? Home?

The clinic was the only home she had known.

Besides, she had a plan. All she needed was a who and a where.

All the time she was in Larksford, she had been told that her family had been killed by the serial killer. Her whole life up to that point was to find the killer and bring them punishment.

And now. She had found out they were alive.

But the question remained: whose voice had she heard and what had they done?

Melanie experienced a mixture of feelings. Happy her family were alive, but also sad that they had left her here. She was also angry. Angry at the person who had done this to her.

Melanie knew she couldn't tell anyone what had happened to her. Not even Toby. Besides, who would believe her? She was in an institution for people who had their own little worlds. She would be scoffed at and told to be quiet. And nobody even knew she existed in the other wing until the other day.

And even then, the professor probably said she was from somewhere else, passing through or some bullshit like that.

But then the nurses didn't really care. If she had been anywhere else but Larksford, there would have been questions. But not here. Melanie was sure the professor hired them because of their lack of empathy or capability to give a crap.

Melanie had slowly developed some kind of strange relationship with Toby, but she still didn't fully trust him. She began to realise the only reason she felt this way about him was the dreams, and that wasn't even him – it was someone else.

Melanie finished her shower and towelled off. She was glad of the mask as it hid her face and emotions.

The nurse brought Melanie back to her room and locked the door behind her. Now Melanie was alone. Alone to think things through, plan.

Despite everything, she was still going ahead with what she had been planning for years. Now she had a little more information to work with. The person she was looking for was somehow connected to her family, possibly a family friend or work colleague.

Melanie would have to wait until after dark to get to the office to use the computer. There was a connection between her family and Professor Hicks. Trouble was she didn't know what her family name had been – she wasn't even sure Melanie was her actual name. She had been in the clinic for so long her past was a blur. But she had a thought about how to get the information. Melanie knew she had been there the longest, so that meant records. She just hoped that they had put it all on the computer, and it wasn't a paper trail. If the information was only on paper, that meant files in an office she would never get into.

Hicks' office.

Ever since she was little, Melanie had the feeling something was wrong. She had *seen* something. At first, she thought they were all right. That she was indeed crazy and a danger to others.

And then the dreams came, and the flashbacks.

The doctors had put it down to multi-personality disorder. However, she began to know different. As the years went on, she had grown more aware of her surroundings and the people within. She'd learned how to manipulate and camouflage herself using their perceptions of her. Melanie had broken out so many times it was a regular occurrence. In fact, so much so staff came to think nothing of it.

They never worried because they knew she never left the grounds. After years and years of breaking out, it became normal – a regular occurrence. Constantly breaking out to stand by the fountain and the pond, *never* leaving the grounds.

After all, she had never done so before.

Or so they had thought.

CHAPTER TWENTY-NINE

DI Richard Platt and DC Kate Summers were on the road again after meeting up at the station at 6:00 on the dot.

Platt had been there ten minutes earlier. A force of habit had installed into him by the army. 'Ten minutes before parade' had been drilled into them from basic training.

As Kate walked onto the station's parking lot at the side of the building, she saw the Jaguar with Platt sitting inside on the passenger side, the seat folded back as far as it would go.

She figured Platt was either waiting patiently – or sleeping. She couldn't be sure.

Summers noted how peaceful he looked. She thought about not disturbing him – giving him five more minutes of peace.

She smiled when electronic whirring sounded as the passenger side window was lowered.

'Don't worry, Kate, I'm not dead. Not yet, mores the pity. I might get a decent kip then, without people gawkin' at me through windows,' he smiled.

Summers laughed and shook her head as she walked towards the driver's side.

'Sleep OK?' Platt asked, noting her fresh, rested complexion.

'OK, I guess, guv. And you?' she asked, returning the pleasantry more out of politeness than actual inquiry.

'What's sleep? I think I did while watching some God-awful programme on the telly, somethin' about some TV people stuck in a house together. Bloody crime scene waitin' to happen there to start with,' he laughed.

Summers smiled, knowing exactly what he meant, except she loved that show. As she sat on the soft leather on the driver's side, the smell of food filled her nostrils. She sniffed – what was that? Bacon? Summers followed the scent to the back seat and saw a plastic carrier bag. She looked over at Platt, who sat with a stony expression. 'Breakfast?'

'The six Ps, my dear – the six Ps,' he said with a smile. Then folding his arms around himself as though he were hugging himself, and closed his eyes.

In confusion, Summers mouthed the words he had said. 'What the hell are the six Ps?'

'Planning Preparation Prevents Piss-Poor Performance,' Platt recited, as if they were words to live by.

'Sounds like an army thing,' she said.

Platt nodded and waited for his order to arrive.He had brought two bacon sandwiches and a flask of coffee for the trip, knowing it could be a long day, and he didn't know where the cafés would be.

'Where to, guv?'

Platt thought for a moment, weighing up his options. Earlier, he'd gotten a text message from Elford: *I'm in Notts, found a possible connection.*

He had thought about heading down to Nottingham as well, but Dave had that covered. Besides, Platt had other plans. They were going to another crime scene.

'We're goin' to the last victims' house before the Thomas's. I wanna test a theory,' Platt said, his eyes still shut tight.

Summers sat for a moment, thinking. She had no idea of the address. Suddenly, a post-it note was waved in front of her face. Platt had noted down the address for her.

Summers looked at him in wonder – how the hell did he know?

————

According to the report, the Bolders had been a quiet family, very happy and pleasant people. They lived in a small town just off the A59 York Road. Unfortunately, the Bolders had been murdered the month before – or to be precise – three weeks before, and to Platt, it was still fresh.

The place hadn't yet been taken over or sold, and everything had been left as it was for the time being. But Platt knew he would have to let it go at some point, and the evidence would be lost as fresh coats of paint were brushed on walls and new carpets laid.

Again the mother and daughter were found bound and slaughtered. The husband, Jerry, was found in the corner with his throat slit. Every aspect of the attack had been the same MO throughout. Of course, CSI had done a complete sweep of the place and found nothing – just as before. But now Platt and Summers had a fresh perspective.

They were looking for cameras.

CSI had found several wi-fi cameras at the Thomas residence, mainly in the parents' and daughter's bedrooms. Just as Platt had suspected. The monster had been watching them, and that was also how the killer knew that Summers hadn't been home that day.

Platt had Tech check out the devices. If they were short-range, at least that would give them something to work on. Perhaps a car or van that had been parked outside for a length of time? It had been a rough night at the last crime scene for both of them – Summers in particular. Platt understood her pain, even though his wife and daughter had survived, in another way, they hadn't. He still had no idea why they had been spared. If anything, killing them would have been a more compelling statement? Instead, his wife was left in a withdrawn state. She would look at him as if he wasn't there. As if nothing was real.

His daughter had taken her own life.

The reality of it all had been too much to bear.

As they drove, Platt stared at the photo of him and his family. A sad and lonely look carved itself onto his long, thin face. His weathered skin showed signs of stress and quick dinners. Possibly supermarket microwave food. The photograph sat between two fingers of his large hand, which displayed scaring.

'What happened to them, guv ... if you don't mind me asking?' Summers asked.

He smiled. Impressed at her skills at reading people. But then he figured everyone knew at the station, and she was just being comforting.

'I was in London at the time. There had been another killing up north, but I was sent down south to track down a bollocks lead. The killing up north had the MO and everything. Dave was got sent to the scene to check it out while my illustrious leader sent me on a wild goose chase; personally, I think he just wanted to see the back of me,' Platt smiled wearily. 'The second murder was the Brooks family. I had been there for four days when I get a phone call. It was the nick at Leeds where we were stationed with the task force. Someone had broken in and assaulted my wife and daughter,' Platt explained, his gaze fixed out of the misted-up window next to him. Using the back of his left hand, he wiped away the condensation, leaving a streak of clear glass.

'Someone ... you mean the killer?' Summers asked.

'He'd left them alive, raped them in the same manner as the others, but left them alive.' Platt choked back emotion.

'That's good, right – they survived?' Summers asked, trying to see the bright side.

'My wife and daughter were admitted to a local clinic. My wife stares out of a window all day ... doesn't say anything to anyone.'

Summers was almost afraid to ask. 'And your daughter?'

'She ... she killed herself two days later, hung herself in her room. The clinic had failed to put a suicide watch on her,' Platt said, his eyes burning with anger.

'So, what are you after, guv? Revenge?' Summers was confused at her boss's motives for being on the case.

'I just want stop this bastard from destroying more lives. I wanted revenge to start with, but a good friend taught me that was never the answer ... that once that need was gone, I would feel empty and have nothing to push forward for. I want justice, sure. But I think seeing this son-of-a-bitch rot in jail is more satisfying, take his life away day after day, not the quick way out,' Platt explained with a broken smile.

Summers nodded and returned the smile.

'Sounds good to me, guv; let's get this bastard. For both our families.' The rest of the way, the two sat in silence. Wondering if their lies had convinced the other of their intentions. They both wanted the killer dead.

As painfully and as slowly as possible.

CHAPTER THIRTY

AFTER THE SHOWER, MELANIE HAD DRESSED AND SITTING in her chair, facing the window, watching the change in colours. The burnt orange was being replaced by a pale blue with mountainous clouds. Another nurse had brought her breakfast. But Melanie never asked why Tony had not brought her the meal, as he had so often done this past couple of weeks.

She guessed it was another one of Professor Hicks' games to get a reaction from her. So she sat in silence.

The nurse went directly to Melanie's bed and found the secret place where she kept her lockpicks. The tall thin man smiled as he displayed the thin strips of metal and placed them in his pocket. As he left the room, Melanie leapt after him, but she was too late – the door had already slammed shut. She heard the man's laughter as he walked down the corridor. It was a cruel laugh that echoed in her ears.

Under the mask, she smiled. Knowing what he had found would prove as useless as a chocolate fireguard – her real picks were in the heavy Russian book Tony had flicked through on their first meeting.

For a while now, she had suspected her room was being spied upon. And not just by Eric and that stupid camera. She had felt the eyes upon her – distant, leering eyes.

Melanie sat back in her chair and looked at the bed. She began to think over the nurse's actions. He had gone straight to the bed and to the place she'd previously stored the picks. How the hell did they know they were there? A camera from above wouldn't show the hiding place. The walls were too thick and with nowhere to hide a camera behind made hiding devices at that level impossible. As for the door, she always had her back to it when she got them. The only answer that made sense was they had found the picks long ago, maybe when she was less cautious. Whatever the case, they had taken the picks, or what they had thought to be them.

The question now remained: why take them now? Had it been something she had said or done? Whatever the case, she knew she had to be careful when she retrieved the actual picks.

On the plus side, though, she had an alibi for when her plan came into action. The fact was she couldn't get out of the room, so how could it have been her?

Toby looked at the two hairpins the nurse had taken from Melanie's room. He smiled as he tossed them into the waste-basket near the coffee fridge. The nurse had no idea what they had been for, nor did he ask how Toby knew they were there.

Toby grabbed the two coffees he had prepared and carried them to the monitor room that sat between the two wings. As he approached, Eric opened the door for him, then locked it behind.

'Did I miss anything?' Toby asked as he handed Eric his mug of black coffee.

'Nah, sod all. Another quiet day at the farm,' laughed Eric as he sat on the office chair and blew on the hot beverage.

Toby looked over at the monitor that showed the car park and front entrance. 'Looks like the good professor is heading out again.' Toby nodded at the screen.

'Twice in so many days. Probably got some tart on the side,' laughed Eric.

Toby looked closer at Hicks through the camera. His face showed more signs of concern than anything else; this was not a man heading to a cheap hotel to get his leg over. This was a man with something darker on his mind.

Hicks had climbed into his car and had sped off down the long driveway. Toby rocked back and forth. Where was the man going in such a hurry, and why had he taken a medical bag with him?

Elford stood in front of the rundown old house. The garden was overgrown, so much so that Elford had trouble following the path. He shivered as he looked at the crumbling wooden doorframe. The thought that homeless people would stay out in the cold rather than set foot inside chilled him.

He took out a key and tried it in the Yale lock. There was a click as the bolt released. Elford took a deep breath and pushed the door open. The old hinges creaked with age as he stepped inside.

He struggled to find his handkerchief and quickly retreated. The air inside was dank and thick. The smell of death was potent.

Elford stood outside and sucked in lungfuls of fresh air before coughing. He quickly searched his pockets, found the fresh cotton handkerchief, and held it to his nose and mouth.

As he re-entered, he stopped for a moment. The house was dark save for streaks of dust-filled beams of light which had broken through gaps in the boarded windows.

Elford pulled a small torch from his pocket and switched it on. The powerful lamp lit up the hallway and stairwell with bright blue as a thousand lumens cast the darkness aside.

'Bloody hell,' he swore as he shielded his eyes, forgetting the lamp was on the full-beam setting from the last job they had been to.

Quickly, he clicked the ON switch to change the settings and dim the light. Elford stood still but moved the flashlight around to get a feel for the place. He stood in a long corridor with a door at the end. A stairwell ran up against the left hand wall but before that was another door. Elford moved towards the door and pushed it open with his right foot. The aged door creaked on the stiff brass hinges. The room was large, with a double window next to the door and a patio door at the end. It was a long room with a living room and dining room combination. The furniture still sat on what was once a red carpet. Cobwebs hung from the corners and shrouded the furniture. Thick layers of dust covered every flat surface. A house lost in time, forgotten but left intact. Not as it was a shrine, but because nobody wanted to set foot in the place.

The owners were dead, and the banks didn't want it. Who would want to buy such a place? Tearing it down wasn't an option because it was a listed building. Elford looked at the photographs that sat on shelves or hung from the walls. A happy family. A family with a blonde mother and daughter. Elford moved slowly through the dining room and into the kitchen. Less for the dust and cobwebs, the house was spotless, no clutter or plates was lying around, everything was in its place.

Elford figured that the wife had been house-proud and was the sort of person that kept an orderly household. Either that or they were expecting visitors. Elford thought back to his mother and how she used to run around the house tidying before someone came around. He smiled as he could almost hear her voice yelling orders.

But this was different, almost as if it was always this tidy. A house-proud family. A happy family. The kitchen was of average size, with enough room for the usual amenities. Elford figured that they all sat at the dining area's small dining table, as there was no room to sit in the kitchen. But that's who these people were. A tight family who had meals together. Breakfast, Sunday roasts and evening meals at the table together.

The kitchen gave away nothing, but he took his time. Almost as if he was trying to put off what he had come to do. Go upstairs to the bedrooms. He swallowed hard and pushed through the door to his right, which led back into the hallway. He held the handkerchief tight to his mouth and nose. This was more out of comfort than anything else. Elford had seen the photographs that the coroner's office had taken, and had seen what this monster had done to the poor woman.

Now he was venturing up the stairs, taking his time with each step. Flashes of awful images came back to him as he saw things he recognised. The bannister rail that still had blood on it. The white carpet that displayed bloody drag marks in the parents' bedroom. The scratch marks on the wallpaper where the woman had tried to cling onto some-thing. Scratches that soon became smears of blood as her nails were ripped out.

Elford stopped at a broken mirror that hung on a wall and stared at the spiderweb pattern caked in blood. The killer had smashed the woman's face into the mirror to shut her up. The autopsy photographs showed marks on what had once been a pretty face, and Trace had found pieces of the mirror in the wounds.

Elford headed for the parents' room at the end of the hallway. He felt his stomach churn at the thought of what had happened. He had not been on the case at the time; he and Platt had been assigned later on, after the original investigators had been retired for health issues. They had been brought on after a killing in a small village near Exeter, the third murder, or so they thought. Platt was unsure, and Elford now shared that feeling.

This house was classed as an unrelated killing, burglary gone wrong they said. But the more Elford looked at the evidence in front of him, the more he was sure it was the same person but during an infant state of their wicked, violent spree. This could have been the first or second ... a burglar turned to murder quite possibly ... or something made to seem that way. The killer was smart even back then.

Elford stood in front of the door to the parents' room. His eyes glued to the blood smears on the white paintwork and the door handle. He nudged the door open slowly, as if expecting to see a body laying there, courtesy of photograph flashbacks. He held his breath, waiting for the worst but only found more bloodstains on the carpet and furniture.

He edged his right foot forward, pushing the door fully open. His heart pounding in his chest, his breathing laboured. The room was almost completely covered in blood, the bed and carpet showing outlines of where bodies had been. With a gloved trembling hand, Elford held onto the door for support; his weight was too much and it caused the door to hit something behind. It fall onto the carpet.

He jumped backwards and swore loudly as something fell - something big, like a body.

'Jezus,' Elford yelped. He stepped forward slowly, holding

his breath and the flashlight as if it were a club. 'Yah bastard,' he muttered, trying to get his breath back.

His hands gripped his knees as he leant forwards, laughing, and shaking his head as he saw it was just a coat rack. Standing straight, he bounced on his heels and shook his hands. Trying to get the blood circulating again after his fright.

Finally, he moved into the room. The flashlight lit it up like a searchlight, causing long shadows. The beam reflected off mirrors and glass, sending back a blinding glare. As he moved it about, he caught a glimpse of something, but didn't know what – a person, maybe an animal?

He went to move the torch, but something struck him on the back of the head – hard.

Bright flashes of light danced before his eyes and he felt sick and dizzy. The room began to spin – and then he fell. His unconscious body lay in a pool of his own blood.

———

Hicks hadn't told anyone where he was going; he felt what he did or where he went wasn't of anyone's concern – after all, *he* was the boss.

'I'm going out on business,' he had told his secretary as he'd left his office and ambled by her desk.

Not that she was concerned where he was going; just the fact he wasn't going to be there was all she was interested in. The secretary had figured a long time ago, the more he was out, the less she had to do.

The secretary, Brenda White, was in her thirties. She had long brown hair and wore dark-rimmed glasses, which enhanced her large brown eyes. She had a round figure but wasn't overweight, which was surprising, considering how much the woman could eat. She was not a looker, but she had an explosive temperament, perfect for keeping out undesirable people.

Hicks had left early that morning straight from the office. He had things to arrange.

The news of the latest murder was unsettling, and the police were showing no signs of giving up the chase. Still, he had kept up with the cases since they had started all those years ago, but he knew that the police would be no closer to catching the killer than during their previous attempts.

Hicks had found it interesting that Platt had taken the case, a man with a definite personal interest for sure. However, Hicks wasn't concerned about the police and the killer. After all, there was no connection between Larksford and the killer. But he worried all the same. He knew if it came out about Melanie, he would be done.

Hicks had big plans for Melanie, but she had to tow the line, and so did this Toby fella. He was close to a breakthrough with his other patient, but everything hinged on Melanie. His other experiments had not been fruitful, but with Melanie and the woman he had hope. If not, then they were of no use to him and would be lost in the system – disappeared. The families needn't know; after all, it had been years since they had had visitors. Hicks had seen to that. Soon, Melanie's parents would no longer be a concern and he would be free to do as he liked, without hindrance.

The woman in the room next to Melanie's was in the same state as Melanie all those years ago. Quite unresponsive, trapped in her own little world. Vacant expressions, but troubled by nightmares.

But Melanie had been a child, and the woman was not. Melanie was unresponsive to everyone except Toby. Maybe this woman also had a trigger? But maybe it was too soon; after all, it had taken Melanie ten years. But he couldn't wait that long; he needed answers and fast.

Hicks had travelled south to Nottingham, where he had unfinished business. A loose end that needed tying up, because the last thing he needed was the police or the press digging into his past – or his recent venture.

CHAPTER THIRTY-ONE

It was ten past seven when Summers drove the Jaguar to the Boulders' residence, located in the town Bolder-on-Green, which lay between Harrogate and York off the A59 York Road.

A quaint place with about six hundred residences, most of which were retired army officers, locals, or a few who'd had enough of city life and had sought refuge in the country. A few surrounding farmers produced dairy, crops, or pigs and poultry for the local butchers and shops. It had a local pub that acted as the local hotel, a village green, small supermarket, post office, doctor's surgery, and the local church.

DI Platt nodded to DC Summer's to indicate the vicar on his bicycle as they passed the church. The priest was a thin man in his fifties, with black hair and a smile for the world. Platt took note of the vicar. If anyone had known the victims, it would have been him. In his experience, Platt had found that the local spiritual leader was a wealth of knowledge when it came to their congregation.

Platt watched as the vicar waved to a middle-aged couple

pushing a blue canvas-covered pram. They smiled and waved back while yelling a greeting, 'You alright there, vicar?' The man was short with a round build and thinning blonde hair. He wore jeans and a grey-and-white pullover; the woman was taller than him and slim. Her long brown hair fell onto the shoulders of a short summer dress.

Platt had to concede they were an odd couple visually as they couldn't be any more different, but then the heart wanted what the heart wanted.

'Small villages give me the creeps,' Summers said, shivering.

Platt wasn't sure if it had been for effect or she had genuinely shivered.

'Why's that then?' Platt looked at her with interest.

'Well, I mean, everyone one knows everyone's business. I don't think you could fart without someone knowing about it in an hour,' she said.

Platt had noted an angry undertone which he couldn't understand. She had come from the city, so how would she know about village gossip? He let it lie but made a mental note of it; everything was important.

They drove through the sleepy town, past the local shops and pub. Platt raised an eyebrow as they passed a classic car dealership from what he could see. He gazed at the Jaguars and Minis, MGBs and old Rovers, and wished he could spend a moment checking out the cars.

They drove to a quieter part of the town. Platt suspected this was where all the money came to roost. The houses were all big and surrounded by sturdy fences and high walls. The driveways were long, with no parking spaces on the curb.

'We're here, guv,' Summers said, looking at the navigation system which was displaying a chequered flag symbol on the digital display.

Platt noticed that the Boulders' house had a long front garden and hedges that acted as a wall. The front gate was made from dark-stained wood. An old, large stone wall ended where the gravel path began. By all accounts, the house was secluded and hidden from view. Perfect for the killer's needs. The last thing needed was for someone to see the goings-on through the windows.

Platt and Summers sat for a while, and stared at the old place that may have been built in the thirties. Despite the modernisation, the designers had adopted the aesthetics of the town. Even the double glazing was made to look like lead windows.

'We not going in, guv?' she asked, looking at Platt, who was still staring at the house.

'Not yet. I'm just hoping to get a feel for the place. Try and see what the killer saw,' Platt replied. His unblinking eyes regarded the house and grounds, his thoughts slipping somewhere else as he attempted to put himself into the killer's shoes.

'Hello, can I help?' asked the vicar, rapidly tapping on Platt's window.

'Jesus!' Platt yelped.

The sudden interruption made both Platt and Summers jump with fright. He coughed, as if trying to calm himself and not seem as appear as if he'd filled his underpants. He gazed forward as he coolly rolled down his window using the button. 'DI Platt and this is Summers; we are investigating—'

'The murders, I know. I saw you and the other man on the telly,' said the vicar in a semi-excited voice. 'You don't seem to be doing very well, do you?' He offered a solemn shrug.

Platt's gaze fell onto the vicar with little emotion, prompting the man to step back and laugh apologetically.

'We're here to look over the Boulder place,' Platt said. 'Double checking if the killer left something, or somebody missed something. Perhaps one of your parishioners had seen something, and forgot to mention it to the investigators?' He stared at the man as if hoping the man would give up something of note. After all, a local vicar would know everybody and their little secrets. An occupational hazard some might say ... or just being plain nosy others might declare.

'Maybe you know something, sir? Perhaps we should take you down the local nic and have a chinwag?' Platt's slowly spoken words were laced with suspicion.

The smile fell from the vicar's face and he shook his head so much, Platt though he would shake it loose at any moment.

'What? Me? Heavens, no. No ... I'm afraid not, oh gosh ... is that the time?' He asked, looking at his watch. 'Well, I wish you luck, constable,' he said with a nervous smile.

'Thank you, rabbi,' Platt shot back the intentional inaccuracy.

The vicar gave Platt a confused look and went to correct him, then realised his own error.

'Oh ... uhm, good day,.' He seemed taken aback as he rode off on his bicycle.

Platt smiled at the man's discomfort and got out of the car.

'So, what's your beef with the church, guv?' she asked, puzzled at Platt's attack on the poor man.

'Nothin' much ... just it's all a load of bollocks,' he scowled, then shrugged. 'But hey, I guess if you believe, you believe, and I'm the last person to say ya can't.'

'I take it you're an atheist, then?'

'Call it what you want, luv. I just can't believe there is this thing up there watchin' all this shit that is goin' on down here, and he's doin' bugger all, It just seems ...'

'Messed up?' she suggested.

'To put it politely ... yeah, *messed up*.' Platt gazed back at the house.

. . .

Summers followed Platt and pulled her coat tight around her as a sudden cold wind brushed past them. She felt a shiver run through her body, not just because of the wind, but the feeling she got from the house. As they approached the front door, Platt noticed there were bits of police tape still hanging from the corners of the doorframe where most of it had been quickly removed.

Platt reached into his pocket and pulled out the door key he had gotten from Evidence. He inhaled deeply and held his breath for a moment before turning to Summers.

'You ready for this?' he asked, exhaling as he spoke.

She gazed at the door and nodded. It usually wouldn't bother Platt, entering a crime scene. But these were a little close to home, more so for Summers. But they both knew, to catch the killer they had to do things that were less than comfortable.

Summers followed Platt through the front door and into a long hallway. The air was thick and musty, and the stench of crime scene chemicals and stale air made them cough.

The ground floor was made up of two doors on his left and right – possibly the living room and dining room – and one at the end, which was the kitchen.

Along the right-hand wall was a staircase which he figured led to the bedrooms and bathroom. The wallpaper was egg-white with swirls; the skirting boards and doors glistened with glossy paint. A thick red carpet ran along the floor and up the stairs. Brass light fittings hung from the ceiling.

There were faded squares on the wallpaper along the stairs where framed photographs had stopped the bleaching process. Platt looked at the stairs and noted where the cleanup crew had sought to clean the wallpaper, but the blood had clung to parts of the graining.

Platt turned to Summers and she nodded as if to confirm that she was OK.

Platt nodded in reply and pulled on a purple nitrile glove before reaching for the door handle of the room to the right. He slowly inched it down until it clicked open.

They stood in what appeared to be the living room, a large space twenty feet long and twelve feet wide. At either end was a window; one showed the front garden and the street, the other showed the backyard. Platt noted that the green velvet curtains and lace nets had been left up and closed, keeping out the sun and possible prying eyes.

All the furniture was gone, but marks remained on the thick carpet where things had once stood, probably for years – the only sign that remained of the owners.

As Platt looked around, he could visualise the sofa, the sideboards, the bookshelves all placed as they were in the photograph. Summers was unsettled by how calm and focused Platt was, but then he had been on this case for a long time and had probably learned how to numb emotions.

They stood on a dust-filled beige carpet that ran all the way to the patio door. The place had been modernised at some point, possibly in the last ten years. Walls had been knocked through, but the supporting walls left untouched. The house inside was much larger than it appeared to be from outside, as the creepers and vines that covered the house from view made the place look smaller.

Platt stood in the centre of the living room and slowly peered around, taking in every detail, then referred back to the crime scene photos. Taking time to confirm in his mind the relation between the room he was in and the photographs. He had to admit the photos were good high-definition glossies and the photographer hadn't missed much.

Platt packed the pictures back into the file and Summers followed him as he headed for the second door that had been on their left. The room was a mirror image to the living room, except at the end, instead of a patio door, there were a double window and the entrance to an open-plan kitchen.

Platt noted dents in the carpet, the same thick beige as the living room. There had been a sideboard along the left-hand wall gauging from the round divots left behind, a long dining table, and enough seating for fourteen people. It had identical green velvet curtains and lace nets, and wallpaper. They headed slowly for the kitchen. The light from their touches was the only illumination, less for cracks of sunlight where the curtains didn't close. Platt needed to see just how the killer may have moved in the dark.

The kitchen and dining room were separated by an archway and breakfast bar. This detail was obviously added later to modernise the home, which opened out into the twelve-foot square kitchen area. The backdoor was to the left and a door that led to the hallway on the right. The floor was grey tile and the walls were a mix of white-and-grey stone.

Platt sauntered towards the kitchen and rested his hands on the marble breakfast bar to support himself as he took in everything. He wished the furniture had still been there, but it had been three weeks since the murders. There had been crime scene photographs, but he preferred to see the rooms as they were.

The crime scene cleanup crew had done an excellent job, as there were no signs of the blood visible in the photographs. However, he could see it in his mind's eye ... as if the red streaks, smears, and splashes were still there, covering walls and floors and furniture.

The husband had been killed in the living room, stabbed twenty-seven times with the family's kitchen knife. At the time, the investigator put in the report that he believed the husband had disturbed the killer as they broke through the back door. A reasonable theory, but why use the kitchen knife?

From what Platt had seen in the photos, the knife block had been nowhere near the back door, so it wasn't a weapon of opportunity. The killer had chosen the twelve-inch blade for a purpose. But how did the killer know that the family had that particular knife? There had been other knives in the block, but they had specifically chosen the twelve-inch Japanese blade. It was definitely more robust and sharper than the rest, but not the largest.

Platt moved toward the kitchen and stepped before the back door, unlocked it, and went to pull it open. The door was stuck. He lifted the door slightly using the handle and then pulled gently, on the off chance the frame was warped. The door swung free and gave a low *creak* as he nudged it open.

Summers watched as Platt looked about the kitchen. He stood in the centre of the room and only moved his head, his body as still as a statue.

In his mind, he began breaking down the room into sections. He started at the wall near the door and looked toward the sink, then to the cooker to the work counter near the large standalone fridge-freezer combination – until l he'd mapped out the whole room.

Platt took out the photos again and searched through them to find the kitchen pictures, and held up one set of photos. Summers couldn't get a good look because of the reflection of light from the torch. He looked towards the ceiling, then directly at Summers.

She saw the look of confusion on his face; something was wrong, but she had no idea what. What had she missed?

Platt ran towards the hallway door and then the stairwell, with Summers close behind.

'What is it, guv?' Summers yelled. Her heart was pounding heavily in her chest. He was making her feel nervous.

What had he seen that she hadn't?

She found him in the parents' bedroom. The room had been cleaned but hadn't been repainted. Again, Platt looked at the photographs. This room had been not used as the killer had done previously. The mother and daughter had been taken to the spare room at the back. The question: why break the MO?

'What are we missing, Summers?' Platt asked, standing at the door with a puzzled and frustrated look.

'What do you mean, guv?'

'This house breaks all the rules that we have come to know about the killer. He always brings his own weapons, but here he uses a kitchen knife that belonged to the family ... and he always takes the wife and daughter into the parents' room. In this case, he uses the spare room.' Platt shook his head, perplexed.

'Maybe this wasn't planned like the others. Spur of the moment?' Summers suggested with a shrug.

'No, this was planned, just like the others,' Platt declared

'We don't know that.'

'Yeah, they knew to lift the back door, or it wouldn't open, they knew that the family had that particular knife and where it was—'

Suddenly Platt stopped and his gaze fell to the bedroom window. Slowly, he moved forward and stopped at the curtains. As he turned, he wore a broad grin on his face.

Summers stared, feeling unsettled.

'Now, I see,' Platt said, walking from the room.

Summers looked at the door and then the window. She ran over to where he had stood and looked out.

'Son-of-a-bitch.' She peered back at the door and smiled, then looked out the window and onto the houses opposite, focusing on the old people's home where a group of onlookers were standing before a window and waving happily at Summers. She waved back and shot off to see where Platt had gotten too.

'Man's a bloody genius,' she said under her breath, wearing a silly smile.

She found him in the back bedroom, once again looking at crime scene photos. He took his time, mapping out the room in relation to the images in the photographs. Both the mother and daughter had been found in the room. Bound and gagged. Killed slowly after been subjected to god knew what horrors.

Platt had wondered why the husband had been killed downstairs. He had, like the other detective, thought it was a mistake. The husband had caught the killer off guard. But as he studied the photograph and room, he suddenly figured it out.

'There wasn't enough room,' Platt said, his voice quivering with excitement.

'For what, guv?' Summers asked, confused, like someone walking in at the end of a conversation.

'I was wondering why the killer had changed his MO,' Platt said quietly, his forehead furrowed. 'Why did he use the back bedroom and why did he, or she, kill the husband downstairs?'

'Well, we know why he chose the back room; the bedroom had too many eyes on it. As for the husband, maybe it was like the detective who had done the report had thought. Perhaps the husband had surprised the killer?' Summers said, but she could see he had another theory.

'This room was too small to get everyone into it.' His tone was filled with excitement. 'Sure, it seems large now, but look.' He handed her the photograph.

Summers saw what he meant. With the dresser, wardrobe, the double bed, there was very little room for the killer to have three bodies in the room.

'But why downstairs? I thought the MO was the killer liked to make them watch the men die?' Summers was confused at the sudden change in the killer's way of thinking.

'Maybe the killer did show them,' Platt said, taking another photograph from the file. The crime scene photographs showed there had been a flat-screen TV opposite the bed.

Summers smiled and nodded as she suddenly understood. 'The bastard filmed it?'

'What if the killer *always* filmed the killings, the men and the women?' Platt asked, tucking the pictures back into the file. 'We had wondered why the killer never took trophies; maybe the films are the trophies?'

'Guv, if we can find the killer and he has those tapes?' Summers said, her eyes wide with excitement.

Platt nodded. The tapes would undoubtedly lead to a watertight conviction. 'Yeah, all we have to do is find the bastard first.' But I still don't get how he knows everything about these peoples lives.' Platt suddenly sounded frustrated.

'What about the cameras we found in the other place?' Summers asked.

'There were none here. I had CSI sweep it yesterday and they found nothing,' Platt's words sounded deflated. His idea that the killer used cameras to spy on the families was shot to pieces.

They moved downstairs and stopped at the breakfast bar. He took out the photographs and spread them out. A morbid collage to be sure, but somewhere in the pictures lay another puzzle or answer. They stared hard at the rooms themselves and not the blood and gore.

'This husband sure was safety-conscious,' Summers laughed.

'What do you mean?' Platt tried to see where she was looking.

'All the bloody fire detectors. I mean really, in the bedrooms? I thought they had to be outside the rooms?'

Platt laughed and gathered up the pictures.

Summers looked shocked.

The man danced towards the front door. 'Come on, Summers; we have to find out who fitted those alarms.' He sounded excited.

Summers ran after Platt and locked the door behind her. He was already in the car when she arrived. Buckled up and staring at the pictures using his cellphone as a magnifying glass.

'How do we know the husband didn't fit them himself?' Summers asked, clicking the seatbelt into place across her body.

'Because these aren't battery-powered ones.' Platt pointed to one of the devices. 'These are wired into the mains, so there is permanent power. I saw an advert on TV for them once.' He showed her the expensive-looking device. 'This was done professionally.'

'OK, so if that's the case, why are they not on now?' A puzzled look crossed her face.

'Exactly,' Platt said with a grin.

CHAPTER THIRTY-TWO

THE SUN SHONE BRIGHTLY THROUGH THE DOUBLE security window and bathed Melanie's room in a honey glow, making the room warm and rejuvenating. She sat in her chair and read a book on the wildlife and fauna of Britain. Taking note of the flowers and plants, what was edible and what was poisonous. The book was full of photographs and detailed instructions where the plants or fungus could be found, so people knew what areas to avoid while hiking.

Melanie had figured hospitals had seen more than a few hundred cases of people picking and eating mushrooms, only to be rushed to the emergency room later.

She turned the pages slowly, taking in the pictures, but concentrating mostly on the poisonous mushrooms, their shapes, colours, any distinguishing features they had.

The room was quiet and she felt the warmth of the sun on her skin – she smiled contently, Melanie liked the quiet and had no time for that world outside her window. But still, she needed to get out into the chaos she had seen on the internet;

there was no way she would be able to find her answers in Larksford, not in her tiny room.

For years, Melanie had studied the web for information on what lay beyond those large stone walls. She had learned about money, shops, libraries, bank accounts, slang in different areas – everything that people who lived in that world took for granted.

Melanie's mentor had taught her everything she could before she left, but Melanie was able to build upon the rest. Her mentor had told her that before Melanie left Larksford, she should know everything about that world or it would swallow her up. To use her instincts and not to trust anyone straight away – trust had to be earnt.

Days later, her mentor was gone, and Melanie was alone. Still, she had everything she needed to survive inside Larksford, but she was nowhere near ready for the world beyond the wall.

Melanie was enjoying the solitude, but she also missed Toby. What had happened to him? Had he been let go after failing to get whatever it was the professor wanted from her? A pity she thought, but she had survived without him before and she would again. But it was curious. First, he stopped the visits and then her picks had been taken away. She had noticed that someone was visiting the room next door more frequently, which in itself was the most strange of all. Whoever was next door hadn't had this much attention since their arrival four months ago.

Melanie looked over at the table that held the tray with the empty breakfast plates and empty warm milk mug. Next to it was a list of books that she was allowed to get, with small tick boxes to the side of each suggestion so Melanie could put in a tick or cross, marking her choice. The list was broken into a choice of genres, such as thrillers, nature books, astronomy, maths, etc. She would get the list every so often, but she was only allowed four books every two weeks. The list was limited but held some books of interest. And if she wanted something particular, there was room at the bottom to request a specific type of book; then it was down to whoever to find a suitable one.

Melanie left the list blank. She already had enough books for now – most of which she intended to read again for clarity, despite her extraordinary memory.

A noise outside caused Melanie to stand and peer out the window. One of the patients was having a meltdown and he was running across the lawns towards the pond. Melanie watched with her heart in her mouth. He was heading for the fountain. Darting here and there, as if something or someone were after him. He fell to the ground but scrambled up again, screaming for somebody to get them off him. As he changed direction, Melanie began to breathe again.

She watched as some of the other patients ran away in fear, a few laughed and pointed, and others ignored him and went about their business.

The man fell again, but as he rose, he headed back towards the fountain. Melanie stood, fixed to the spot, unable to move. Her eyes were transfixed on this delusional man who was about to ruin everything. She sucked in a breath as he drew near. Suddenly, he fell to the ground screaming as he held his head in his hands and curled up in a ball, shouting for help, for *somebody to get them off*. Suddenly, there was a cloud of people in white descending on him while several nurses rushed to sedate the man and take him back to his room.

Melanie exhaled the breath she had been holding; she could feel beads of sweat running down her back and forehead.

'Shit, that was close,' she murmured, grasping the table.

'What was?' asked a familiar voice from behind.

Melanie spun to see Toby stood in the doorway. 'Oh ... one of the patients was having a bad day,' Melanie said. 'He was heading for the pond. They stopped him.' She pointed a thumb in the direction of the water. *The pond.* The name made her laugh. The damned thing was almost a lake. 'But they got him, no big deal.' Melanie shrugged as though it was nothing. *Thank goodness for the mask.* Her facial expression would have told him she was lying.

'Yeah, he probably didn't like the pancakes this morning,' Toby laughed.

'There were pancakes this morning?' Melanie asked with a shocked and disappointed tone.

'You have no idea what they are, have you?'

'Not a clue,' Melanie said, anticipating his answer.

'You never had any when you were a kid?' he asked, finding hard to believe.

'No, we weren't allowed things like sweets and stuff. Mom said it would ruin our teeth.'

'Well, I guess you won't want this then?' Toby took his usual spot at the table.

Her eyes lit up as he placed down a mug of hot chocolate. It had cream and tiny pink and white things on it.

'What are those?' she asked, somewhat suspicious.

'These, my dear Melanie, are marshmallows.' He pushed over the hot beverage. 'Careful, it's hot.'

Melanie went to grasp it and then stopped as she touched her mask. 'Maybe later, I have some reading to catch up on,' she said hesitantly.

Toby nodded.

'So, what are you reading today?' he said, looking at the book cover. '*Plants and Animals of Britain.* OK, that's cool,' he said, puzzled as to why she might want to know about plants.

'It's interesting ... a little sad though,' she said, settling in her chair.

'How do you mean?'

'Because I will never get to see any of the things in the book, but I like the pictures,' Melanie said with remorse.

Toby said nothing, merely gave her a sad smile and picked up the tray with the breakfast plates on it.

'Who knows? You'll get out one day ... hopefully soon,' he smiled.

'Maybe. Like you said ... who knows?' Melanie's voice held a curious tone.

CHAPTER THIRTY-THREE

DS DAVID ELFORD WAS WOKEN BY SOMEONE SHAKING HIS shoulder. His head hurt like hell, and the room was spinning.

'What the fucking hell happened?' Elford tried to sit up.

'Take it easy now, sir,' said a deep booming voice. Elford's vision was blurred. All he could see were shapes in front of him. 'You've had a nasty bang to the head.'

'Nasty bang ... some bastard clobbered me,' Elford growled, disorientated.

'Do you know your name, sir?' asked the voice.

Straight away, Elford knew he was talking to a local policeman. 'Elford. I'm working with Platt on the murders.'

'Now, take it, easy sir, we are waiting for the ambulance to arrive. You may have a concussion.'

Elford was suddenly confused at the way the man was speaking to him. He checked his pockets. His wallet and ID were gone, and so were his car keys. 'The bloody bastard has nicked my stuff, I kill him,' Elford said and winced. 'Ouch.'

He patted himself down again and smiled. His mobile telephone was still in his pocket. How the mugger had missed that he had no idea. Suddenly, there was a burst of chatter over the policeman's radio. One of the other officers had caught a homeless bloke trying to buy booze with stolen ID – one DS Elford's ID to be precise.

'I'm not going to hear the end of this, am I?' Elford asked the smiling constable. His vision was starting to return.

'Fraid not, sarge, but that was a hell of a blow you took by the look of things, all that blood,' said the officer.

Elford touched the back of his head, then checked his hand. 'But I'm not bleeding.' He was puzzled.

The white-haired constable smiled as he drew out a huge kitchen knife from behind his back and embedded it into Elford's chest.

'Shit!' Elford yelled as he woke with a start.

He touched his chest where the blade had been plunged into him, and let out a gasp of relief as he found nothing. No knife and no wound.

The dream had seemed so real – too damn real for his liking.

He was sat in a local hospital with a bandage wrapped around the top of his head. He had taken a hell of a knock on the head, enough to knock him unconscious for a few hours. A postman had seen Elford enter the house and a few moments later another man ran out. The postman had figured something was wrong when he had not seen Elford run after the man.

He peered across the room and saw Platt in a chair, reading a file. He was alone, which meant Summers was doing the legwork somewhere.

'Glad to see you're still breathing, I'd hate to be the one to tell your mother,' Platt said without looking up.

'Why? Because she'd kick the shit out of you?' laughed Elford, wincing and trying to sit up straight.

'You're not wrong. I've seen that sweet old bat clobber a few skulls in my time, but best pub landlady I've seen come out of the East End for a long time. Besides, Spain is a bit out of the way for a home visit,' Platt laughed. 'So, what happened?'

'Not sure ... walked into the house, nothing seemed out of the ordinary, no windows broken or doors kicked in from what I had seen. I made my way into one of the bedrooms to check out the scene. Suddenly, someone belted me from behind and the next thing I know, I'm here,' Elford explained. As Platt closed the file, Elford saw it was the one he had taken into the house as a reference.

'It was a homeless man. You surprised him,' Platt said simply.

'Not half as much as he surprised me, I bet,' Elford laughed.

'Probably. Anyway, the local police caught up with him and he's in questioning now,' Platt said with a smile.

'You think someone else may have come to the house before?'

'His reaction to you was one of utter fear; I think someone kicked the shit out of the poor bastard before,' Platt explained.

'At least he'll get three squares and a bed to sleep in, I guess.' Elford smiled, almost feeling sorry for the bloke. 'He didn't take my ID and wallet did he?' Elford asked, remembering the dream he'd had.

'No ... why?' Platt asked curiously.

'No reason, just some weird dream I had while I was out.'

'Well, you rest up, and I don't want to see you back until you're fit,' Platt advised.

'Thanks, guv,' Elford said with a nod, prompting him to wince in pain.

'No, seriously, when we catch this bastard, I don't need the defence to use you as a get-out-of-jail-free card,' Platt said solemnly. 'Besides, you look bloody stupid with that soddin' bandage on your head; you look like the fuckin' mummy,' laughed Platt.

The two men said nothing further. Just a simple nod and then Platt left. Elford sat back and looked out the window and watched starlings dart here and there in a clear blue sky.

And all he could think of was the dream. What the hell did it mean?

CHAPTER THIRTY-FOUR

THE BREEZE BLOWING THROUGH TREES AND THE CHATTER of birdsong filled the air outside Larksford House, but Melanie couldn't enjoy them. She was being kept in her room with frequent visits from different nurses who would bring her food and take away the empty trays. It was to be an ordinary day for her.

Toby had been in earlier for a brief moment, but then Eric had come and whisked him away. That had been about an hour ago, and she figured he wouldn't be back. *Fine, more time to read.*

Melanie gazed out the window and began to wonder where the professor had gotten too. His car wasn't outside and hadn't been all morning. Perhaps he was taking one of his mornings out?

The time went slowly, and the frequent visits by the nurses had gotten less frequent. In fact, Melanie was beginning to wonder if they had forgotten about her. She looked at the sun's position over a tall tree in the wood line, taller than the rest but enough for her to call a focal point. Usually, when the sun was over the tree, there would be a face at her door window, or they would enter just to disturb her reading, but there was no face at the window. Melanie placed down her book, rested her masked face against the glass, and looked up and down the corridor. The long stretch of corridor was empty.

Melanie started to worry about what might have happened – perhaps something terrible? She rushed to the table and stared outside, onto the gardens and driveway. But all was the same as always, with patients wandering about or sitting on outside chairs. Then Melanie started to think about Hicks and his games. The change in routine could be an order from Hicks to mess her about for the day, knock her off balance. That would explain the nurse taking the lockpicks and the lack of visits from Toby.

Melanie still couldn't figure out what Hicks wanted from her; she was no one, just a piece of the furniture that had been left behind – the forgotten child.

Then she looked at the wall on the left-hand side. The person next door – someone was spending a lot more time with them. Could it be that she and this person had something in common? Melanie definitely felt as if she was being tested and toyed with the past couple of days.

She went to her door and looked out the small window as best as she could. There was nobody there to be seen, but then the cameras were in the corridor. Before she could move about freely, nobody seemed to give a damn as long as she never got out, and even then they knew she would never go beyond the pond. Why should she, and where should she go? Or so they thought. Where indeed? That was precisely what she was working on.

First, however, she had to find who had put her in here, then find the person whose voice still bounced around in her head.

'They are going to die, and I will take pleasure in it.' Who the hell were *they* and why would *anyone* take pleasure in it?

Melanie thought back to the woman called Karen – her mentor. Karen was tall with a slender figure and long blonde hair. Her eyes had been pale pools of blue. She wasn't pretty or ugly; some would say average.

Karen used to break into Melanie's room and they would sneak about the old mansion. At first, Melanie had been surprised that this strange woman knew the old place so well, as if she had been there forever and knew every little secret.

Not long after, Karen had shown her how to use a computer, and Melanie had started doing her own detective work. Delving into her past, hoping to get answers why she had been brought to the clinic in the first place.

Melanie had told Karen her story, how she had been shipped off because of something she had said. Karen had found Melanie interesting, mostly because she believed little Melanie wasn't a crazy killer, merely a victim of circumstance. While they were messing about on the internet, they came across a story about a killer. This had been long before the family killer, but something had rung familiar to Melanie.

Then years later, the family killer started. And then, old man Hicks went and died, and Junior took over. That was when things changed.

Next came the refit and the cameras, keycard entrance doors, and security. After that, Melanie learned to be docile and plain – not a nuisance to anyone.

The place became a business. People were paying big money to put loved ones into a safe and caring place. Caring ... that was a joke from the start.

Larksford House wasn't a place of compassion ... it was a

moneymaker. Hicks didn't give a crap about the patients ... only their cash. He hired the cheapest nurses, regardless of their past – hell, some had done time or been sacked for previous mistreatment of patients. But Hicks didn't care as long as the public didn't know about it.

Hicks made sure that those allowed to wander about were doped up to the eyeballs. And those rebellious enough got put into the loud wing.

Melanie had no idea why she was still there at Larksford. They had shipped off Karen as soon as they found out she had no family and the government wasn't willing to pay the outrageous sums of money to care for her. After Karen left, Melanie had the idea that Hicks had lied and that she indeed had a family. The question was, why had he told her they were dead? But then – he hadn't. She had never met Hicks Junior. It was the red-haired nurse who had told Melanie. Maybe she had lied, and Hicks had no idea? Melanie doubted that. She had seen the two together. Two peas in a pod.

Melanie sighed, her warm breath fogging up the armoured glass. She knew that it would make no difference as it disappeared as quickly as it was formed. It had been more of a rebellious gesture than anything.

She needed to get out. Get to the computer in the break-room down the hall. But she knew the camera would spot her. Before had never been a problem, but now they thought they had her lockpicks; if she left now, they would search her room to find the actual picks and find other things she had hidden away and other stuff. No, she would wait for an opportune moment. She just hoped one would turn up soon, as she had too much work to do.

Melanie was close to tracking down the person she was

after … close to tracking down this family killer. She was convinced that the person had something to do with why she was here – even if indirectly.

Melanie used the nights to do her computer research. The staff never used the bottom breakroom after nine o'clock at night; they had a better place to go at the far end, away from the patients. There were no cameras there. Besides, for those who used to take longer breaks than usual … the loud wing wasn't the place. The people on the desk would notice the nurses' comings and goings. And it was restricted to only individual staff members.

She had planned to go to the breakroom later and catch up on something she had been working on. The latest killing had sparked her interest, as had the others, but this one most of all. She had seen a photograph in one of the tabloids that had an internet page. The photograph showed two police detectives and a crowd behind. In truth, nothing out of the ordinary – after all, she had seen plenty of these throughout the killings. But this was different. In the crowd were two figures she recognised: one was Hicks and the other was a man she had known from her childhood, but couldn't put her finger on a name.

He wore a blue pinstriped suit with razor-like creases and a brown trilby hat.

CHAPTER THIRTY-FIVE

MELANIE HAD TIME TO KILL, SO SHE WENT BACK TO HER book. Occasionally she would gaze dreamily out of the window. Thinking about the wind brushing against her skin and fluttering through her hair. The warmth of the sunlight, the chattering birds as they swooped and danced in the sky, the smell of the freshly mowed grass.

She knew the time she had been let out was more of a training exercise than anything. Possibly to be used as a reward for good behaviour, but she wasn't that kind of girl, circumstance had seen to that. Melanie was smart, rebellious, and tricky.

Her large blue eyes scanned the page, but she wasn't taking in any of the information. Her brain was too busy working on other problems. One of them was how the hell was she going to get out of the room unnoticed?

A diversion would be brilliant, but she couldn't do much from her cell. A squeak of metal signalled the door being opened, prompting her to look at her visitor. It was another nurse, one she had never seen before. This was a sizeable chubby man with black hair and obvious issues looking at women; either that or she scared the shit out of him. She hoped for the latter. The man walked over and placed a tray on the table that had toast with marmite and a cup of hot chocolate.

'Hello, not seen you before,' she said, her voice chirpy with a hint of playfulness.

'I'm not meant to talk to you,' said the man, who was in his late forties, mid-fifties. His skin was pitted and it appeared he couldn't grow facial hair. Sweat glistened on his forehead and nose.

'Well, you did a great job of that so far,' Melanie laughed.

'What do you mean?' he asked in panic, then slapped his forehead with an open palm hand after realising his mistake.

'Don't worry ... I won't tell if you won't,' Melanie said in a low, secretive voice.

The man nodded and placed a finger to his lips as if to say shush.

Melanie smiled under the mask. Where had they found this guy? And what was he meant to accomplish? She let him go on his way. His movement was sluggishly awkward, like an ageing walrus.

She picked up the hot chocolate and went to take a sip when a squeak of metal made her turn to face the door he'd closed behind him.

The door swung open slightly. In the man's haste to get the hell out of her room, he hadn't adequately secured it. She had a way out.

Melanie grinned under the mask and slowly eased herself out of the chair. She took a sip and then drew the mask back down over her chin, her eyes transfixed on the door. All the while, her brain was telling her it was all too easy, that something was wrong – *seriously* wrong.

In the control room, Toby stood watching the monitor that

was facing Melanie's corridor. He sipped his hot chocolate, eyes glued to the screen as if he were worried he would miss something if he closed them for even a millisecond. The nurse who had just been in Melanie's room walked into the control room and wiped the sweat from his forehead.

'Do you think she bought it?' Toby asked the man who wasn't as nervous as what he had made out.

'Fuck knows. I guess we will find out soon enough,' he said in a broad Scottish accent.

Melanie reluctantly reached for the door. Her arm stretched awkwardly, as if a great weight were attached to it. As she grew near, she could hear voices in her subconscious screaming, 'Don't do it; it's a trick!'

Her hand reached for the door, and sweat began to cascade down her back and face.

Toby paused as he went to sip. He had seen the hand inching out of the doorway. He held his breath. What would she do? Close the door or step out into the corridor? Suddenly more of her arm stretched out, then the rest of her arm, a shoulder. Then her face. Toby smiled.

He had her ... hook, line, and sinker.

Toby's smile fell away as Melanie looked up at the camera and extended her middle finger.

'I guess she's smarter than the boss gave her credit for,' chuckled the nurse who had just walked in. He sat and reached for the small doughnuts that sat on a small table away from the equipment.

Above the table was a sign in large black bold lettering: FOOD AND DRINK TO BE CONSUMED HERE ONLY AND NOT AT YOUR DESKS.

Toby had often wondered about the sign until he had seen how some of his other colleagues ate.

'Or she's just being her usual charming self,' laughed Toby.

'Why are we doing this again?' asked the chubby nurse before stuffing a fist-sized doughnut into his mouth.

Toby cringed and shook his head in disbelief before turning his focus back to the monitors. 'Beats me. Something the professor wanted us to do. Fucking cruel if you ask me.' His tone was filled with pity.

'I got no idea what's up with the professor lately. It's since this last murder, he's gone all weird.'

'You mean weirder,' said a thin male nurse who had just come in from doing his rounds. 'But you're right about there been a link to the killings.' The nurse made a beckoning gesture, as if trying to huddle the others together in a secret chat. 'You know that woman in the room next to Melanie? She was a victim of the killer, but she survived.'

'Nah, that's just tales, that is,' replied the chubby nurse, shoving another doughnut into his maw.

'No fucking word of a lie. I was here when they brought her and her daughter in,' declared the thin nurse.

'Her daughter?' Toby asked, the hairs on the back of his neck standing on end.

'Yeah, her daughter. Pretty young thing. Completely messed up she was; didn't help much that one of the other nurses took a shine to her,' said the nurse sheepishly.

'You?' Toby asked with a scowl.

'No fucking way; the poor little cow had been messed up enough,' said the thin nurse, his gaze falling on Melanie's room.

'So, what happened to her?' Toby asked.

'The girl committed suicide. Hung herself. She used the bed and a sheet ... or so they say,' the thin nurse explained.

'There was an 'Internal Investigation' ... of sorts.' The man laughed drily, as though what had happened was absurd.

'But you don't think she could have done it?' Toby asked.

The nurse shook his head. 'She had put the bed on its end and hung herself ... so how did she get up there? She was only five-six or somethin', and off her head.'

Toby nodded, seeing the nurses point. A five-foot-six girl hung herself from a six-foot bed?

The thin nurse said, 'Swept it under the carpet they did, told the father it had been suicide, left out the bit about the assault though.' He wore an angry look on his face. 'Guess Hicks didn't need the coppers making a fuss, lookin' into things he didn't want them too.' He shook his head.

'When was this?' Toby asked suspiciously.

'Oh, I don't know ... six years now.' The nurse's face went pale as a shot of realisation crossed his mind. 'You don't think?'

Toby reached for the phone and started to dial a number.

'What you doin'?' asked the chubby nurse.

'Phoning the cops – they need to know this,' Toby said, confused.

'No they don't,' stated the thin nurse.

'And I suggest you quickly forget about it. The last thing we need is the fuckin' copper's knockin' on our door.' The chubby nurse's eyes were wide, anxious.

Toby knew he couldn't have had anything to do with it; the bloke was too young. But that didn't mean there wasn't something else he was hiding, something he didn't want the outside world to know.

CHAPTER THIRTY-SIX

THE BRIGHT SUNNY MORNING HAD BILL IN GOOD SPIRITS. The night before, he and his family had enjoyed a fantastic meal and watched a little TV together. He missed those family moments every time he went away. Admittedly, the conversation was always one-sided. One spoke and the others sat and listened. 'Ah, families,' Bill would sigh with a broad grin.

He had driven to work early, leaving his family to rest while he hit the road. The company he worked for was five miles away from home, so it wasn't too bad of a commute.

Bill whistled along to a tune on Radio 2, an oldies song that he hadn't heard for ages. 'Just another reason to smile,' he thought. Today was going to be a good day. He'd put in his final figures, make some calls, check out new clients, and hopefully finish around five. Nothing could spoil his day. He pressed his foot on the accelerator a little.

As Bill pulled into the local filling station, he was still whistling. He filled up the tank with petrol and went into the kiosk, which was in fact a small shop. Bill picked up a couple of pork pies from the refrigerator and a fizzy drink to wash them down with. In front of him was a little old lady who was often there.

She only came to the shop because it was closer than the big supermarket that had opened two miles away. But Bill didn't care, he had time to spare. That was when he saw the news. **Policeman attacked in murder house?** said a texted news flash scrolling underneath the story they were showing.

Bill's eyes fixed on the story. He felt his mouth go dry with fear. Panic flowed over him, and he tossed some cash at the small, slim man behind the counter.

'Ah, hang on Bill! Don't you want your receipt?'

'Sorry, got to go! I'll be late for work,' Bill lied.

But he wasn't going to work; he had to find out if it was the same place he feared it was.

———

Platt met Summers in a local coffee shop. He was sitting in a corner with the full view of the doorway and all those who came in.

Summers smiled as she approached. Before her chair sat a latte with caramel flavouring waited for her. 'Thanks, guv. I've been gagging for this all morning.' She took off her coat and settled into the chair on Platt's right. It wasn't that she wanted to get cosy; she just knew sitting in his line of sight of the door would drive him nuts. 'How's Dave?' she finally asked.

'He'll live. Gonna have a helluva bump on his head for a while though,' Platt smiled.

'Did the homeless guy say anything yet, like why he was there?'

Platt shook his head as his gaze fixed on a group of young lads who'd entered. The usual poorly dressed kids, but harmless enough. Platt figured they were there for one of the girls behind the counter. A sweet blonde thing with too much make-up and a cheeky smile. The three lads laughed and joked before buying a couple of coffees-to-go and some sausage rolls.

'No, not yet. One thing bothers me though,' Platt said, taking a sip of English Breakfast tea.

'What's that, guv?' She wiped the creamy foam from her top lip.

'Dave said there was no sign of breaking and entering. All the windows and doors were secured. He used the key he had gotten from Evidence, so the locks hadn't been changed.'

'So, how the hell did our homeless guy get into the house?' she asked, perplexed.

'Exactly,' Platt smiled, not just because she had figured it out, but because they had a new puzzle to solve. 'Was he there because he was homeless? In truth, I wouldn't be surprised if he wasn't at all. In fact, from what Dave was saying, it was more like he was looking out for the place.' Platt leaned back into his chair.

'You mean the homeless bloke was guarding the place?' Summers said, unconvinced of his theory.

'Well, let's look at the facts. Everything was locked up tight, no signs of a break-in. So, what does that tell us?'

'The man was locked in, or he had a key?' Summers took a long sip.

Platt looked at his watch. It was nearly twelve o'clock. They had travelled down to Nottingham after hearing about Dave's hospitalisation. At first, he had thought Elford was at death's door and sped there as quickly as possible, leaving Summers to check out a few details on the present case. She had travelled down later on the train, seeing no sense in taking two cars back to North Yorkshire.

'We need to check out that house,' Platt stated, his mind spinning with too much information about too many things.

'You think Dave was on to something?'

'I'd say our unexpected guest in cell three answers that one, don't you think?' Platt smiled wryly and took another sip of tea.

CHAPTER THIRTY-SEVEN

MELANIE'S REFUSAL TO PLAY THEIR GAME HAD AMUSED
Toby. He had known that she wouldn't have gone for the door.
He still couldn't figure out what Hicks hoped to accomplish
with all these games, or his interest in the woman in the room
next to Melanie.

Toby reached into his pocket and took out the two strips of
metal and held them flat in his outstretched palm; he knew that
they were not Melanie's actual lockpicks, merely two hairpins.
They would have done the job, but not as effectively as she
obviously had.

He started to understand how tricky Melanie could be,
possibly more than those who took her at face value. A big
mistake, by any accounts. She had an agenda; he knew that. He
just didn't know what it was. Toby figured Melanie was going
to try and escape Larksford – and who could blame her? From
what he had seen and understood, he didn't believe she should
be there in the first place. There was something wrong with the
entire tale of her incarceration and the way Hicks hid her away.

Toby made a choice; he was going to help her. But he didn't

know how just yet. There would be a lot of planning. But then she probably already had a plan, Melanie certainly had the time to get something in place.

The only problem was Hicks and Eric; between the two, they had her on constant surveillance.

He smiled as a simple idea came to him. Why not just ask her what she wanted him to do?

———

Melanie looked out of the window. Her gaze locked onto the fountain and the pond. She was angry; the problem was she had no idea with who. The years of planning and slipping out had all gone to waste. Her investigation into the killings and murder before had given her something to focus on.

She had discovered that years before the family killer had surfaced, there had been a murder in Nottingham. Once again a family, but this time they were all dark-haired, not fitting with the family killer's MO. She had also found out that the wife in that attack had been married to an abusive husband. After a spate of beatings, he was jailed. She had divorced him and remarried after moving away.

After hacking into the prison database, Melanie found that the man had been released six years prior to the family killings. Unfortunately, all trace of the man after that disappeared. He was in the wind with a new name, new life, and possibly a new lust for killing.

However, Melanie did know that the man came from North Yorkshire, and she had traced some of his old pals. All of which had disowned him when they had found out what he had done. In the years that the man had spent in prison, they'd all moved around. Some had stayed in Yorkshire and others had moved to London or the Midlands.

However, they all too had disappeared off the face of the earth.

Melanie did have a hunch, but one she couldn't prove while she was confined to her room. Suddenly, for the first time in a long while, she felt lost and powerless. Melanie had to admit she needed help.

But *who* could she trust?

There was a creak of metal as the door slowly opened. Melanie turned around to see Toby in the doorway. She smiled underneath the mask, but it quickly faded as she began to wonder why he was there.

'Come to take my books away now?' she asked in a bitter voice.

He shook his head and pulled the door shut slightly, leaving a centimetre gap between the frame and the door. 'I've come to help,' he whispered.

'Help? Help me how?'

'You're looking for something ... someone. I wanna help you.' He moved forwards quickly, as though someone had pushed him from behind.

'You want to help – ha! That's a new one. You've done nothing but play me ever since you got here,' Melanie hissed, wishing she could take the mask off to show him how mad she was.

'I was only doing as I was told. I never understood before,' Toby said, his voice wrought with regret.

'Understood ... what?' Melanie asked suspiciously.

'That you're not a patient. You're a prisoner,' he declared solemnly.

CHAPTER THIRTY-EIGHT

THE BLUE SKIES HAD QUICKLY BEEN REPLACED BY GREY, angry-looking clouds, the storm the weather girl had predicted was on the way. The constant high front that had consumed Britain for so long was going to be met by a swift cold front from Europe. From the woman's description, it was going to be four days of rain and high winds, creating a weather front of biblical proportions.

Hicks looked up through his windscreen at the dark looming clouds and shook his head. He didn't need this, not now. Torrential rain would slow him down, even force him to stop. He was a couple of miles from Nottingham, with another six miles until he got to the old house. He began to curse himself for that quick detour he had done, but it had been necessary. Even though he had left early, he had another matter that had sought his attention.

He had found a suitable person to take Melanie's place in another care facility. The director there owed Hicks a favour, and now he was collecting. The new girl would be there by the time he arrived back from his business in Nottingham.

Hicks had left instructions with a nurse he trusted. The girl would be given a room down the hall from Melanie and dressed up like her. Of course, she would be sedated up to the eyeballs, just in case. This girl had a violent history, sad really, but it would put the icing on the cake.

Hicks thought about the attack on the policeman. He wondered if there would be more police at the scene; after all, it was now an active crime scene again. He had no idea they had caught the person who had assaulted Elford; all he knew was it had happened in an old house in Nottingham. And that was enough to get him panicked.

The sudden small splashes of water droplets impacted Hicks' windscreen, causing the wipers to brush them away. The droplets increased in number, then turned to a massive downpour. The rainstorm hammered down as if Hicks were going through a carwash. Quickly, he adjusted the heater onto the windscreen as it began to fog up and swore under his breath, then yelled at the radio as the guy reading the weather warned everyone about a sudden rain shower.

'Too late, you silly arse,' Hicks screamed as he slowed the car.

In front of him, the only hint of traffic was the red glint of some backlights. He knew if this deluge continued, he would have to leave at the next junction for the rest stop. His eyes weren't as young as they used to be and were straining under these intense conditions. With luck, it would only be a quick shower.

But the dark heavens above showed no signs of letting up. Hicks swore again as he saw a sign for a rest stop. A cup of coffee and time to rest his eyes was probably the best decision. Not that the weather gave him much choice. He swore angrily as he turned off and made his way onto a large parking area. All Hicks could hope for was that the rain would stop, and the idiot hadn't left anything incriminating lying about the old house – especially something that could lead back to Hicks.

He found a spot near an entrance and got out of the car and ran over to the mall-type complex as fast as possible, locking the car with the key fob as he went. The lights flashed on to signal the vehicle was locked and secured. The compound held shops and a restaurant –everything a person needed on a long journey. He headed straight for the restaurant. The smell of freshly cooked food made his stomach rumble, and idea of just a coffee left his mind was replaced with the lust for a full English breakfast.

As he looked out of the large windows, he realised he had time. The rain was getting worse, with no signs of slowing. He would be there for a while.

He placed an order and waited for the pre-cooked food to be plated and handed to him. He had to admit the picture on the advert looked better, but then, his smile and charm had gotten him an extra sausage and piece of bacon. *Oh, the joys of knowing how to manipulate people.* The coffee smelt strong and required more milk and sugar than usual.

Hicks found a table away from everyone and the towering windows. He needed time to think, plan. He had sorted out the Melanie problem for now and hoped the person he had entrusted to take care of things could follow it through if the Freemans turned up suddenly in his absence.

Hicks had arranged for them to visit the next day, as he would be out of town. He knew they were impatient and had anticipated any pre-emptive move on their part. He had been able to hold them off for all these years, and *now* they start making this fuss.

Hicks settled down to his breakfast. It wasn't the warmest of meals or the most appealing to look at, but he had to admit it tasted good. His eyes kept drifting to his mobile phone that lay on the beige plastic tabletop, almost hoping it would ring with some kind of news. Whether it was from his trusted nurse saying the Freemans had been there and were satisfied, or even the moron from the house saying how he had gotten away. As time went by, his fear of both cases going wrong grew stronger.

After an hour of drinking too much coffee and staring at his phone, the weather died down to a light shower and sunshine, and Hicks was back on the road.

———

Jason and Abby Freeman waited for Danni to come downstairs for breakfast as they wanted to speak to her about some things – things she probably wouldn't like.

'Morning,' Danni said, bouncing into the kitchen with a refreshed look on her face. Her face was red from a hot shower and facial scrub. Her smile faded as she noticed her parents sitting in the open-plan part of the living room. Danni felt a chill come over her. Last time they did this, they had found a joint in her room.

'Danni, sit down a sec. We need to talk to you,' Abby said, her voice trembling with emotion.

'I'm sorry, I won't do it here again; am I in trouble?' Danni blurted out, not thinking.

'No, I fear we are ... wait ... 'do it' *what?*' Jason asked, hearing the admission of guilt for something.

'It doesn't matter,' Abby interjected. 'We feel it's time to come clean about something,' She saw relief and also puzzlement on her daughter's face.

'What ... what is it?' Danni sat crossed-legged on the big armchair.

'It's about your sister,' Abby started.

'Sister? I don't have a sister,' Danni said, her eyes wide with confusion.

Abby and Jason sat quietly, the unmistakable look of guilt on their faces.

'You told me she was dead.' Danni suddenly felt a cold chill run down her spine.

Abby and Jason said nothing.

'When I was in the hospital – after that accident ...' Danni's voice was hoarse; the tears began to stream down her face. 'You said she had *died* in the accident?'

'No, not quite ... dead ... just...' Abby struggled to find words.

'Just ... what?' Danni asked, her voice low with anger.

'She's ... uhm ... in a hospital,' Abby said softly.

'Is she sick ... in a coma like I was?' Danni's tone expressed concern.

'Not really sick, as such ...' Jason said, trying to choose the correct way of phrasing it.

Danni looked at her parents and the penny dropped.

'Oh, that kind of hospital. You mean she's frigging bananas,' Danni replied, the anger coming back in her voice. 'So, what did she do? Talk to herself, behead dolls or something?'

'No, she said she was ... going to hurt us,' Abby said, choosing to bend the truth to protect her daughter.

'Hurt us how? You mean, kill us?' Danni asked, dazed and confused, standing up and taking a step backwards. 'I ... I don't believe you.'

'It's true baby, she threatened to kill us all,' Abby explained.

'No, I mean I don't believe you would lie to me about my own sister,' Danni growled and tears began to flow down her face. 'How long?'

'Ten years,' Jason said, his voice full of regret.

'Ten fucking years?'

'Watch your mouth, young lady,' Abby yelled.

'Or what? You'll lock me up too?' Danni yelled back.

Abby slapped Danni across the face so hard, it left a red mark. There was sudden silence as the realisation of what had happened sunk in. Abby went to say something, but no words came out; her mouth, like that of a fish lying on the bottom of a boat, flopped open and shut.

Abby went to reach for her daughter, to pull her close and hug her. But Danni had already bolted for the door, holding her anguished, sobbing face. 'I hate you! I hate you! I wish you were both dead!'

The door slammed shut, and Abby felt her knees buckle. Jason caught her as she started to fall. The drama had been too much and she had fainted. He placed his wife on the sofa and looked at the closed door, his gaze full of tears and rage.

'Hicks ... I want my family back,' Jason growled.

CHAPTER THIRTY-NINE

'A prisoner – really?' Melanie asked as if testing his sincerity. She didn't move or attempt to stand. She simply glared at him through the slits in the mask.

'Look, I don't know what Hicks is up to. It's like he's made some sick sort of collection of people. He has a lady next door to you locked up as well, but then she's not really the sociable type from what I've seen; she doesn't move, just stares out of the window,' Toby explained, his gazed fixed on the wall that separated Melanie from the other patient. 'Apparently, she was the victim of the family killer or something.'

'What woman?' Melanie stood.

'I don't know her name,' Toby said. 'From what I got from the others, she and her daughter survived the killer's attack. Not sure about the full story, but I do know that Hicks has turned all his attention on her, and somehow you're involved in his plan.'

Melanie folded her arms across her body, as if in a self-hug.

'What plan? What has she got to do with me, or I with her?' Melanie asked, her words cold and emotionless. She needed time to think, but she also knew that Toby's arrival would stir up trouble. She looked at Toby, her gaze a splinter of ice which made him shiver.

'Did you tell anyone you were coming to see me?' Her voice was stern, severe.

'Well, not exactly ...'

'How *exactly*?'

'I said I was doing my rounds. Why?' Toby asked, puzzled at her reaction.

'Then go and do your rounds – the longer you are here, the more suspicious people will become,' Melanie said as she went back to her chair.

'Shit, you're right. Damn, they would have seen me coming here,' Toby murmured.

'Then go,' Melanie instructed. 'But when you come back, make sure you have a drink and a snack or something with you. To make it look as if you came to ask me if I wanted anything.'

Toby thought about it and nodded, conceding it was a good plan.

'But check the other rooms here first, as though you truly are doing your rounds,' Melanie said without looking at him, her gaze engrossed on the cover of the book she had just picked up.

Toby went to speak, but changed his mind and waved as he closed the door behind.

She had been correct in her assumption. He had to make it look like he was doing his job and not rushing straight to see her.

Toby checked the other rooms and their occupants. Most ignored him, others snarled and gave verbal abuse. The Loud Wing. The name made him laugh. These people were probably the sanest in the building and that included the staff.

. . .

Melanie put down the book, *A Guide to Wild Plants of Nothern Britain,* and smiled. Why she had picked up that book and pretended to be interested in it she had no idea — either way, her plans were going to have to change. She would have to get out of the estate sooner than she'd previously thought. No matter. Everything had been put into place; all she needed, of course, was the final piece to the puzzle and, apparently, it had been sitting next door to her for months.

Melanie smiled at the irony of the situation. All the time she'd been breaking out to go to the staffroom, checking the internet for clues, she could have saved herself time and befriended her neighbour. However, it wouldn't have been that simple. She had read about trauma cases; people who had gone through something like what she had endured were more likely to shut down. A simple 'Hi, I'm your new neighbour' wouldn't get the responses she was after, if it got one at all. Plus, Melanie had no idea what the hell Hicks had been doing to the woman, the cruel bastard.

She peered out the window and across the grounds. The rain became a slight drizzle. Small lakes had formed near the driveway and on the lawn, courtesy of the earlier deluge. Above, there were now patches of blue peaking from the mass of grey clouds. Still, it was a miserable day, cold and wet and un-inviting for people to venture out in. *Perfect.*

CHAPTER FORTY

'You've got to be kidding me,' moaned Bill as he crouched down to change his tyre. Luckily the rain had stopped him from going too fast. He had heard the thump-thump-thump of the slow puncture as he had left the petrol station.

A large nail protruded from the rear right tyre. He cursed his luck. He could travel back to the petrol station on it and change it there. Bill kicked it and jumped as he forgot his footwear's thin material and metal hit nail, bone and flesh.

'Oh, for fuck's sakes,' he cursed again. Mumbling to himself, he limped around to the rear of the car. As he opened the boot, he stared at an empty well. The spare was missing.

He slammed down the lid and mumbled his way back to the driver's side. He was cold and wet. At least the heater worked. As he sat on the comfortable seat, he thought back to where the spare wheel could have gotten to; then he remembered one of his work colleagues had borrowed it.

'That idiot Barry said he had put it back, lying little toad.' Bill cursed again.

Then he remembered he had the other set of tyres with

rims at home. He'd always meant to swap them over. A new set he had gotten on the off chance these had become too worn. People had said he was nuts. That he was too organised, too finicky; everything had to be meticulously planned out. He laughed. *Who's laughing now?*

Bill put the heater to full and slowly turned the car around. He would go back home and put the new wheels on. *Not a problem, everything will be fine.*

Danni walked about in the rain for a while, using bus stops for shelter. She had tried to contact her boyfriend, but he wasn't picking up. She needed someone to talk too – someone who would understand. Her friends would listen to her, but that would be as far as it went. 'There, there' wouldn't make the pain go away, nor would alcohol. That was when she thought back to Uncle Bill. They didn't live that far away.

She looked at the list of buses that would pick up from here. She smiled. The next bus would stop not far from her uncle and aunt's house. Danni needed to talk to Aunt Ann; she would know what to say. Maybe she even knew what had happened. Danni couldn't see her parents right now, possibly for a long while. She tried her boyfriend's number again, but it just went to voicemail. She'd try again later.

Fifteen minutes later the bus arrived – a half-full double-decker with room enough on the upper deck. Danni pulled out her MCard from her purse and swiped it against the reader; it beeped to confirm the transaction, then she raced to the upper deck before the transport pulled away from the pick-up point.

Danni felt alone. She was hungry and angry. Perhaps she was angrier because she was hungry? Danni didn't know. She didn't know anything at that point, just that she had to go and see someone who cared.

· · ·

The bus ride took almost an hour with all the pick-ups and drop-offs, but Danni didn't mind. She had started to dry out as well as calm down. Danni had been listening to music on her phone through her earpieces, cordless things that flashed blue from time to time. Danni started to see houses and buildings she recognised. They were close. She got up and headed for the steps, holding onto seats and handrails to steady herself as the bus's momentum knocked her off balance from time to time. For her, it was part of the fun, not falling flat on her face or down the steps.

The transport heaved to a stop and the doors hissed open. Danni pulled her coat tightly around her before thanking the driver and stepping onto the pavement. The paving slabs were filled with oceans of water, and the street looked more like a canal.

'Bloody weather,' she groaned as she played hopscotch, trying to land on a piece of paving that wasn't under water. She had stormed out of the house wearing trainers, not realising a monsoon was taking place. But then who made a dramatic exit *after* they had sorted out what to wear?

Aunt Ann lived about half-a-mile away from the bus stop and, in that weather, that was half a mile too long. Danni avoided getting too close to the cur;, there was always some silly arsehole who thought it was funny to drive through the puddles at high speed and drench people. She'd had enough experience with that. One old guy had done it while she was wearing a white dress; it became almost transparent with the drenching. Thankfully, karma had been a real bitch that day and he had crashed his car into a police transit van that was parked a little further down.

. . .

Danni thought about phoning ahead to see if they were in, but then her uncle had said they had been under the weather of late so she figured someone would be home. Danni hurried down the street, hoping her quick movement would somehow make her less wet. The house was down the road on the left and, at her present speed, two minutes away at the most.

Danni ran onto the driveway and down the path that next to it. Thankful for the small covered entrance, she shrugged off as much water as she could before ringing the doorbell. She waited for a moment as there seemed to be a lack of noise from within.

She rang a second time. Again, nothing. Danni knew she had to get dry before she caught her death.

Ann had shown Danni where the spare key was kept – just in case of emergencies, and as far as Danni was concerned, this was an emergency.

She made her way around the back of the house and to the garden shed. The key was underneath a statue of a fat frog with light-up eyes. She grinned happily at the fact it was still there and headed for the front door.

Inside was cold and gloomy with a heavy smell of something ... something she couldn't quite place. She made her way to the living room. The place was as she remembered it. Neat and tidy, not a thing out of place.

'Hello Aunty Ann, Uncle Bill, anyone?' Danni shouted, expecting a mumble or even a cross word. However, silence filled the air. She shouted again but failed to get a response. She figured they had gone to the doctors or they were feeling better and had all gone to work.

Danni went into the kitchen, expecting to find food that had gone off, but again, everything was pristine. She shrugged off the feeling something was off and clicked on the kettle, and searched for the tea bags and mugs. They were in the same cupboard they had always been. The tea was in a tin second from the left and the mugs were on the right.

While she waited for the kettle to boil, Danni head into the utility room and switched on the light. Inside were a washer and a dryer, also a basket with some of her cousin's clothes. Danni held up a bathrobe that seemed to be the right fit and stripped off her damp clothes, then stuck them in the dryer. She knew her aunt wouldn't mind and neither would Uncle Bill. Setting the dryer to the quick-spin cycle, Danni went to check on the kettle's progress. Small plumes of vapour rose from the spout. She poured the water over the teabag and left it for a minute before putting in the milk and sugar, then removing the teabag.

The mug was warm as she cupped it with both hands. She blew on the liquid before taking a sip. As she moved into the hallway, the smell hit her again – a pungent smell of what she could only explain as dry rot or something. Perhaps a pipe had burst and they were spending time in a hotel while it got fixed. It was a definite possibility; after all, the weather had been worse than usual the past couple of days.

Danni took another sip from the tea and looked at the staircase. She was curious to know what had happened. With another sip, she ventured up the stairs. Ageing floorboards creaked with each step. When Danni reached the landing, she stopped. The mobile telephone that she had stuck into the pocket of the bathrobe had buzzed, letting her know there was a message. She took it out and checked the alert – it was from her dad. She wanted to ignore it, but the time on the bus had calmed her. She was still mad at them, but she guessed she understood their motives. With a smile, she pressed the call button. After several rings, she heard her dad's voice.

'Hey, Danni, look sorry it took so long to tell you, sorry ... well, just sorry really.' His words were soft and sincere.

She smiled again and wiped away a tear from her cheek.

'It's OK, Dad. I'm still pissed at you and Mum though,' she said, trying to sound tough.

They both laughed.

'Look, why don't you come home, and we can try and sort things out.'

'Sounds good, but you'll have to come and get me though,' Danni said, unconsciously opening doors to rooms.

'OK, no problem ... where are you?' Jason realised that should have been the first thing he'd asked.

'I'm at Aunty Ann's ... it's weird though.' The smell was getting worse.

'Weird – how do you mean?'

'Nobody seems to be—' Danni froze.

The mug of hot tea smashed as it hit the floor. Her eyes widened, her mouth tried to release a scream, a cry out, anything, but nothing came. She was frozen in fear.

'Don't disturb them, they're sleeping,' said a voice from behind.

Jason Freeman heard the piercing scream before the strange sounding voice of his brother-in-law. His blood ran cold and he yelled before the line went dead. Still shouting, Jason felt his knees buckle, and all he wanted to do was throw up.

'What is it? What's wrong?' yelled Abby as she ran over. She began shaking her husband.

'Call the police! Something's happened to Danni!'

CHAPTER FORTY-ONE

It was 12:45 in the afternoon when Platt got the call to go back to North Yorkshire. The text message had read: two bodies found with a possible link to your killer. Vague to say the least, but nevertheless a lead. He had Summers spin the car around and told her to head back. Platt had let her drive while he looked through Elford's files on the old house and the killings. Apart from the type of women, the MO seemed the same. Possibly the killer had found a new infatuation with blondes of athletic build.

Summers had engaged the sirens and warning lights, blues and twos all the way. Platt could see her expression was one of concentration and suddenly cracked a smile of enjoyment. He had to admit she was a hell of a driver, but then she was also half his age, so her reaction time was twice as sharp. In his youth, Platt had been just as good, with that same look. Now, he was tired of it all. The case had taken too much from him, but he still had his soul.

Well, up until he caught the bastard ... and then it might be a different story.

The drive up north would take an hour at least, as long as the traffic stayed steady and there were no jams. Time enough to catch up on Dave Elford's file and see how he thought it tied in with the recent killings. At first, Elford had thought it was a waste of time – after all, it had been Summers who had found out about the house and done most of the research. But Elford had followed the investigation through – and got a nasty smack on the head for his trouble.

This wasn't some blind alley, shot-in-the-dark theory; it was a lead, possibly the best they had up to now. Like Elford had said, 'Maybe this was where it had all started?'

Platt pulled out his phone and dialled the number for the local police in Nottingham. The phone rang twice before the desk sergeant picked up.

'Sergeant, this is DI Platt. We will be late getting to the house and the interview with the man you picked up. Yes, sorry about that ... we got a call. They've found another family,' was all Platt had said before disconnecting. He didn't feel he needed to say more, nor did he feel compelled to give a shit what they thought. He had a job to do, so to hell with the rest of them.

'So, Dave thought that this might have been one of the first murders by our killer?' Summers asked as she wove between cars.

'It was a theory; I could see where he may have thought so too. The wife was found brutally stabbed, the ex-husband – who ended up a suspect, may I add – he was a wife-beater, that's why they split.'

'So, the detectives at the time liked the ex-husband for the murder because he was an arsehole? Makes sense,' Summers said, her tone ringing with sarcasm. However, in a murder investigation, she also knew the spouse or ex-spouse was always top of the list when it came to suspects. 'Did he have an alibi?'

'At work, he travelled a lot apparently,' Platt murmured, gazing once more over the file.

'What happened to him?'

'We don't know; he's in the wind. He did time for assault and after that, gone.' Platt went through the particulars of the case.

'Gone? How could he just disappear?'

'Change his name, skip the country, who knows? All we do know is he wasn't happy about being sent away,' Platt said as he flicked over an incident at the courtroom. 'Apparently, he told her in open court that she was, 'A lying bitch that would one day get what was coming to her,' or so the report says.' Platt tapped a finger on a highlighted part of the report.

'So, he tracks down his ex-wife and daughter, finds out they have a new life and what? Goes bonkers and kills them?' Summers shook her head.

'And so, still filled with anger, he kills one family a year.' Platt's voice sounded as if he was narrating a play or audiobook. It lightened the mood slightly. 'No, you're right, of course, this wasn't a random killing, no more than the others we are investigating. A man like an ex-husband would have been more savage, dare I say, and to kill his own daughter? I can understand the wife, but *his own kid*? No, it doesn't add up,' Platt closed the file and his eyes.

Summers knew he wasn't taking a nap; he was sorting through the facts in his head.

CHAPTER FORTY-TWO

MELANIE HAD TO BE ESCORTED TO THE BATHROOM BY A small-framed man. She had smiled when she'd seen him; he was thin with a large head and squinting eyes that sat behind huge round glasses. He had looked like a mole from one of the storybooks she had read, or perhaps it had been a cartoon she had seen on the internet.

They had walked there and back in silence, and afterwards, he had scurried away – just like a mole. As Melanie entered her room, she looked at her table. There, in the centre, was a cup of hot chocolate and a plate of chocolate digestive biscuits.

Melanie had started to wonder why she had gotten such a treat so early in the day – and then it came out.

'Melanie,' said a soft but powerful voice. It was Eric and he was sat in her chair, reading one of her books. Which surprised her as she had no idea the man could read, let alone tie his shoelaces. 'At some point tomorrow you'll be going for a walk with Toby – you can go where ever you want.'

'Wherever I want? *Really*?' Her voice rang with suspicion.

'The only thing is that you can't come back in here, and you can't go round to the front of the hospital,' Eric said in a slow tone as if she were a slow person.

'So, you want me to get lost for the day while you do some freaky shit with my room?' Melanie picked up a biscuit.

'No, it's just we have some people from the health department coming, and you are ... well ...'

'Not here!' Melanie lifted her mask slightly and bit into the biscuit.

'No ... no, you're ... well ... special, and the professor is afraid they might want to take you away.'

Melanie was about to call him a lier, but then she thought back to her mentor. She had disappeared not long after a visit – by who Melanie had no idea, but what Eric said held a frightening truth. Because if she were taken away, she would have to start all over and she had no idea what the new place would be like. At least at Larksford, they didn't care enough about what she did.

'Fine, but I want to be allowed to leave my room like I used to before,' she stated, hoping to strike a deal.

'I never knew you used to leave your room,' Eric said with a shocked expression, placing the hairpins onto the table before walking towards the door. 'It may be a short notice thing, so ...'

'Yeah, no problem, I'll make sure I'm out of your hair as quickly as possible,' Melanie said, sounding uninterested.

However, she was *very* interested. Why did they want her room? For the moment, it was none of her concern. All she knew was she was able to leave at any point just like before. Melanie smiled. She had to hand it to them, using her lockpicks as a bargaining tool was brilliant. She just hoped that she'd played dumb enough for them to buy it. But before she left the room, she would have to make sure her secrets were well and truly hidden.

Melanie thought about why she had to avoid the front of the building. The crap that Eric had said about the people from the health service doing a check was stirring her interest. In the years she had been at Larksford, the people doing the checks had only been there once and a few minutes, and only once had they ever visited the Loud Wing.

Then there was the question of why her room? Sure, hers was probably the only one that looked as normal as you could get, given the fact they were in a hospital. She considered her family. Were *they* coming to visit ... was that it? Was she being taken out of her room because Hicks didn't want them to see her?

The was a loud beep and then the sound of the metal security door opening at the hallway entrance. Melanie moved closer to her door and tried to look through the small window to see what was going on. She could hear footsteps of two people approaching – Eric and the nurse with the red hair.

'The professor wants the women swapped as soon as possible – this *can't* go wrong,' Nurse Hawthorn said.

'Don't worry. I've talked to Melanie, she's cool with it,' Eric laughed.

The footsteps approached the room next door, then stopped.

'Is he sure she knows something?' Eric asked.

'He's not sure, but he can't risk it; that's where Melanie comes into it. She broke out of her catatonia, and he is hoping it will help this one to do the same,' Hawthorn explained.

'So, what's all this government grant crap he is looking for?'

'The professor thinks if it helps her, it can help others ...a breakthrough in medicine,' Nurse Hawthorn explained, her tone was full of sarcasm.

'You mean he's hopin' to get rich outta this?' Eric chuckled. 'And they call me an idiot.'

'You *are* an idiot, Eric. But you are *our* idiot.' Her tone was full of fond sentiment.

Melanie shot back from the door, as though she'd gotten an electric shock from it. Her eyes fixed on the door in shock, unable to comprehend what they were planning. She felt her breathing getting heavy, as if there was no air in the room, and her heart began to pound in her chest. She grabbed the sides of the mask, ready to rip it from her face as she felt the walls closing in on her. The feeling of fear was beginning to consume her, a feeling she hadn't felt since that day ten years ago when ... Melanie stopped, her breathing slowed, her heart returned to its usual rhythm. The last time she had felt that kind of fear was when she had heard that voice in a dark room.

She was starting to remember.

Melanie was too far away to hear what the red-haired nurse and Eric were talking about. Undoubtedly, more plans and arrangements for her leaving her room. But she still had no idea why, just that Hicks needed her gone. Then she remembered what Toby had said, how she was relevant to the professor's research into the person next door. Which fitted what Eric had just been speaking about to the nurse. But how was *she* the key? She was nothing special, just a woman who had been there since she was a child.

Melanie rushed towards the door and eased her masked face against the glass once more, hoping to catch more of the conversation.

'I hear the prof got a phone call that freaked him out?' Eric asked.

'People talk too much in this place.' Hawthorn's words were harsh.

'So, it aint true, then?'

'He got a call from the parents. They want to see her. They can't be permitted to do that as you well know; that is why we have to exchange the women,' Hawthorn explained.

The pieces started to fall into place. Her family was coming to visit for the first time. But Melanie knew that wasn't going to happen – how could it? After all, they had told her that her family was dead. And as for her parents, what had they said to them to suddenly warrant a visit?

Melanie knew if he was planning on staying, Hicks would have to lie to her parents, trick them somehow. Maybe he had told them she had gone mad and was some kind of psycho killer, which would make sense if they came to Larksford and saw how she lived now. They might possibly attempt to get her out – but Hicks needed her.

Maybe they would show Melanie's parents the woman next door and tell them she was Melanie. Which would work if she was in a catatonic state like Toby had said. They'd think twice about removing Melanie from specialized care.

But something in the back of Melanie's mind told her that wasn't enough. Maybe if they swapped her with someone dangerous, angry, aggressive, that would scare them away for good.

She realised with horror that if her family thought she was still a threat, they would leave her here and forget she ever existed. Then this prick, professor Hicks, could do whatever he wanted.

She glanced at the thick wall that separated her and the other woman. If this killer had gotten to her, why had she and her daughter survived? *This woman knows something, something that's driven her over the edge.*

Melanie needed to get to a computer. She had to learn more about this woman and, hopefully, more about herself. She still had no idea where she had heard those words that rang in the back of her head: they are going to die, and I'm going to take pleasure in it.

CHAPTER FORTY-THREE

It was 2:15 when DI Platt and DC Summers arrived at the address he received by text. The local police were there. They had cordoned off the driveway and blocked off the street to keep the public back far enough so those wanting snapshots using their mobile phones would not be able to do so.

The road was illuminated with an eerie blue from the police cars' lightbars. Platt pointed to an empty spot next to a police patrol vehicle parked on the other side of the street. Behind it were several onlookers gazing out their front windows with wide, expectant, and inquisitive eyes.

'Pull in over there will you,' Platt instructed.

Summers stayed silent and manoeuvred the vehicle.

'That will be twelve-fifty please, guvna.' Summers laughed at her terrible Cockney accent.

'Put it on my tab, I'm good for it,' joked Platt as he unclipped his seat belt, seeing officers at the front door, chatting amongst themselves while shaking their heads in disbelief.

'Looks like it's a bad one,' she said, leaning forwards and looking past Platt.

'They all are, but it looks like there is something different this time,' he stated solemnly and placed a hand on the door latch.

'Only one way to find out.' She opened her door.

Platt watched Summers exit the vehicle. He took a deep breath and joined her. She was fresh-faced and enthusiastic; Platt couldn't remember the last time he was either of those. The truth was, he couldn't remember the last time he slept properly – or at all. The most he was managing was twenty-minute catnaps here and there.

As they walked towards the residence, Platt had the feeling all eyes were on him. Not judgemental, but questioning. *Why?*

The press had been kept well back as per hiss instructions. The local medical examiner was at the rear of his Volvo, filling out the report. In front of the Volvo was the black transit van from the morgue, the doors open to accept the bodies of the latest murders.

'I can't believe there was another murder; I thought this guy was on a cycle?' Summers said as she manoeuvred past the crowds before getting to the police tape.

The constable on barrier duty recognised Summers and nodded before lifting the tape to let her through. A set of photographers tried to dart under the lifted tape. But they were quickly met by another police officer who had foreseen their mischief.

'Well, it looks like our killer can change their MO at the drop of a hat,' Platt said grimly. 'I mean, look, the first victim was dark-haired and now, he or she, has a taste for blondes.' He gazed around the scene outside the house. 'So, what's to say that they feel that only killing once a year is no longer enough? What if our killer has gotten a real hunger for it?'

'DI Platt and this is DC Summers.' Platt showed his warrant card and then took the sign-in sheet from a bright-eyed constable. He signed in and handed the sheet to Summers, who did the same. 'I take it the bodies are upstairs in a bedroom?' Platt asked knowingly.

The PC went to answer but failed to find the words, so he merely nodded.

'Don't worry, son, it gets easier,' Platt said with a wink as he handed back the clipboard.

'Not like this it don't, sir,' the PC responded, causing Platt to shoot the man a strange look before racing up the steps with Summers close behind.

'What's wrong, guv?' she yelled after.

'I don't know yet,' Platt answered, his tone filled with fear. How could this one be worse? They pushed past two officers and entered the parents' bedroom.

Platt and Summers just stood at the entrance, their mouths hanging open. He had seen some horrendous sights on this case, but nothing like this.

On the bed lay what had once been a mother and daughter. Platt could only assume it was the two women but couldn't be sure. Not because of the wounds but because of the amount of decomposition of the bodies.

'How long does the doc think they've been here?' Platt asked one of the officers.

'Can't be sure, but months I'd say, due to the bodies are turning into soup,' came a tiny voice from behind them.

Summers and Platt turned to see the ME they had seen outside.

'Doctor Foster,' said the man as if to introduce himself. 'And yes, I know, so keep the jokes for another time.' He was a small man in his fifties with grey hair parted to the side and a clean-shaven red-cheeked face. A pair of gold-rimmed glasses covered his pale blue eyes. He wore a blue suit with a brown knitted waistcoat. 'I won't know exactly until I get them back to the lab.'

'This is DI Platt, and I'm DC Summers,' Summers announced to the doctor.

'Charmed,' Foster said with a gracious smile.

'No sign of the husband?' Platt asked, pointing to an empty corner of the room.

'He's outside in a patrol car, sir,' said one of the policemen at the doorway, but refused to enter, his head turned to the side, looking away from the two corpses.

'He's alive?' Platt asked, his tone both shocked and confused.

'Yeah, and that's not all,' said the other, beckoning them to follow him downstairs.

Platt and Summers followed the older cop down and towards the kitchen. There they found a young blonde woman surrounded by her parents. The girl was crying uncontrollably, rocking back and forth, mumbling something to her mother, who held her close to her. The policeman stopped Platt and Summers, forcing them to turn their backs on the family.

'The young woman, she found the bodies,' he said in a low tone.

'Was it a robbery gone wrong?' Summers asked, thinking the teenager had broken in for money or stuff.

'No, she's family; she had an argument with her parents and thought she'd come here to hide out for a bit. She used a spare key to get in,' replied the PC. 'Her name is Danni Freeman, eighteen years old; the parents are Jason and Abby. One of the victims was Mrs Freeman's sister, Ann, and the other was Deborah, the daughter.'

'And the husband?' Summers asked, shocked that he could do a Norman Bates and nobody noticed.

'Oh, him, yeah. His name is William Brown, or Bill to his friends. A security camera salesman who travels around a lot,' the PC answered.

'I can see why,' Summers said, her black humour not going down well with Platt or the PC.

'Take the husband back to the station. We'll have a chat with him later,' Platt instructed the PC, who nodded and headed for the front door.

Platt looked over at the family. He was used to giving bad news; the old sorry for your loss speech, but this seemed different ... this *was* different. In truth, he had no idea where to start. Platt took a deep breath, exhaled, and headed towards the Freemans.

'Mr and Mrs Freeman, I'm DI Richard Platt, and this is DC Kate Summers,' Platt introduced them both. His voice was calm, and he spoke in a gentle yet commanding voice.

Years of experience of doing this, Summers thought.

'I know it's not the best time, but we have to ask you some question, is that OK?'

Summers noted that Platt's comment was more towards Danni, but he directed the question towards all of them.

'Did he kill them? Did ... he do that to them?' Danni asked, forcing back tears.

'We don't know anything yet,' Platt replied.

'He said they were sick, he said ...' Abby's emotions took over and she held her daughter tight.

'We hadn't seen them for months, at least six, I think,' Jason said, then shook his head, unable to comprehend what had happened to his sister-in-law and niece. 'He came around the house the other morning, he seemed ... dare I say ... normal,' Jason explained.

'Why did he come around?' Summers asked suspiciously.

'He was checking on the security system his company had installed,' Abby said, blowing her nose on a handkerchief.

'Did he come over often?' Platt asked, making notes in a notebook he'd removed from his inside jacket pocket.

'No, he did the paperwork months ago. Then last month a team came around and fitted it. We hadn't seen him since then ... well, until yesterday, when he came to inspect the work,' Jason explained.

Abby nodded as if to confirm what he had said.

'I know he goes around all the properties to ensure every-thing is working. Customer relations and all that bull.' Jason's tone had turned sour.

Platt made more notes and waited. He knew this next ques-tion would be difficult, but he had to ask it. 'Danni, can you tell me what happened?' Platt asked, his voice gentle.

'I'd had an argument with Mum and Dad,' she said softly.

'What about?' Platt hoped it was relevant.

'Just family stuff,' Jason answered, hoping to stop Platt's fishing expedition.

'OK, so you left the house; how did you get here?' Platt gave Jason a cautious look.

'It was pissing down, so I caught the bus. I just wanted ... needed ... someone to talk too. Aunty Ann was always there when I needed to get shit off my chest,' Danni explained. 'I got to the front door and tried the bell, but nobody answered. I was cold and wet, so I needed to get dry. I knew where the spare key was, so I let myself in.' Danni paused, reliving that terrible moment. 'When I came in, I smelt something weird.'

'Weird?' Summers asked.

'Yeah, like mouldy eggs or something damp,' Danni explained, a curious look on her face as she thought back.

'Go on,' Platt instructed.

'Like I said, I was cold and soaked to the skin, so I went to the kitchen to make myself a cuppa and dry my stuff off. I found a bathrobe in the utility room and put my stuff in the dryer. I found it odd nobody was home. After a while, I got bored and went for a look around.'

'And that's when you ...' Platt urged.

'I'd just had a call from Dad; we were talking and he was saying how sorry he was, and that's when I walked into—' Danni broke down.

'Is this necessary?' Jason barked.

'With all respect, Mr Freeman, we have discovered the bodies of your family who have been dead for some time, possibly killed by your brother-in-law. I appreciate this is hard, but it *is* necessary.' Platt's voice was calm but stern; he was bored of people getting in his way or whining instead of helping.

'Dad, it's OK. I want to do this. I have to do this for Aunty Ann, Deb and Mel,' Danni said, giving her father's hand a squeeze.

Jason nodded and smiled proudly.

'I walked into the room and saw them; I've never seen anything like it. The smell was unbearable. I went to scream, but nothing came out. That's when I heard him, Uncle Bill. He stood behind me and told me, 'Don't disturb them, they're sleeping.' He was looking at them at them as though they were people and not ...' Danni sounded confused. Her eyes stared into space as she tried to comprehend her uncle's actions.

'He was probably in shock,' Summers said. 'People react differently to such things.' She glanced at Platt whose demeanour was calm – possibly too calm – considering the situation. She remembered when she had heard about her family; she had hit rock bottom fast. Drinking to excess, sleeping with anything that breathed. She'd been a mess. But she had gotten through it with the help of a friend – a professor, in fact. A man her family had known for a long time. Her mother and father had gone to university with him: Professor Albert Hicks.

———

William Brown was taken to the local police station to undergo a psychological examination before he could be interviewed. Summers had recommended it due to the circumstances.

Of course, Platt had to agree it was a good idea. The last thing he needed was any evidence being thrown out because Bill Brown hadn't received proper treatment or an assessment of his state of mind beforehand. Hell, if the man was that far gone – he still saw his family as they had been and not rotting corpses – anything he said would be questionable.

Platt had left it with the station to sort out a doctor who could check Bill out. He had enough on his plate. Dave Elford was still in the hospital and they hadn't checked out the old house that Elford had been attacked in; they were against the clock until the killer was due to strike again. In terms of Bill, they had time – he wasn't going anywhere.

If the killer held to a pattern, an area, then it would make things easier. They could at least keep tabs on the women that fitted the description. However, this bastard moved around, not sticking to anything apart from his type of victims. But that led to another question. If these people were so spread out, how was he choosing them? It wasn't like he could go to a website.

Platt eyes flew open. Summers was driving them back to Nottingham to speak with the homeless guy and check out the house. They definitely had time.

CHAPTER FORTY-FOUR

'POLICEMAN'S WIFE AND DAUGHTER SURVIVE INTRUDER' read the headline. Melanie read through an article she had found on the web search. The story was five months old and didn't give much information, just that the policeman's name was Richard Platt. His wife and daughter had been abused but left alive. The police took it as a warning – or worse, a taunt. Of course, Platt wasn't investigated as he was in London at the time, looking into the family killer.

Melanie finished that article and found another. This reported the suicide of the daughter while in care. Melanie's eyes widened. The daughter had been at the same clinic as her mother: Larksford House.

Melanie read on, but the information was vague, to say the least, due to the clinic giving as few details as possible. Melanie looked at more articles, this time on the killer and the policemen in charge: DI Richard Platt and DS David Elford.

Of course, the papers were less than kind, saying that the police were incompetent because the killings were going on so long without a hint of an arrest. But the more Melanie read, the more she found the press guilty of immortalising the killer.

'Talk about giving the bastard an ego boost,' Melanie said, shaking her head.

She wondered why the killer had spared Platt's wife and daughter. They were both blonde, athletically built, everything that the killer was looking for in his prey. So why them? Maybe the killer thought that letting them live would be more hurtful than killing them, that the thought of them reliving that day over and over would do more damage – knock Platt off his game even.

But that made no sense. If Platt were unfit, they would just assign another DI. In fact, how had he managed to stay on the case, considering what had happened?

Melanie imagined that Platt was the sort of man that could convince the powers that be he was still the right for the job, but chances were that nobody wanted this case. It was a career maker or breaker, and the way the odds were stacked against the police, no one would commit that sort of career suicide. She imagined there were plenty of people waiting to take over the case if it started to look promising.

Melanie leant forward as she started to read another page, this about another murder by the family killer, this time it was the family of a PC. The family had all been killed less for her as she was in London at the time. They showed a photograph of the family using an old still the press had been given. Again, all the women were blonde, less for the PC who had dark hair.

Melanie took a bite from one of the cheese-and-onion sandwiches she had found in the fridge, which had been marked several times with Eric's name. As if his name had been a warning to ward off anyone who thought about taking them. As if that was going to put her off eating it. If anything, it made it more of a dare.

The story was a short piece that was concentrated more on the victims than the PC. Possibly a precaution by the police to keep her out of the public eye. A wise move, Melanie had thought, due to the unwelcome publicity she might receive. Melanie cleared the user history and closed down the internet before stretching off. Scanning the web had made her eyes burn, and she had a slight headache starting.

She had lost track of what time it was – not that she ever needed to know before. Time seemed irrelevant to her. All she knew before she had found the restroom was it was either day or night. She looked at the clock on the wall. It was half past two. *Time to go, I guess.*

Melanie stood up and put the room back together as it had been, ensuring it looked as if she had been resting on the sofa. Changing the channel on the television to something she may have watched.

As she left, Melanie turned off the lights and headed for toilets. She didn't need the toilet, but it seemed less conspicuous if she went somewhere else than the staff room. As good a deception she could muster, given the circumstances. Melanie knew they had her on camera, so if she could make out like she was going to the restroom to watch TV and sleep, then it was better than no explanation at all.

As Melanie left the room, she stretched her arms high, as though she had been sleeping, and sluggishly headed for the toilets, the camera in the corridor following her every move.

CHAPTER FORTY-FIVE

AGAINST DOCTOR'S ADVICE, DS DAVID ELFORD discharged himself from the hospital. The news report on the bodies found in North Yorkshire had shaken him from his bed rest. The news report had been vague, saying the victims' father had been taken in for questioning, but not much else. From the picture the media was painting the guy had killed his own family and was possibly the family killer.

'Bloody animals,' Elford had said as he watched the report. Knowing full well the poor bastard had just lost his family, and now they were already hanging the noose around his neck.

As he walked erratically outside, he saw a taxi pull up. He let the old couple get out and shot in behind the driver. 'Local police station, please mate.'

Elford checked his pockets to see if he had his wallet and ID. He sighed with relief as he felt the stiff leather from a warrant card and the thick bulge from his wallet. Inside, he found a twenty-pound note and a tenner. More than enough, he thought or, at least, he hoped. In his jacket pocket he found a piece of paper. It was the address of the house he had been checking out.

'No, wait! Take me to this address?' Elford requested, handing over the address.

'Yeah, wherever,' said the cabby, tapping it into his satnav.

'How much?' Elford asked.

'Thirty quid?' the cabby replied after brushing his hand over his jaw.

'Police business.' He showed his ID, knowing the cabby was pulling a fast one.

'OK, a police discount; ten quid,' the cabby said begrudgingly, as if he were doing Elford a favour.

'Done. Now, drive.' Elford sat back as the man put his foot down.

The desk sergeant had trouble finding the usual doctor to look over Bill. The clinic where he worked said he was busy and would be unavailable until that afternoon. The clinic had said they would send someone else in his place, which made the desk sergeant more than happy; the last thing he needed was the DI breathing down his neck. The sarge knew Platt was covering his bases; he couldn't blame him. A case like this, you had to make sure some smart-arsed lawyer didn't get the killer off on a technicality. Not that Bill was at present a suspect as such; he was simply helping them with their inquiries.

He loved that saying. It made the public think you were guilty before they had even started with the questions. The sarge made a few notes on a large A4 pad and went back to reading the paper.

. . .

At three, Platt sat opposite the homeless man in one of the interrogation rooms. It was an eight-by-eight box with a thin, grey wiry carpet and white plasterboard walls. Against the left-hand wall, a table sat lengthways to accommodate four chairs, two on the left and two on the right. The table had a blue-grey top with a single pillar support, which sat in the middle and was bolted to the floor. Above was a single halogen strip-light that made the room bright and uncomfortable. The duty sergeant had made sure the man had gotten a shower and was a given a jumpsuit to wear while his clothes were examined by forensics. Platt had also left instructions the man should be fed and given plenty of water – after all, you got more flies with honey.

The interview was recorded using four high-definition cameras placed in the corners of the room. The use of tape recorders had long since passed; now the detectives could see the people and hear them whenever they needed. Platt had welcomed the change but still wasn't entirely sure how it worked.

He went through the usual formality of saying who was in the room, who the interviewing officer was, who was being interviewed, along with the date and time. Platt was ready to ask questions.

But he simply sat and stared at the man. Not in an angry way or any way that could be classed as threatening. In fact, the look had no emotion at all. It was like being stared at by a doll or picture. And this made the man feel even more uncomfortable than if Platt had brought in thumbscrews.

The man began to fidget. Even though the pause had been for a few seconds, to the man it seemed like an eternity. Again, Platt had done nothing that was threatening or could be classed as illegal. However, the man was beginning to sweat buckets.

'I trust you had a good meal?' Platt asked, his voice soft and calm.

The question made the man stop fidgeting and stare at Platt in confusion. 'Uh ... yeah ... thanks,' the man replied, gazing around the room. He peered at the long mirror that sat on the opposite side from them and stared at their reflections for a moment, weighing up who sat beyond that two-way mirror.

'It must be tough, living on the streets I mean; of course, I have been lucky and have no idea,' Platt said, pouring a glass of water from a plastic bottle he had brought in.

'Uh, it's OK, I suppose,' said the man, confused at what was happening.

'So, how long have you lived out there?'

'Dunno, ten years I suppose. I forget.'

'I guess all the shelters are full. Lots of homeless people at the moment due to the army cutbacks, I guess.' He stuck his fingers in his trouser pockets, then rocked back and forth on the back legs of the grey plastic-coated chair, feeling the grey cushioned material against his back.

'Tried um – too many bad people wantin' to nick ya stuff, fuckers,' muttered the man.

'Terrible, bloody terrible,' Platt said, shaking his head, sounding concerned and not patronising. 'I bet that house you're in changed all that ... bet it was like winning the lottery. A nice roof over your head, comfy, warm ... safe?' Platt's voice turned to a whisper, as if it were a secret.

'Oh yes, sir,' the man said with a broad grin that showed off a set of poorly kept teeth.

'I mean, when you were offered the chance to stay in a house and look after it, it must have been like a dream?' Platt added, throwing his arms about as if he were happy for the man.

'You're not wrong there, sir, that it was ...' The man stopped, a puzzled look on his face.

'And then that man broke in, started looking through your house. I mean, how dare he?'

'Yeah, the bastard was snoopin' around good he was, bastard. In *my* house,' the man said, banging his fist on the table.

'Bloody snooper,' Platt said, banging the table as well, as if joining in the man's distress.

'Yeah, bloody snooper.'

'And I bet you kept that house all safe and sound for all that time, no snoopers until him. Yeah, and I bet the person who paid you to look after the place, I bet he didn't even appreciate what you'd done. I mean, he isn't even here for you now, bastard.' Platt banged the table again.

The man roared in anger and banged the table and sat back and folded his arms, sulking. The act of aggression was more towards the man's benefactor Platt surmised.

He nudged the plastic glass of water over to the man, who took it and emptied the glass quickly. A disgruntled look still etched onto his face.

Platt cracked a smile. *Got ya.* 'The house must be pretty special if you're taking so much care of it?' Platt slowly poured another glass of water.

'Not really, not to me anyway. Just a place to keep warm, dry and safe, plus it pays,' the man said and began to squirm. His eyes fixed on the cup; the sound of the water had him needing to take a piss.

'Yeah, but an old place like that, you'd think someone would want to do it up, put it on the market?' Platt put down the bottle – to the man's delight.

'Didn't ask, didn't want to know, still don't. All I know is it's a roof over me head and I ain't gotta go searchin' for fuckin' food,' the man replied in a huff.

'So, what's in the place?'

'What ya mean?'

'You know, furniture, things … anything?'

'There's some sofas and stuff, the kitchen is still there, nothing works though, no power ya see,' explained the man.

'Seems a bit unfair, you watching over the place and there's no heating, electricity?'

'Ah, it's worse on the fuckin' street. Besides, the geeza has a heater for me, little campin' stove thing, sweet as houses it is,' the man said with a proud wink.

'So, the man buys things for you?' Platt said with interest as he leant forward, planting his elbows on the table. A crooked grin formed.

'I never said it was a he,' said the man with a sudden, surprised look. 'No bloke would smell like that.'

Platt's mouth fell open. He looked over to where Summers stood in the doorway – only to find an empty space.

CHAPTER FORTY-SIX

THERE WERE BLOOD SMEARS ON THE WALL AND THE METAL mirror had been dented in several places. A trail of blood went from the toilet cubicles to the sinks and then out the door.

Melanie sat in the staff room. The first-aid kit in front of her on the table. She was carefully wrapping a bandage around her right hand. She had scrapes to her arms and legs.

Melanie had no idea it was a nurse. It didn't register. All she knew was as she had stood to pull her knickers up and someone punched her in the face and sought to tear off her pants. They were going to rape her – or so she thought. Why else would they have done all that?

The nurse had moved fast and had waited until she was in a vulnerable state – so he had thought. Either way, it was a bad move on his part.

There were loud shrieks and flashing red lights as the alarms sounded. The man who'd been watching the security cameras had sounded the alarm. But only when Melanie had walked out of the bathroom covered in blood.

The corridor was filled with the sound of people running

towards the bathroom. Then came a couple oh-my-Gods as the staff went to help. But nobody entered the staffroom. Nobody thought to check on Melanie – nobody except Toby.

'So, what happened?' Toby asked calmly.

'The bloke slipped I guess ... dangerous places, bathrooms,' Melanie replied, her voice calm and emotionless.

'Luckily, he appears to be alive.' Toby grabbed the bandage and finished the job.

'Only because the voices told me to stop,' Melanie said, her own voice sounding strange, as if crazy.

'You didn't bite his dick off?' Toby asked, thinking back to the story Eric had told him.

'Nah, broke his jaw – bastard,' Melanie said, her tone now angry.

'What happened? Did he try to rape you?'

'Either that or he's got a thing for fresh stinky underwear,' she said, pulling her hand away as soon as he had finished taping off the end.

'How can you be sure? Maybe he—'

'Because he punched me in the face, then tried to rip my knickers off. I'd say that was a pretty big clue. Besides, there are no males allowed in the ladies' bathroom. He entered, or at least tried to. Got what he deserved, if you ask me,' Melanie declared flatly, stretching her bandaged hand.

'There is that, I suppose, but he could say he was passing and heard you cry out.'

'Really, and the security tapes will what? Disappear, get wiped by accident?' Melanie laughed.

'What do you mean?' Toby asked, confused.

'The camera is on this corridor, filming everything, and nobody noticed the guy enter the bathroom?' Melanie frowned.

'Perhaps he missed it?'

'Didn't miss me coming out though, did they?' Melanie was

suspicious at the slip-up. 'He' and not 'they'? Did Toby know there was only one person in the security room? She realised Toby knew the man lying face down in a pool of his own blood. He was the other guard who was supposed to be in the booth.

Melanie didn't think her retaliation had been over the top; in fact, the bastard probably got off easy. The odds had been against her. The guy was about two-hundred pounds to her one-twenty; he was bulky where she was athletically thin. She hadn't heard him enter the room. In fact, it had been a shock when she opened the stall door and found him there. When the man had punched her in the face, the mask had taken most of the impact, but it was still enough to send her backwards.

As she fell back onto the toilet seat, Melanie kicked up with both feet, catching the man in the throat. This had winded him enough for her to rush past and kick him under the groin, knowing this would hurt worse than a kick to the balls.

As he went down, she had kneed him in the face. But as he flew back, he had flicked up a hand and caught her across the face. Fortunately, again the mask had taken most of the impact.

The man roared in anger, but she was quick and nimble. As he swung again, she rolled and swiped his legs, causing him to lose balance and fall. Too bad the sink had been there to catch his fall … too bad for him anyway. The was a sickening crack as bone met ceramic. This knocked out some teeth and broke his nose, as well as dislocating his jaw.

Melanie froze as the blood-soaked nurse stood up like some beast from a horror movie. The man lifted his arms like a bear and lunged at her. The fact he was still conscious had stunned her for a blink. However, that had been a blink too long.

The nurse had grabbed her and thrown her against the mirror. She let out a cry as she smashed against it, then fell down onto the blood-soaked sink. The man came again, but he was slower this time, as if he had expended all his energy on the last attack. But she was also winded and could do little as he picked her up from the ground by the throat as if she were a rag doll.

Melanie could feel the air being choked out of her. She could feel her limbs becoming weak from the lack of blood and oxygen. But she mustered enough strength to lift a hand and apply enough pressure on to his injured nose to cause him to scream in pain and release her.

Melanie coughed and sucked in air. But she couldn't afford to pause. Not before this beast had been put down. She ran at him again and jumped, using a double kick. He smiled and sucked in a lung-full of air; he wasn't going to be caught unprepared this time.

However, Melanie wasn't aiming for his chest. The double kick landed with full power onto the man's right knee. There was a cracking sound and the man screamed, grabbing his injured limb. He stumbled to steady himself but slipped on his own blood. He came down hard and smashed onto another sink. This time the ceramic sink broke away from the wall, and deep red fluid began to fill the floor around him.

Melanie was surprised – and impressed – that she had actually caught him in the knee. She thought she might come up short and catch his upper thigh, but luck was on her side. She lifted the mask and spat on him as she walked over his limp body. She left the room with a hidden smile. *Let the bastard bleed.*

Toby stood speechless. He didn't know what bothered him more; the fact one of the nurses tried to rape a patient or the fact Melanie had explained the story so emotionlessly. She had no guilt, anger, fear.

A noise in the corridor made him look out the open door. Four nurses were wheeling the bloodied mess of a man towards the security door. Outside, an ambulance waited to take the man to a hospital: Leeds.

'Bloody Hicks is going to shit himself when he hears about this,' came a familiar voice from the corridor. It was Eric and another man. Eric looked into the staff room as he walked past.

'Bet you didn't get that on your little camera?' Melanie shouted. This time there was a hint of sadness. She had been betrayed by someone she had considered a friend for years: Eric and that stupid camera.

Toby saw something in Eric's eyes; they were cold and dark. Not like before, not like they used to be. Was this the true nature of the man?

Eric walked past without a word, not even to ask how Melanie was.

'I've made sure a female nurse takes you to the showers so you can clean-up,' Toby said with a sigh. He was confused about the hospital, the people and most of all, Melanie. Of all the patients there, she showed the least signs of mental illness; yes, sure, she had issues. But she had been placed into care and left for ten years. Who wouldn't have issues?

'Thanks,' Melanie said gratefully.

'I have to go out ... got something that the clinic wants me to take care of, but I'll check on you later,' Toby smiled.

Melanie smiled back and nodded.

A knock on the door made them both look over. There stood a brutish looking woman over six-feet tall and built like a Russian shot-put athlete. Melanie looked at this beast of a woman and smiled to herself.

'My protection, or you just don't want me coming on to any more nurses?' Melanie laughed.

'Possibly a bit of both,' Toby smiled, shaking his head.

Melanie walked up to the woman, who was called Heidi, and looked at her up and down. 'I don't know; she's kind of cute.' She slapped the nurse on the arse before heading to the shower room.

Heidi's eyes opened wide with shock, and then mellowed as a cheeky smile formed.

'Oh, Jesus,' Toby said, again shaking his head, this time with disbelief. 'Don't get your hopes up, Heidi; she's not your type.'

Heidi's smile faded.

'Or I'm just not yours,' Melanie shouted down the corridor.

Heidi's eyes lit up again, and she followed slowly down the hallway.

Toby looked at his mobile telephone. There was a text message from a number he knew well. It merely said: things are getting out of hand, end it now.

He placed the phone back into his pocket. He would reply later. But first, he had business to attend to.

CHAPTER FORTY-SEVEN

BACK AT THE POLICE STATION, PLATT HAD CLOSED DOWN the interview and rushed outside after Summers. The only question on his mind was where Summers had disappeared too? Platt found it odd – but also disturbing – that Summers had left just as the homeless guy had said that the house owner could be a woman.

The desk sergeant had said she had rushed out, but he never asked where she was going because cops came and went all the time.

Platt was pissed because all he could think was she'd had something to do with the whole damned mess – or at least been part of it. But there was another part of him that refused to believe that. The more he thought about it, the more sense it made. She was working on a high profile case that was more close to home for her than anyone.

Platt questioned whether it had been a good idea to have brought her on to the case. After all, it had been his recommendation that had gotten her on the team. He'd followed her career and had seen something promising, so naturally he had taken this woman under his wing. Dave was due for promotion, and he'd already told Platt he was looking at going back to London at some point, so that would leave room for a new DS.

Platt stood outside and felt the crisp air on his skin. It made his skin tingle after been stuck in the building too long. He breathed in fresh, unpolluted air, then exhaled slowly. Summers had gone, and there was no call for irrational behaviour. One way or another she would be back, or they would catch her, he had no doubt of that. Just another problem for another day. He had another problem for now: he needed to be at the old house. And he needed a car and driver – because his driver had legged it with the car.

Platt was about to turn and go back inside to talk to someone about getting a new vehicle when a squad car pulled up and two officers got out.

'Are you pair off duty?' Platt asked brashly.

'Uh ... no guv, why?' said the taller of the two.

'Because I need to get to the house where they found Elford.'

The two smiled and nodded, anything to get out of doing paperwork.

'Hop in, guv,' said the shorter of the two as he slid onto the back seat, giving Platt room in the front.

There was only one place Summers would go if she had something to do with these killings – that house.

As they drew near the old house, a black bellow of smoke plumed over the roofs. Suddenly Platt had a bad feeling and told the driver to floor it.

Pulling onto the street Platt and the officers saw what Platt had feared: bright orange flames clawed through the windows like a mythical beast trying to escape. The squad car came to a screeching halt, and Platt rushed over to the blaze while the officers began to keep people back. The taller officer radioed through, requesting back up and emergency services.

'Bollocks,' Platt shouted, kicking the ground. 'Fuckin' bollocks!'

As he turned to face the people, he saw the familiar faces of Elford and Summers, each one stood at either end of the crowd, regarding the blaze. Platt stood with the inferno warming his back, anger welling inside of him. He was tired – tired of chasing his tail and having the carpet pulled from underneath his feet every time they had something to go on.

Dave Elford had asked him if he thought the killer was a cop; now he was beginning to feel as if it was. The worst part was it could be either of the two in front of him right now.

In his rage, Platt never saw the car leave down the street.

A silver Mercedes-Benz GLE.

Platt spotted where Summers had left the unmarked Jag and marched over there, hoping that Elford and Summers would follow. He didn't have to look around to know they had anticipated what he wanted.

He stopped and stared at the pair. He didn't want a scene. Not with so many mobile telephones connected to the internet. His outburst earlier could be put down to anything, written off by a media statement. But him ripping into two officers, especially one that had just come out of the hospital, would look bad and he didn't need that right now. The press would have a field day and Platt would be replaced – or worse.

'Get in the fucking car you two,' Platt growled under his breath as the street filled with more police and fire trucks. He gave instructions to one of the officers as he pulled up. 'Hold the press off, and get the arson unit up here. I'll be back at the police station with these two.'

The officer nodded and started with the cordons for the public. Platt jumped into the back seat and told Summers to drive.

'Where we going, guv? Back to the station?' she asked, starting the vehicle.

'No, not yet,' Platt replied, sitting back and massaging the heels of his palms into his eyes.

'Where to, guv?' Elford asked suspiciously.

'We're off to jail; I want to know more about this husband who disappeared off the planet after spending five years inside,' Platt said, still angry. He had questions for them, that was for sure. But they could wait. He was mad and tired, not an excellent mix if you wanted to think rationally.

Platt knew the prison was about an hour away. He nestled down in the back seat and closed his eyes. 'Wake me when we get there, and there is *no* rush. Nobody's going to burn down the prison ... I hope.'

Summers put her foot down on the accelerator and gave it some gas. Elford looked back at his boss using the mirror on the sunblind. Platt seemed peaceful, but Elford knew he would soon be screaming and waking up from nightmares. He had seen it before. Platt was hurting. He never got to say goodbye – not like the others had. Sure his wife had survived, but she wasn't alive as such; she was more like a zombie, as someone had once said. It was hurtful to hear, but correct for the better part. And that was what the killer had intended. Constant pain to put Platt over the edge, to make him make mistakes.

Platt was strong, however, determined, an asshole for sure, but a hell of copper. If anyone was going to catch the killer, it was Platt – and that scared the shit out of Elford.

CHAPTER FORTY-EIGHT

At Larksford, the air was tense, but things had got back to normal.

Melanie had showered and changed; her old clothes would no doubt be burnt rather than laundered. Sending blood-drenched clothing to the laundrette would raise too many questions.

As the heavy door closed, Melanie sat in her chair and looked across the lawns to the fountain and pond. She knew she had to leave soon, but she wasn't ready yet; she didn't have all the facts. Especially one – a name.

She had to see the woman next door. This mysterious woman might hold a key to who she was looking for; after all, she had come face-to-face with her assailant, the killer.

Melanie had no idea how she would accomplish this; those damned cameras were always watching, even if the people in the booth weren't. Her gaze wandered about with nothing particular in mind to look at.

The same view every day, less for the change in weather. That said the last couple of days had been slightly more unusual, with people's comings and goings. Most of all, Hicks – where had he gone? His usual pattern was upset by something, that was for sure.

A canvas of white, friendly-looking clouds replaced the dark, angry ones. The storm had passed, blown over to the east. Blues skies peeked through gaps in the blanket of white as the clouds passed by like a massive wave of cotton. Melanie liked the rain; it was cooling, refreshing and, most of all, it hindered people.

Melanie's plan was all hinged around a storm that was coming. There had been other storms. However, she hadn't been ready. Not that she was ready now, but things were getting weird – even dangerous.

For a start, she didn't believe the attack in the bathroom had been merely an intended rape; someone wanted it to look that way. But she was in a secure wing; it wasn't as though they could say one of the other patients had gotten off of his meds. Then she remembered the guy down the hall. A real piece of work that one. He was brought in around five years ago, after telling everyone he hadn't killed his family, his ex-wife, kid, and new husband. At the time, the police didn't see it that way because he was covered in blood. They brought him straight to the clinic for a psych evaluation. Hicks had said he was a danger to himself and others, and locked him up. At the time, the local judge read the professor's report and ordered that the guy spend the rest of his days confined there.

Swept under the carpet and lost forever, or forgotten about. For years, Melanie had to endure listening to the guy rant about his innocence. That was until Professor Hicks Junior had the guy pumped full of meds to calm him down. There was no messy trial as far as people were concerned, and the taxpayers weren't charged a fortune for a pointless trial.

It had been swept under the rug. There was nothing much

in the papers about a trial. Only that the family had been killed in their home. That was one hell of a rug.

Melanie looked at the stack of books and chose a crime novel set in the Caribbean. The back cover blurb had seemed fun, so she thought she'd give it a go. Who'd have thought there would be so much death in a paradise like that? The first chapters were amusing, which gave her cause to continue. She smiled under her mask. Not just because of the novel, but that she realised she had someone else she had to speak to.

CHAPTER FORTY-NINE

Summers watched sympathetically as Platt had one of his nightmares. He had to endure the recurring hell every time he went to sleep, or rather when he did sleep. Luckily, Summers had already parked per Elford's instructions. He had seen the nightmares before and knew being on the motorway when Platt came out of it was not the place to be.

Summers looked at Platt with compassion as he roared and thrashed about. Elford had opened the doors, so his boss didn't hurt himself or they had to explain why windows had been smashed.

'Is it always—'

'The same ... yeah, pretty much, poor sod,' Elford replied before Summers could finish.

'Maybe he should see a psychiatrist?' Summers suggested.

'Seriously? You do know what happened to his kid in one of those places, and his wife ...?' Elford shook his head. 'The boss would rather go bonkers than let those bastards near him.'

'I know a good doctor, a professor actually,' Summers said, ready to pull out a business card. She froze and inched her hand away from her pocket as Elford shot her a look that pretty much summed up what he thought.

'Don't even mention it to the guv or I guarantee you'll be working in some shithole in the middle of nowhere,' Elford said.

Summers gulped and nodded quickly, as if to overemphasise her understanding of the situation. 'Do we wake him?'

Elford looked at Summers with a surprised look. 'I really wouldn't ... but then again, be my guest.'

She went to lean in and shake Platt's leg to wake him, but jumped back as Platt kicked about, nearly smashing her in the face.

'I see your point,' she said, shocked. 'How do you ...?'

'Wake him? You don't. Let it take its course; if you don't, he will never forgive you,' Elford said simply.

Confused, she began to ask, 'I don't understand. If it's so painful, why—'

'Jeez, you're full of bloody questions, ain't ya?' Elford exploded and stepped away from her. 'Just leave him in peace will ya, fuckin' 'ell.' He walked around in small circles, as if to calm himself down.

'I'm sorry.'

Elford gazed at her and saw the way she was holding herself. Standing straight with a bowed head, almost as if she had been trained to seek forgiveness that way. Not from school, no, something more like a parent or guardian. But what parent would make a child feel such shame from doing something wrong, even the slightest thing? Elford was confused at the display. This strong, confident woman had been brought down by an authoritative voice. *Strange.* Then he paid it no further heed.

'Look, I'm sorry for shouting; it's been a shit week and ... well, I'm sorry,' Elford said, patting her on the side of the arm.

She flinched slightly and stepped to the side.

'You OK?' he asked, concerned.

'Oh, it's nothing ... bruised my arm doing sports, that's all,' she smiled uncomfortably.

'*Sport ist Mord.*' Platt sat upright.

'What?' Summers asked.

'Sports is murder ... sports will kill you,' Platt said, extending his shoulders and legs, releasing fatigue. 'Good job with the doors, Dave, don't want to fill any more forms out.' Platt touched his shins with his palms.

'No prob, guv,' Elford replied, wincing at the cracking sounds that emanated from Platt as he undid the knots in his body.

'So, what now, guv?' Summers asked.

Platt crossed his right arm across his chest and held the elbow with a flat palm, pushed while looking the opposite way. 'The prison can wait for a bit. There's a service area over there; we'll grab a coffee and then we can have that little chat,' Platt said with a severe expression.

They made their way over. It wasn't ideal, but the last thing Platt wanted was a yelling match at a police station full of strangers. Besides, he'd had time to calm down ... of sorts.

Yes, he was still angry as hell, but not as much as he had been. He had – as it always was – had time to run through things in his mind while he slept. What he never told anyone was he did it by having a conversation with his wife. Generally, in a café or restaurant, sometimes by a beach in some sunny land. He had no idea why; repressed regrets about the places she wanted to go to perhaps, but he'd never had the time, save for the moments they were there alone, having a meal or walking barefoot in the sand – that was until the dream turned ugly, as it always did.

Platt would find himself walking into their bedroom. He

would see his hand reach out and push the door open gingerly – as though he was being forced to, despite his fighting against it. As he entered, he could feel the cold of the room, and watched as his breath turn to mist as he breathed. The heavy stench of copper and rotten eggs, the smell of body fluids and decay, filled his nostrils.

Inside, the room was dark less for the small lamp on the nightstand, which provided enough illumination to reveal the blood smeared across the walls. Platt looked up and saw his daughter hanging from the ceiling; as she swung like a pendulum, she sang a lullaby she had learnt as a child.

Platt would turn to run – to head for the door and escape, but his wife would be in the doorway, standing there dressed in a torn, bloody nightgown. Her lips would be blue and her eyes would be rolled back into her skull, showing only the whites of her sclera. Then she would reach for him, her mouth opening and closing but no words coming out. As she drew nearer, Platt would wake.

He had never told anyone of his nightmares. Why should he – what business was it of theirs? But he needed them, in a way, because they kept him sane.

The roadside café was virtually empty, with only a few customers sitting in scattered locations. It was a small place with cream-coloured walls and a red vinyl floor. There were two rows of eight tables with a walkway down the centre. At the end were the kitchen and register.

They found a spot away from the door and a possible draft every time someone entered or left. Platt found a place with his back against the wall, facing the door. The tables were long enough to seat four people and were held up by a long stainless-steel shaft, bolted to the floor. They sat on wooden chairs with PU leather cushioning, which looked like something left over from the sixties or seventies, but they did the job. The tabletop had a fake marble pattern to it – the best that money could buy. It was empty, less for a stainless-steel caddy that held salt and pepper cellars and bottles of ketchup and vinegar. Next to these were a couple of menus –printed pieces of long, laminated cards. There wasn't an extensive choice, but enough for hungry travellers, most of which were variations on the English breakfast combination.

Elford smiled as Platt quickly looked around to assess the place and people. As they sat, a happy-looking blonde waitress walked over to take their orders.

'Hi, I'm Denise. Do you need a moment, or can I get you anything?' she asked in a bubbly voice.

Platt hadn't needed the card, and neither had they. 'Three coffees please.'

'Is that with or without milk?'

'Can you bring some and then we'll decide?' Platt asked with a fake smile.

The woman nodded and gave an uncomfortable smile before heading off to get the order.

'But I wanted something to eat,' Elford said, holding his stomach.

'And I wanted this friggin' killer months ago and to see what was so bloody important about that old house. So, I guess we are both disappointed, eh Dave?' Platt growled.

Elford went to speak, but his brain stopped him just in time.

Platt went to speak but was interrupted by the waitress as she brought the beverages. 'Oh, go on then Dave, fill your gap.' Platt shook his head, not wanting to listen to Elford bitch about how hungry he was or to listen to his stomach growl all day. He rolled his eyes when he saw the needy look on the face of his DS.

Elford smiled like a child and ordered a bacon sandwich. Platt didn't know whether it was the smell in the café, the fact he hadn't eaten for ages, or it just sounded too good, but he ended up getting one as well. Summers declined the meaty feast and asked for buttered toast instead.

'OK, now that we've ordered and are all comfy, would you two like to tell me what the bloody hell you were doing at that house and more importantly, DC Summers,' Platt's large brown searching eyes staring at her, 'why you took off without consulting me or taking me with you?'

'It was something that homeless bloke said, guv, something about that he 'never said it was a *he.*' What if the bloke never saw who delivered the money? What if it was just drop-offs?'

'Go on,' Platt said, realising he'd had the same thoughts during the interview. He had to admit she was turning out to be a better copper than he'd first imagined.

'The whole thing about the killer is a misdirection,' Summers explained. 'Like the autopsy report not being able to determine if it was a man, or something was used to penetrate the women. Most serials take trophies, this we know, so what if our killer *leaves* something?'

'What? A kind of sick 'catch me if you can' thing?' Elford asked with a furrowed brow, pouring milk into his coffee.

'Yes, but CSI would have found something out of the ordinary,' Platt explained, trying to figure out where this was going.

'What if it wasn't out of the ordinary? What if it was something so *normal*, it would be missed unless you *knew* what you were looking for?' Summers asked before blowing on her black coffee.

'The killer left something at your house that night, didn't they, something you couldn't explain until now. What was it?'

Platt asked, hoping that whatever *it* was he had the same thing at his place, and the other crime scenes did as well.

'I found yellow flowers in the bedroom in a vase,' she replied.

'Yeah, so, your dad bought your mum flowers, so what?' Elford was confused at the relevance.

'I found a thistle in a glass of water ... thought my daughter had picked it up and gave it as a present to my missus,' Platt said, staring into space as if remembering.

'Sorry, you've lost me?' Elford sat back into his chair and shook his head.

'A thistle? Oh, that's a bad one,' said the waitress as she placed their orders onto the table.

'What the fu-heck are you talking about? It's just a flower,' Elford said, pulling his plate closer.

'It's a warning,' the waitress said, nodding warily at the group before leaving.

'And this yellow flower?' Elford asked, but Summers was already on her mobile telephone, checking the web for a name and meaning.

'It's Locus Corniculatus, commonly known as Birds-foot trefoil, and it means revenge,' Summers said, shaking as a shudder ran down her spine.

'Revenge for what?' Elford asked with a mouth full of sandwich. 'And how the hell did you get to flowers from what the bloke said about it not being a *he*?'

'If our homeless guy thought it was a woman, then there must have been something to make him think so, correct, less for seeing the person that is. But our killer is smart. Why would he or she reveal themselves to a bloke who has no real commitment to the person? You heard him, sir, to him it was just a job,' Summers explained.

'So, what made him think it was a *she* and not a *he*?' Elford asked.

'Perfume?' Platt said shrugging. 'If they left money and items, it could have smelt like perfume.' Then his eyes widened. 'No ... flowers. Our homeless guy thought he smelt perfume. Instead, he was smelling *flowers*.' Platt sat back and clapped.

'Great, so we are looking for a botanist or a flower shop,' Elford muttered, still lost at the theory.

'So, what makes you think of the house?' Platt asked, turning back to Summers.

'Our killer has to grow the shit somewhere; why not an old house that nobody visits?'

Platt smiled to himself, impressed at her thinking, but kept it hidden. 'No, the homeless bloke would have found them,' he said, dismissing the idea. He got on his phone as something occurred to him. He looked up the yellow flowers that Summers had mentioned. A smile crossed his face.

'What is it, guv?' Summers asked, but Platt raised a hand to quickly silence her while he waited for someone to pick up the phone.

'This is DI Platt. The homeless guy, can you ask him a question for me?' Platt's tone carried a mix of excitement and uncertainty. 'Yeah. First off, did he find any locked rooms in the house or basement? Also, had there been times when he'd to be *out* of the house? ... What? ... Yes, I'll wait,' Platt said to the custody sergeant.

Summers and Elford angled forwards, eager for the response.

'Hello? Yes, I'm still here. What was that?' Platt nodded and chewed his bottom lip. 'Yep, OK, got it. Cheers sarge.' Another smile crossed his face.

'And...?' Elford asked impatiently.

'It appears there was a room upstairs that was always locked. Apparently, our homeless guy was forbidden to go into it, and get this.' Platt smiled with satisfaction. 'He had to be out of the house from eight in the morning until midday.'

'Which means what?' Elford urged.

'Kate, the yellow flower you mentioned, it's full of hydrogen cyanide.'

'So, it's a poison?' she asked.

Platt shook his head. 'Not particularly; it's used mostly as a sedative.' He displayed what he had found on the web page.

'OK, so someone left weird plants at the scenes. Doesn't mean anything?' Elford said, unsure where this was going.

'It wouldn't usually, but don't you find it odd the killer can subdue the families without any fuss?' Platt asked, thinking more about it as he spoke.

'Killer could have used one of the kids as a hostage,' Elford said.

'The first time definitely, the second possibly, but after that – doubtful. The killer had a reputation by then. The mother or father would have fought like crazy because they knew what was going to happen – no, they were drugged somehow, got to have been,' Platt stated, shaking his head.

'OK,' Summers said. 'How? You have to be pretty close and comfortable to slip someone a mickey.' Then she thought about Platt's initial theory and smiled. 'They *knew* the killer!'

'They knew the killer,' Platt repeated, confirming her thoughts.

'But where did he – or she – get the toxin?' Elford asked.

'Well, he had the plants, that's for sure, because he or she had left them at the scene. What's to say he didn't do it himself? I mean, with the crap on the internet, we can learn how to paint a room, rebuild a car, refit electrics in a house.

Why not how to make stuff from plants?' Summers asked with a shrug.

'It's possible, I guess, if they had the right equipment. Why not? Avoids those awkward questions at the chemist, like what do you want with all this hydrogen cyanide?' Platt joked.

'The bastard had a distillery upstairs; you think our killer went back to burn down the place to hide evidence?' Elford asked, feeling the massive bump on the back of his head.

'Yeah, because you found their base of operations ... you made the bastard nervous enough to torch the place. All we have to do is find out if anyone saw someone hanging about the place – apart from you two of course,' Platt said, giving Elford and Summers a squinty-eyed searching gaze.

'Yeah, cheers, boss,' laughed Elford.

'So, why were you there?' Summers asked, turning to Elford who now had a piece of bacon hanging from his lips.

'I saw the report on the news,' he replied while fighting to talk with red-hot bacon in his mouth. 'I figured there must have been something fuckin' important in there for someone to be watchin' over the place. So, I did a runner from the hospital and went over. A bit too late though,' Elford said, swallowing his food and taking a quick sip of coffee to wash it down.

'Or just in time?' Summers asked, causing Elford to shoot her a nasty look.

'What you mean? *I* lit the fire?' Elford barked.

'No, what I mean is, you weren't in there. If the killer was that intent on destroying evidence, they wouldn't have been bothered who was inside, that's all,' she explained defensively.

'Yeah, guess you're right ... sorry,' Elford apologised with a crooked smile.

'But then – come to think of it – you did have time,' Summers joked, looking upwards as if pondering the matter.

'Fuck off,' Elford laughed, giving her a friendly slap to the arm.

'Look, the fact is our killer is now nervous. He or she is panicking and that means they will ultimately make a mistake; we just need to be ready for when they do,' Platt said.

'What's your plan boss?' Elford leaned back into his seat and pushed the empty plate forwards.

'We turn up the heat on this bastard, but first we go to the prison. I want to know more about this husband who disappeared,' Platt said, his brow furrowed, and sporting a strange grin of satisfaction.

CHAPTER FIFTY

It was nearly five o'clock when Hicks made it back to the hospital; he'd heard the news about what had happened to Melanie. He had called for Eric to be in his office as soon as possible. In fact, the correct words involved: your arse, my office, now.

Even though Eric was a big man, possibly a foot or two taller than Hicks, Eric feared the man. There was something about Hicks that put the fear of God into people when he required something.

'So, what happened?' Hicks started before Eric had time to close the door to the office.

Beads of nervous sweat began to collect on his huge forehead. 'In truth, Professor Hicks, I'm not sure. One of the nurses broke into the female toilets and tried raping Melanie.' Eric played with his hands like a naughty school kid.

Hicks scowled at him. 'Who was it?'

'George, sir.'

'Oh, for fuck's sakes, not again. That sick bastard should

have been thrown out of here years ago, especially after the incident with the girl who hung herself. Shit.' Hicks rocked furiously in his chair. 'Did he ...?'

'No,' Eric answered with a grin. 'She kicked the shit out of him, and he's in the clinic recovering.' He hoped it was the correct answer.

'Good,' Hicks said, assessing the situation, trying to find the best solution to the problem. Then a smile came over his face. 'We tell the Freemans they can't see their daughter because she attacked another one of the nurses and we fear for their safety.' He laughed. 'Maybe the idiot wasn't as useless as we thought.'

'And what about George?' Eric asked with a shrug. 'Pay him off?'

'Nah, the bloke is a leech. He will threaten to spill the beans, and he'll blackmail us for cash every chance he gets.'

'Even at the risk of admitting what he'd done?' Eric asked, puzzled.

'I said he was a leech, not a smart man. No, people like that need to be handled properly,' Hicks declared.

'You mean, taken out? That's cool. I know a bloke who will do it for a bag of jellybeans if you like,' Eric said with a proud shrug.

Hicks stared at him open-mouthed. 'What kind of a ... never mind. That's not what I mean, but just keep that thought in the back of your head, just in case. No, I have something else in mind.' Hicks grinned wickedly. 'See to Melanie; make sure she is fit and well, and give her time outside with that moron Toby.' He stood and headed for the drink cabinet.

'He's not here. He had to go out on an errand or something,' Eric explained.

'Very well, when he gets back then,' Hicks said, pouring a large whiskey into a cut-crystal glass.

'What about the other girl – the stand-in Melanie?' Eric asked before turning to head for the door.

'Ah, yes, I forgot about her. Keep her sedated and out of sight; she may still come in useful,' Hicks stated.

Eric nodded and left Hicks with his thoughts.

CHAPTER FIFTY-ONE

At the same hour, Doctor Sarah Owen pulled up to the local police station of the small Yorkshire town. As the local GP, she had been brought in to examine Bill to make sure he was OK physically, and a psychiatrist had been called to check his mental health.

The desk sergeant thought all the fuss was for nothing, but he knew Platt wanted to cover all his bases. Owen locked her golden-brown Range Rover and made her way inside. All the local coppers knew her, so she was greeted with hellos and pleasant smiles. Of course, she got a second look from most of them, which she found flattering. She was a stunning redhead with a fantastic figure shown off by a fitted black trouser suit.

'Hi Derick,' she said in a low husky voice.

'Morning Doc, here to see the nutter?' the desk sergeant smiled.

'If you mean the poor man that lost his family, yes,' Owen replied, giving him a scolding look that she couldn't hold and cracking a friendly smile.

'He didn't lose them – they were still fuckin' there, rottin' away, so they say.' The sergeant shivered at the thought. 'Man's bloody barking if you ask me.'

'Well, luckily, that's not for us to decide. I've asked an old friend to come and examine him,' Owen said with a glint in her eye.

'What, that bloke they got me to phone from the hospital?' he leant back in his chair. 'Waste of time if you ask me. Killed um he did, fact. I bet he's this pigging family killer,' the man said, striking the desk.

'Again, we won't know until the other doctor turns up,' she said with a shrug.

'So, how do you know this bloke then Doc? An old flame, a school chum, some bloke from med school?' he asked with a smile.

'All of the above and not in that order,' she laughed.

'Good bloke, is he?'

'He's alright ... father's a bit of a prick though,' she laughed again. 'When's he due here?'

'The clinic said he's on route,' the sergeant said, looking at his watch.

A red Aston Martin BD5 pulled up outside the local police station where Bill was being held. The sun reflected off the deep coloured paintwork, making it glisten as if it were made from coloured glass. A classic to be sure and not a cheap one at that. The door opened and a man got out. He wore a blue pinstriped suit and brown brogue shoes and had greased-back hair to give that distinguished look. He was of medium build and height and had an air about him.

His heels clipped on the floor, making a metallic tap-tap-tap sound as he sauntered towards the entrance of the police station. The man introduced himself at the front desk and was ushered through the security door. He thanked the desk sergeant and proceeded towards the cells and the custody sergeant.

Doctor Owen stood waiting with the sergeant. She looked at the man as he approached, and her smile grew at the sight of him.

'I take it that's him then, Doctor Owen?' asked the custody sergeant.

'Yes, that's him,' she replied with a soft angel-like tone.

The man walked steadily, with a swagger.

'It's been a while,' she said.

He sauntered up to her and shook her hand before kissing her on the cheek.

'Too long,' he replied in an American accent.

'Sergeant, this is Doctor Tobias Longford ... he is looking at buying Larksford House,' she said.

'Please – call me Toby.' With a pleasant smile, he shook the sergeant's hand.

CHAPTER FIFTY-TWO

'Only a few days to go,' Melanie said to herself as she made a mental note of the date. It was less than a week before the storm. From all accounts, from what the weather people had predicted, it was due to be horrific – just what she needed.

Her plan was simple enough: slip out as she always did and find her parents. She had gotten their address from the internet, using maps to pinpoint a location. She had to search her memories for clues, the type of house and its features.

Melanie remembered it had been a big house with a long driveway and it was the last house on a single road or path. Once she had a rough location, she looked up the address and then the online telephone directory. She found a family called Freeman lived there. From there, she went onto social media and hoped they had an account, which the daughter Danni did.

Melanie's mouth dropped open as a bombardment of feelings overtook her: shock, horror, amazement, joy. The photo of a girl's face could have been that of her own. This was a photograph of her sister Danni. Even though Melanie and Danni hadn't been identical twins at birth, somehow the years had made them so; it was like looking into a mirror.

Danni had posted her life on the web page – revealing all for the world to see, including those excellent little current position markers. These would be followed by a running commentary: I'm having a burger at this restaurant, and so forth. Danni had done one from home, and possibly forgot to turn it off or something. Nevertheless, it showed a location. *Thanks, sis.*

The online maps gave twenty-six miles from the hospital. A long way on foot, but Melanie had a plan – she always had a plan, nothing was by chance or the will of the God, less for the weather of course. Everything had to be calculated, assessed in Melanie's world, and at least three steps ahead. Sure, things would happen, but as long as she could quickly reassess and formulate a new plan, she was OK.

After all, she had a long time to plan the whole thing, and her mentor had given her many great tips as well.

Melanie did miss Karen. She often thought of that dear sweet woman and where she was now. With a sigh, she went back to her book, the massive leather-bound Russian novel, or so people thought. In fact, it was full of printouts Melanie had gotten from the computer over the years. She hoped to print other things, having filled the printer's memory with garbage on the off chance some smart arse might check the last thing printed. If they did, all they would see is holiday information or something along those lines.

As she sorted through the assortment of paperwork, Melanie found a news article on the first murder of the serial killer. The press was convinced it had been a burglary gone wrong, that was until the second attack, the family of a PC. The first killing had been messy, sloppy even. A broken window at the back door, a kitchen knife used from the victim's knife block. The place had been tossed, possibly the thieves looking for items of value. Like the press, the police had considered that the family had woken up and disturbed the thieves, and from then it had gone horribly wrong. A good theory – until they learned of the killer's knack for misdirection. This DI Platt had found this when he was brought on the case after the third set of murders. Still, somehow, he had been ignored, but then he was an outsider to the others because he'd been sent up from London to assist.

Someone had thought he was making progress, because his family comprised the fourth set of victims even though they had lived, but victims, nevertheless. From what Melanie could see from the reports she had retrieved from the Met's secure files, Platt had been sent to London to follow up a lead after the third set of victims had been found. The killer had used that opportunity to get to Platt's family, possibly as a lesson to the others. But why him? He was new there; why not the DI in charge?

Melanie looked back over the article of the first killings. The reporter had either put loose facts down, or the police had given them nothing. There had been a spate of burglaries in the Yorkshire area at that time, so the police's speculation of a B&E gone wrong was possible. There was no mention of who had died, just that a family had been killed. The police's probable tactic was to stop a public panic or see something in the MO, and determined to keep it under wraps in case the killer struck again. A month later he had – the PC's family. Melanie had read the articles many times and had seen no pattern.

She had committed her time at Larksford to finding out who had said those words. Who, in effect, had placed her into this damned clinic, and torn her away from her family?

She had come no closer, or so she had thought. That was until she had learned of two people: the man and woman next door to her. At least one of them had answers; all she had to do was get a chance to ask the question. Melanie worried that her only ally was Toby, a man she hardly knew. Still, there was something familiar about him, something she couldn't quite explain. She sighed. *Great, another mystery to solve.*

Melanie put the pages back into the book and closed it before placing it back onto the bookshelf. She felt tired – lethargic really. Doing nothing all day took its toll and being stuck indoors would most certainly have such an effect.

Melanie looked outside at the trees as their branches swayed in the breeze, the birds chasing each other in the heavens. She missed the feeling of the sun and the crisp breeze against her skin ... the dreams. They had stopped; in fact, the last one was more like a nightmare. Faces of what were once people in a dark room, all huddled together. There had been a smell of something she didn't know or hadn't experienced before. The joys of living in a sterile building: you didn't get to experience many new smells, only bleach and the odd person who had bathed in toiletries.

Melanie smiled at the thoughts of the good dreams, the ones that made her tingle all over. She did miss them, but she still couldn't figure out why the man in the dreams reminded her of Toby. Psychologists would put it down to repressed attraction, which was possibly true, but it felt more than a dream, more like a memory.

The sound of the deadlock being opened caused Melanie to turn.

Eric. He wore a broad smile and held a tray with hot chocolate and a sandwich.

'Is it lunchtime already?' she asked, looking at the position of the sun. She figured it was eleven o'clock at the most, too early for the snack.

'No, we figured you could do with a treat considering ...'

'Considering that I was attacked in the ladies' toilets, and you don't want me to make a scene?' Melanie finished his sentence.

'Something like that.' Eric shrugged, then smiled as he put the tray onto the table.

'What's in the sandwich?' Melanie asked suspiciously.

'Cheese and onion,' Eric answered with a sly smile.

'Don't like onions. Where's my usual?' Melanie asked grumpily.

'What? Oh, sorry, my bad. Got the orders mixed up. This is yours,' Eric said warily.

Melanie knew he was testing her, making sure it hadn't been her that had been stealing his lunch. Whether he bought it or not, she didn't know and didn't care. However, his distraction had been enough to force her to rethink a few things. One of which was where Toby had gotten too?

CHAPTER FIFTY-THREE

At ten-past four, the Freemans had left the crime scene and had been driven back home. A uniform had driven their car while they sat in the passenger seats. The sergeant in charge of the scene had insisted, despite Jason telling everyone he was a good driver. Abby had convinced him it was probably for the best.

Danni was still in shock, wrapped in a blanket, eyes staring ahead as if her gaze still held those horrific images. The medics had said she was fine, physically anyway. Abby sat next to her with her arms wrapped around her daughter. An act of comfort, possibly for both of them. Jason, on the other hand, was angry. Furious that they had argued that she had gone all the way to that house. Furious that he had allowed their contact with Ann and Bill to diminish.

He still couldn't figure out how Bill could keep going like that, as if nothing was wrong? Jason had to agree with the policeman's assumption that Bill hadn't killed them. He would have said the bloke didn't have it in him to kill a fly. But now? Jason had to admit he had no idea who Bill was. Not a killer. In fact, not much of anything anymore. He was well out of it. Reality for Bill had stopped months ago.

Jason looked back from his seat at the front and gazed upon his family – his all, his everything. He smiled at the two women and nodded as if to say all would be alright. Abby smiled and nodded back. She knew it would be. She knew that they would be OK.

―――――

Before Platt had left with Elford and Summers, he'd spoken to the lead CSI at Bill's house. Asking him to look out for any flowers or plants that may have been a gift or placed in what would be considered an unusual place. Platt didn't say what kind, as he didn't know. However, if he was correct, there would be something in that bedroom. This meant his request would be met with a raised eyebrow of doubt, but it was his case, so he got whatever was requested.

The desk sergeant had confirmed a doctor and a psychiatrist had arrived and were checking on Bill as instructed. Platt was happy that things were starting to pan out, even though the others didn't see it that way.

'We have the theory on the flowers; we also know this sick bastard has cameras installed in the victims' houses. And we know that the house of the possible first killing is more than a house. It's something important to the killer,' Platt said before sipping coffee.

'So, what do you hope to find at the prison?' Summers asked.

'This murder at the old house ... we think it was our killer's first, even though it seems like it was more a case of a wife-beating husband getting revenge on his ex-wife and her new husband. However, the similarities in some of the details can't be ignored. The fact the wife was butchered and tortured, and the new husband was killed and cast aside, everything the same,' Platt explained.

'He wasn't cast aside, guv, he was buried somewhere else,' Summers stated quietly.

'That could have been for misdirection, make us think it was the new bloke and not the ex,' Elford said with a shrug.

'Makes sense, but why not do that with the others?'

'Perhaps the killer thought the first husband was more useful missing, then later the killer wasn't bothered about the men. They were merely amusement,' Platt replied.

'Not the only thing that changed about the MO; he went for a change in hair colour as well,' Elford reminded him.

'Yes ... the hair colour, that is a bit of a puzzler, I must admit. Why go from long dark to short blonde?' Platt looked deep into his steaming coffee.

'They could have changed their hair at some point, died and cut it?' Summers asked with a shrug.

Platt looked at Summers, but his gaze was lost in thought. Something she had said had suddenly made sense. 'Summers, the day of the trial for this husband, can you check if there are any photos or news articles?' Platt's gaze was still locked into another place.

'You want to know what colour hair they had,' Summers said, nodding.

'Also, pull up a list of all those involved: jury, judge, even the bloke who cleaned the toilet if necessary.' Platt's eyes had locked on hers.

She nodded and stood, pulling her mobile telephone from her pocket.

'You think this has something to do with the trial of our

missing wife-beater?' Elford asked, thinking it was a little thin, but a definite start.

'I think it started with that, cause and effect if you will. I don't think our missing abuser went on a killing spree after getting the taste for it; if he or she had, why leave my family alive? No, our killer is a thinker, a planner. Sure, there was some sort of catalyst, but I still can't see how it involves our missing bloke,' Platt had to admit. 'To leave flowers that have a symbolic meaning, that takes more than brutish thoughts of revenge.'

'A family member of his?' Elford suggested.

Platt thought for a moment and then shrugged. 'It's possible, but at the moment I'm just covering all my bases.' He smiled.

Summers returned and sat in her seat. 'I phoned around, made some enquires with the courthouse, the records office at the council and the local rag see if they have anything. I gave my email address, so if they find something, they can send me a copy of the photo.' Summers picked up her coffee cup and looked at the empty vessel in surprise, which was then replaced with a depressed look. She couldn't remember finishing the brew, but then it had been a hell of a morning.

The waitress returned to their table with skilled timing, asking if they wanted anything else. Platt usually took this to be a sign from a waitress to say, 'If you're done, move on.' But she seemed happy enough when Summers ordered another coffee. Elford went for a second sandwich while Platt rolled his eyes. He didn't want anything, only to be on the road again, so much he insisted they have their second order to go.

For Platt, time was ticking. The killer was already miles ahead, but they were catching up. A place he'd been once before, and it had cost him. This time he had nothing to lose. This time he wouldn't stop. When the food and drink arrived,

Platt was already in the car. He was driving to free them up to continue enjoying their breakfast – and they'd better enjoy it because he had no idea when they would again get some rest.

———

The interview room had been made gloomy. Toby had requested it, hoping the lack of light would put Bill in a comfortable mood. He had seen copies of the crime scene photographs, a horrific scene if ever there had been one.

Toby had felt his stomach turn at the sight. He was used to treating rich people with teenager problems or teenagers with people problems. He had investigated Larksford House in hopes of buying it. When it was up and running as the best clinic in Britain, he could rub it in his father's face. But he hadn't contemplated that he would become involved with murder suspects. However, there he was.

Bill sat on a chair in front of a long table. The table sat sideways, making room for four people to sit and make notes. At the side was a tape-recording machine and in the centre two microphones that sat side by side, facing the chairs. The room was painted a dull off-white colour with two strip-lights above that were part of the ceiling tiles rather than hanging down – less chance of anyone doing something stupid that way. Bill was quiet, sitting patiently but slightly confused at what was going on.

'So, Doc, do you think he did it?' asked one of the policemen who had brought Bill in.

'Did he kill his family, or are you looking more at did he do the other murders as well?' Toby asked suspiciously. He could tell the copper was itching to book the man and tell everyone he had caught the killer – what a career move.

'Can't say for sure yet. So, you can put that press conference on hold for the minute,' Toby said, causing Sarah Owen to smile and look away shyly.

He walked into the room and stood at the door. Bill looked up at the stranger. A tall man in his late twenties or early thirties, in an expensive blue suit.

'Hi, Bill, my name is Toby,' he said, walking forwards, then standing in front of the chair opposite. 'May I?' he asked, pointing to the chair.

Bill smiled and beckoned his visitor to sit. Toby placed down two coffees and edged one towards Bill. Reaching into his jacket pocket, he produced milk, sugar sachets, and a couple of plastic spoons, and placed them on the table. Bill pulled the porcelain mug close and wrapped his fingers around it, feeling the warmth.

Toby had no notepad, recording device, just a cup of coffee and some biscuits.

'What's he doing?' the copper asked Sarah.

'Building rapport, trust, get him to open up without questioning him,' she replied, staring at the two men through the two-way mirror.

'What for?'

'If he is broken, he will shut down at the first sign of stress. If he did it, he will feel threatened and clam up either way, and you'll get nothing. Let him tell the story in his way and time, and you may have more than you bargained for.'

'So, Bill, what do you do for a living? I know you're a banker or someone important like that?' Toby poured milk and sugar into his cup.

Bill smiled bashfully at the compliment and shook his head. 'No, I'm afraid not. I work in security. That's to say, I sell security systems to homeowners, businesspersons, anyone who needs it really.'

'Well, Bill, I'd say that was just as important; we all need security. To keep our people and property safe.' He observed Bill's expression. The smile had faded; he had hit a nerve.

'You like football, Bill? Or rather, as we call it in the States, soccer?' Toby asked quickly to get Bill back from whatever thoughts he was starting to have.

'What ... oh, yes. Love watching Leeds. Used to go all the time with me dad on a Saturday,' Bill smiled.

'Yeah, I know what you mean. My dad used to take me to ball games back home when I was younger. God, I miss those times,' Toby said with a nostalgic smile as he leant back in his chair and reverted to the original subject. 'So, security. Wow, you must see some weird shit.'

'It's OK, mainly rich blokes spying on the missus to make sure she hasn't got a bit on the side, and stores are the best. Plenty of business there,' Bill answered, his voice holding a calm edge.

But Toby was ready with a diversion question. 'Nice. Company car, bonuses, that sort of thing?'

'The car's mine, but I get a fuel card; as for bonuses, it's mostly if I work weekends, holidays, stuff like that really,' Bill shrugged.

'So, how did you get into a gig like that anyway?' Toby tried to sound interested.

'I was in the army before, and when I left, I caught up with an old pal who offered me a job. Just lucky really,' Bill said with a smile and a shrug.

'Wow, that's one hell of a good friend,' Toby smiled in return. 'The only job I got from a friend was tossing burgers.' He laughed.

· · ·

Behind the glass, Sarah Owen watched patiently for signs that Bill would snap or other issues. While the copper next to her, Geoffreys, was ready to lock up Bill. Sarah looked over at the policeman, his left hand fiddling intently with his handcuffs.

'I glad you police haven't got guns,' she said wryly.

Geoffreys looked at her with a confused look. 'Why's that Doc?'

'Because I'm sure you would have shot him by now,' she replied, gesturing his hand.

'Nah, too quick for a bastard like that,' he said, nodding towards Bill.

'A bastard like what?' she scowled at the policeman. 'We don't even know what's happened yet, and you've already got him with a noose around his neck?' She shook her head.

'He's guilty. Can see it in his eyes. He's guilty of something to do with this mess,' the policeman growled.

———

After a few moments of chitchat, Toby looked towards the two-way-mirror and nodded, hoping Sarah was watching. They had prearranged a signal when she could come in with the file. Toby didn't know if Bill was ready for what was coming, but he had to try. Geoffreys watched as Sarah opened the door to the small room and nodded to a young PC waiting in the corridor. She had been purposely picked to walk into the room and hand over the file.

The PC had short blonde hair and an athletic build – like the victims. As the PC entered, Toby took note of Bill's reaction. She ambled in, placed the file on the table, and pretended to whisper something in Toby's ear. Each movement she made was slow and purposeful. All the while, both Toby and Sarah had a view of Bill.

He took note that Bill gave the PC a onceover; possible fantasies of a sexual nature shot through his mind, but nothing that warranted alarm. Sure, there was attraction but beyond that, nothing. Sarah had waited for Bill to jump over the desk, foaming at the mouth the way Geoffreys had him pegged.

'Would you excuse me?' Toby stood and followed the PC out of the room.

Sarah and Geoffreys looked over as Toby joined them in the observation room.

'I hope this is legal?' Sarah said, shaking her head.

'I'm here to see if the poor guy is bat-crap-crazy or a secret serial killer. We can worry about legal later,' Toby answered, leaning against the wall next to the mirror. All three watched as Bill sat and sipped. Waiting for him to take a sneak peek at the photographs that Toby had left in the file.

'So, what do you hope will happen?' Geoffreys asked, unimpressed with the method Toby was using.

'That,' he said, standing straight as Bill's gaze fell on the file.

Bill sat back in his chair, looking around the room as if trying to fight the urge to look at the file. Corners of photographs peeked out. They didn't show much, but it was enough to beckon a curious eye. Bill looked around the room as if ensuring that nobody was looking and, with his fingertips, inched the file over. As the document lay before him, Bill slid one of the pictures out. He smiled as he gazed upon a picture of him and his family.

He stared at the picture for a time, possibly reminiscing when the photo was taken, remembering the warmth of the weather, the laughter of his family. He was a million miles away. So much so that when he pulled out the next picture, he never noticed the image until it was too late.

Bill screamed and shot backwards, falling over his chair and scrambling for a corner.

Toby rushed into the interrogation room.

Bill was curled up into a ball, screaming at the image burnt into his brain. 'What are you doing to me, you sick bastards?' Bill yelled as Toby grew near.

'You know these people?' Toby asked, picking up the photograph of Bill and his family.

'Of course, it's my family! They are waiting for me,' Bill said, tears streaming down his face.

'No, *this* is your family,' Toby said gently, holding up the other picture.

Bill shook his head and buried his face in his arms. 'No – no – no. I don't know who those peo—things are, but they're not my family. Ann and Debs are waiting for me, I told you,' he insisted.

'What happened to them, these people?' Toby asked, his voice gentle but authoritative.

'You don't understand; these aren't my family, those are … horrible.' Bill hid his face again.

'OK, they're not your family; your family are far away, I get that, but who are these?'

Bill looked at Toby as if he were mad.

'I told you, I don't know. I've never seen them before. Why'd you show me such fucking disgusting things?' Bill growled.

'But they were at your house … in your bedroom?' Toby replied, pointing out the other crime scene photographs showing the dust-filled room.

'No, you're wrong. My family is safe. I've no idea who this is … was,' Bill said, shaking his head. His face was red with anger. 'I was told to do some jobs, and I did them, that's why they're safe,' he stated proudly.

'What jobs?' Toby sat crossed-legged in front of Bill, who remained in the corner.

'Put in cameras like I was asked, did a profile of the clients, that kind of thing, nothing out of the ordinary.' Bill sniffed and wiped his nose on his sleeve.

'Who asked? Who did you do the jobs for?' Toby asked eagerly.

'The clients of course,' Bill answered with a surprised look.

Toby shook his head as if an answer to everything had turned into nothing.

'But the bloke wanted the sender frequency. I don't know what for or why,' Bill continued with a scared look.

'What bloke?' Toby urged.

'The one who said if I didn't do as I was told, he'd hurt my family, but I did as I was told; that's why they're safe,' Bill said with a wink and a smile.

'So, this bloke, who is he?'

'Don't know, just got an email once, thought nothing of it at first, but then things started to happen,' Bill explained.

'What things?' Toby leant forward with interest.

'Don't want to talk about it,' Bill said, burying his face in his hands again.

'OK, so you feared for your family and sent them away?'

'No, he has them; he says I'll see them again soon as long as I do as I'm asked, and I have,' Bill explained.

Toby looked at this poor man and wondered what horrors he had seen to put him so far into denial. 'So, how do you drop off the information?'

'Email mostly ... was told it was quicker and more secure ... we'd never have to meet,' Bill told him slowly.

'Do you have an email address for him?' Toby asked, hoping it would be a clue, perhaps a breadcrumb to a server or provider.

'Not really – they're always different. I'd get a letter put through the post, and that would tell me the new address,' Bill answered with a shrug.

'Bill, how do you know it's a he? You keep referring to the person as a 'bloke', which in my eyes means a man.' Toby wasn't sure he wanted to hear the answer.

'I don't know really, just thought it was, and ...' Bill paused and bit his bottom lip, as if fearful of revealing such information.

'And it's OK, Bill. You're with friends now,' Toby said, resting a gentle hand on his arm for reassurance.

'He said he would do things to my wife and daughter, *bad things*, and he would take his time. He would make them suffer ...' Bill paused again and stared into a void as though remembering. 'He would kill them all and take pleasure in it,' Bill finally said, looking to Toby.

His mouth fell open and he got up to sit in the chair. He felt as if he had just been ploughed into by a train.

Those words.

The same words that he had heard Melanie utter from time to time, as if they were a lullaby. Toby stood suddenly. He was confused, dazed. And he felt sick. Toby slapped a hand to his mouth and ran out as though he were going to vomit.

Geoffreys watched, his gaze fixed on the door Toby had just left by.

'Well, that must have been a hell of a conversation,' he smiled wryly.

Sarah shook her head. 'You can be a real dick sometimes, Arthur.' She headed off to find Toby.

CHAPTER FIFTY-FOUR

'THE EX-HUSBAND OF MURDERED WOMAN DISAPPEARS' the news article heading had read. The page was a printout from the local newspaper's web page, dating back ten years.

Melanie had gone over it three times. The reporter had put forward many ideas, such as the man skipping the country, or having topped himself somewhere. From what she had read, the reporter just wanted to get the story out there. At the time, the dead woman's husband hadn't been found buried – that was in a later edition, written by another reporter.

Melanie set down the page and gazed out the window. The clouds were moving faster now – the storm was on its way. A noise in the corridor made Melanie look at the door. Someone was getting a visitor! But it wasn't the woman; the noise had come from the other side. It was the man, her other neighbour.

Melanie gazed at the wall. If she was right, the poor bastard had been locked up for possibly as long as she had been. Why, Melanie could only speculate. But one thing was for sure; she *had* to talk with him.

Melanie thought about waiting for night, as it was usually

the best time to sneak about. The nurses never bothered with them much after dark; then again, nobody was really concerned about her anyway. Melanie picked up another page and perused the report on the killing in Nottingham, the one the missing ex-husband had been accused of. There wasn't much in the article, just an interview with the local copper that had found the wife's body. But nothing from the investigation team. But then it wasn't the biggest story of the time.

A president was sworn in, a disaster occurred in a faraway land which had left thousands of dead. A couple of actors had died from either natural causes or chemical intolerance. A story about a man killing his family was news for about two seconds.

'Glad people got their priorities right,' Melanie thought aloud as she married up the size of the news reports. The others were large, some with a centre page spread. The murder was almost a footnote on the page, lost in the requirement to sell papers she figured.

Melanie had the police report of that night, thanking the police's need to go digital and back up everything on electronic files rather than just on paper. The back door to the police files had been easy, but she didn't do it too often so as not to raise too many alarms, and they updated their firewall pretty much every month. She'd had trouble enough with this one, but had got there in the end.

The police report had said a woman had been found, but the husband was missing. The woman had been brutalised, tortured before the final stab to the heart. Her body was found in the bedroom, which had been covered in blood. The house had shown signs that it had been searched, but the investigator had put that down to misdirection.

Melanie read through the lines; the police and the reporter suspected the ex-husband for it. And for all intents and purposes, it looked as if this were the case. He'd just gotten out of jail, found she had a new man in her life; he was abusive, jealous, and most of all, he had a temper. Sure, the husband was missing, but the more the police spoke to witnesses and family friends they began to lean towards him being innocent. The man was reputed to be the perfect husband and a good man, whereas the ex was a real prince. No one could explain the fact the husband was missing; perhaps he had run away after the event, or maybe he was on a business trip?

The evidence leant more and more towards the ex. Possibly because he was also missing. An ex-con who'd fallen off the face of the earth was never a good sign, especially the ex-wife having been murdered so horribly. The police and the press had put two and two together and got whatever number they wanted.

That was where Melanie failed to see how it was him. A person with an explosive temper didn't plan; they didn't take their time. They might cause bodily harm, shoot, stab, throw the TV. But breaking in and making it look like it was a burglary? To tie people up, torture them, and most of all, have a clear mind to think about forensics? This was planned and not a split-second decision.

Melanie looked up from her investigation and to the grounds beyond the window. The darkened clouds had all but drifted away, leaving a pale blue canvas. The wind had also died down, causing the tree branches to stop their dancing. The patients roamed freely outside in the enclosed grounds without a care in the world. They were monitored by the nurses – when they were actually paying attention that was, and not focusing on their mobile phones.

Melanie smiled. She missed her little walks, especially in the daytime. She sighed and went back to the pages. Her eyes scanned them for something she may have missed but saw the same information each time.

The first murder in Nottingham had happened when she was little. A coincidence possibly? But then she had never been to Nottingham – not as far as she knew. The second murder happened years later; the year before, to be precise. So, if the killer was the same person, why wait almost ten years? It couldn't have been the first woman's ex-husband because he had disappeared, possibly living a new life somewhere, maybe abroad or something. So, it made no sense that it should be him – besides, what motive would he have to kill random people after such a long time?

Melanie turned to face the wall that separated her and the man next door. She could hear him through the walls. 'Get them off me – get them off me!' he screamed, his voice filled with utter terror.

'Poor fucker,' she murmured.

And the woman next door on the other side, the wife of the policeman, why was she there? OK, she had survived, but why put her into a psychiatric hospital? Melanie remembered looking through the copies of administration orders, something she'd done the day before, when she was looking up Hicks. Both the man next door and the wife had been assessed by Hicks' father; the same went for Melanie. But why? They had nothing in common. Just three random people locked up due to circumstance; the only thing that linked them was Hicks Senior. The guy next door was simply a poor insane bloke, and the woman had been brought here after being attacked. As for Melanie, well, she wanted to ask her parents that very question – *why?*

———

Hicks sat in the office with a half-empty decanter of whisky in front of him. He was drunk and half-conscious. Everything he had worked for was starting to come to an end. On his computer was a page from one of the medical journals – about some hotshot surgeon in Los Angeles had won some prize. But what interested Hicks wasn't the article on the surgeon, it was the mention of his son: Tobias Longford. A big name in psychiatry in the States who was looking at taking over a clinic in Britain. Tobias' name hadn't rang any bells with Hicks at first. Sure, he'd heard of the man, but it never occurred to him that the supposed new nurse was actually this bigwig psychiatrist ... that was until the article had come with a photograph of both father and son.

Hicks had sought to keep the clinic within the family by whatever means necessary, even locking up people that others wanted out of the way, for money. He didn't ask questions, and they had plenty of cash. The money from the health system and private patients wasn't enough, so Hicks had to improvise. And it had worked, he had got rich from it, and the clinic had prospered, but Hicks needed, *wanted*, something more: recognition for his work, a medal, a plaque, an award, something. If Hicks could cure the woman who was next door to Melanie of her psychosis – just as Melanie had come out of hers – he would be set for life.

But there was a problem – a big one.

Someone was blackmailing Hicks to keep the three of them out of the way. They had somehow found out about his terrible little secret. Hicks had thought it odd because the man had been searched for by the police. The girl, Melanie, she was the gift horse. He was getting money for her – a fortune from the father. However, there were strict instructions that no harm should come to here. The woman next to Melanie was also a payday; the husband was paying a pittance, but it was cash. Besides, Hicks couldn't precisely say someone was forcing him to keep her there.

His plan to swap Melanie and the other girl was mostly out of desperation; she was getting too wise, too independent. Sure, Melanie had her moments where people got hurt, like that idiot who tried to rape her, but otherwise, she was as quiet as a mouse.

Hicks was beyond thinking, rational or otherwise. He was drunk to the point he had thrown up on his desk twice while he lay there. He didn't care. If this bastard from the States got hold of the hospital, all would be revealed, and Hicks would go to jail forever. He took out his father's old gun he had found in the desk. It was a .357 Magnum revolver. Its black steel frame and wooden grip gave it an impressive appearance.

'That will do,' Hicks had thought. 'Nice big hole. Lots of mess. No coming back from that.' What he hadn't reckoned on was that he was too drunk to see correctly, too drunk to notice it was a cigarette lighter. All that Hicks had accomplished was burning the side of his head. Luckily, he was too drunk to feel it, but that would change when he sobered up – one last useless gift from his father. The first one, of course, was the failure to keep it up. Hicks' mother had reminded him as often as she could that he'd been an accident – an unplanned and unwanted child.

Something he'd hated his mother for, but at the same time loved her for. Hicks had read in one of his father's medical magazines that emotional stress could lead to physical problems. A statement he hadn't fully appreciated until he tried masturbation – tried and failed. Which hadn't been a big winner with ladies, but something for his classmates to ridicule him about when they had learnt of it.

'Bastards, all of you,' Hicks moaned before throwing up once more, then slowly slid off the desk and onto the floor.

———

DI Platt's stomach rumbled with disapproval. He had followed the satnav that had taken them along the A61 Harrogate Road and eventually led onto the M1 southbound. For Platt, it was a better road than taking the motorway because of the petrol stations.

The new route would take them south through the city of Leeds, but Platt didn't mind the traffic; in a way, he felt safer driving through a town or city rather than an endless motorway with no way of turning off or around if the need arose.

As they drove along Regent Street, Platt noticed the signs for a petrol station which was coming up. The car needed petrol, and he needed coffee and something to tide him over. He pulled into the entrance and parked next to the nearest petrol pump.

'We'll take a quick break here, so get some supplies or go for a piss if you got to,' Platt instructed as Summers and Elford got out and stretched off.

Platt moved to the filler cap, grabbed the nozzle, and began to pump fuel. Platt coughed at the stench of fumes and covered his mouth and nose with his sleeve. He looked back at the other two, who were heading for the service station. Platt smiled as he watched them pushing each other and joking about like kids.

By the time the tank was full, the Elford and Summers were returning with white plastic bags bulging with food and drink. Platt raised an eyebrow, noting Elkford's bag was bulging at the seams. 'Dave, did you leave anything in the shop, ya greedy bastard?' Platt joked.

'Yeah, salt and vinegar crisps,' Elford replied with a frown.

'Bloody hope so, or you're walkin' there, sodden horrible things,' Platt laughed.

Summers shot Elford a confused look.

'He hates salt and vinegar crisps, makes his gums bleed or something,' Elford winked.

Summers chuckled as they headed back to the car.

Platt paid for the fuel and grabbed a BLT sandwich, crisps of different flavours – none of which were salt or vinegar – and a coffee in a to-go cup. Then headed to the toilets to take a piss. By the time he'd got back to the car Summers and Elford had finished most of what they had bought, leaving something for the return journey.

'Right, if we are all fed and watered, let's fuck off,' Platt said, scratching his crotch before getting in the car.

'Nice. Subtle,' Summers said, shaking her head in disbelief.

'What?' Platt asked as if he had no idea what she was talking about.

'Nothin', guv,' Summers smiled. She had known Platt was rough around the edges and an ex-soldier, but she hadn't expected such a don't-give-a-crap attitude, but it suited him.

The HMP Wakefield prison was a massive complex. The first building had been built in the 1500s and, as the years went on, it was added to – including the vast modern-looking stone wall that encircled the complex.

Platt had always found it amusing that it was located down the road from the local train station for easy access 'for all your prison breakout needs.'

The complex was smack-bang in the middle of the city, as though the city had grown around it. Its two entrances sat on the junction of Love Lane and Back Lane. One was the prison's vehicle entrance, which was a massive wooden door at one end, and the public access was through a set of dark blue doors at another. Each was in feet of each other, making it ideal for security reasons.

The prison wasn't like the films, where it was a castle-like structure in the middle of nowhere. Modernisation had seen to that, making it more appealing to the public eye. Across the road was a local brewery and down the street a red-brick railway bridge under which the Back Lane carried on. The nearby buildings looked as though they had been built in the forties, massive, sturdy red-brick places, appearing unchanged and unaltered through the years.

The prison held killers, con-artists, thieves, wife-beaters. The man called William Morris that they were after had been brought in on assault charges almost twelve years before. With good behaviour and a lot of smiling, including keeping his nose clean, he was out in no time.

Platt had studied the man's file. By all accounts, not a bad bloke from what he could see on paper; however, he and his wife were like oil and water. From what the police report had said, the local coppers were always around the place because of a disturbance. Oddly enough, mostly because of her. Platt reckoned one day the bastard snapped and smacked her about once too often. She finally saw sense and had him arrested. Platt had been brought up to never hit a lady, even though many women nowadays were far from ladylike.

Platt had always figured if more people would wake up and realise they didn't get on, the fewer domestic incidences there would be. Giving the police time to concentrate more on the people who really deserved the time, namely those who suffered in silence. The people in fear of their lives because of an abusive spouse.

Platt hated any bloke who beat his missus and kids because he was drunk, or just an arse. As far as he was concerned, these people deserved to be locked up, but that wasn't for him to say, or even prove.

Platt had a picture in his head about this guy. Angry, got drunk a lot, probably hit his missus every time they argued. He'd seen it before, mostly from his sister's old man, that was until Platt had a chat with him to consider the errors of his ways.

Platt was expecting a report from the warden about how this bloke was trouble before he got wise. Probably was in plenty of fights with the other inmates. The picture that Platt had created was one of a man full of hate, revenge. That made things easier.

Platt found a parking space across the street and got out of the car. The other two followed suit. All three looked at the colossal brick walls that had held inmates for hundreds of years.

'Ready?' Platt asked.

The others nodded. As they walked towards the gates, Summers pulled on her jacket and buttoned it up.

'Right, let's get a read on this guy William Morris, shall we?' Platt suggested, his voice sounded tired but determined. His mind was made up. This was their guy, and he wanted him. This wasn't just the murderer of his ex-wife and her husband, but he was also the family killer. Because, if *he* wasn't ... *who the hell was?* Morris had motive, means, and most of all he was missing; if that didn't read guilty Platt didn't know what did.

They stood in front of a set of blue doors. Next to this was an intercom system with a camera. Platt pressed the button and held up his ID, hoping this would cut out any unnecessary chatter. After a short while, the door opened and a guard stood before them – a large-framed man with short mousey hair and a square jaw.

'Good afternoon, the warden is expecting you, Chief Inspector; please follow me,' said the man and stood to the side, allowing them in before closing the door behind them.

CHAPTER FIFTY-FIVE

It was nearly six o'clock when Warden Martin Daniels met Platt, Elford, and Summers at the booking-in desk. A hole in the wall with a thick glass window. This was for visitors and where the inmates came to get logged in and out. The walls were a cold battleship grey with a green floor. Down the sides were two stripes: yellow and a purple. Platt figured one was for heading into the prison and the other was for the exit. It made more sense than lots of signposts.

Daniels was a tall man with a straight back, a side parting in his brown hair, and a pencil moustache. He had a military bearing about him, an ex-officer Platt thought. He was dressed in a blue pinstriped suit with knife-edge creases down the legs and highly polished brown Oxford shoes. Platt smiled to himself as he reconsidered his theory about Daniels' old army rank, and figured he'd come through the ranks. Possibly ending his carrier at captain or a major after a commission from a Sergeant Major's position or, indeed, Regimental Sergeant Major.

'Afternoon Warden, I'm Detective Inspector Richard Platt,

and this is Detective Sergeant David Elford and Detective Constable Kate Summers,' Platt said, shaking the warden's hand.

'Afternoon Chief Inspector, I'm Warden Martin Daniels; please follow me,' Daniels said, his voice deep and booming. He pointed with an outstretched arm, ushering them forwards along the long corridor.

The guard who had let them in tagged along at the back. Platt guessed that this was more a security precaution or someone to show them back if the warden got bored.

'So, you're here about William Morris?' Daniels asked, somewhat surprised.

'Yes, we think he's responsible for the murder of his family ten years ago,' Platt explained.

Daniels smiled and shook his head.

'I take it that comes of no surprise?' Summers said, seeing the man's response.

'Actually, it does,' Daniels said as they moved through a set of doglegged corridors. 'The man was the gentlest soul I've ever known. To be honest, I was always puzzled by why he was even here in the first place.' They waited for a security door to be opened by the guard with them. 'The idea that this man had beaten his wife was ... well, unfathomable.'

'What makes you so sure?' Elford asked.

Daniels stopped and turned to face them, his expression puzzled. 'You better come with me. What do you know of William?' Daniels asked, now looking sad, as they walked along the corridors towards another set of security gates.

'He was a wife-beater, that's what got him locked up,' Summers replied with an angry tone.

'The report said his wife was constantly calling the police about him, saying he'd smacked her around,' Platt added. 'By all accounts, he was not happy in the relationship.' He tried to spin an alternative to what Summers was thinking.

They followed Daniels through several corridors and through three different cell-blocks. Platt and the other two wondered where they were heading, that was until they saw the sign for the rehabilitation block.

'Rehab?' Elford questioned.

'Everyone is entitled to a second chance, Sergeant,' Daniels said with a solemn smile.

'Everyone?' Platt raised an eyebrow.

'Well, we try. Unfortunately, there are those that ... well, let's just say some are beyond being able to withstand temptation,' Daniels shrugged.

'And William Morris?' Elford asked.

As they passed through the next set of doors, Platt noticed they were heading for the art room. 'Don't tell me. He's the next Michelangelo?'

'You'll see, just ... well, follow me,' Daniels beckoned.

The art room was a large open space with easels that sat in a semi-circle around a small table with a bowl of fruit placed on top. The latest model for the students to copy.

'So, Morris liked to paint fruit. Well, that's a case-breaker,' Summers stated drily. Suddenly, she felt a hand on her shoulder and turned to face Elford, who was looking at one of the walls.

Her mouth fell open as she saw a vast two-foot painting of Morris' family hanging above them. The family looked happy, stood in a park with trees and a pond, and a double-tier fountain with a large bronze figure of a woman on top.

Platt looked up in horror. Not at the painting of the family, but of the fountain behind them.

'Is this some kind of sick joke?' Platt grabbed Daniels by the collars of his jacket.

The guard ran forwards to intervene, but Summers and Elford were already on him.

'Let him go, sir,' they both said, prying the poor man from Platt's angry clutches.

'Have you gone mad?' Daniels rubbed his throat.

'Guv, show him the picture,' Summers instructed in a calming voice.

Platt stared into her eyes. Those large blue pools of calming waters. Calmly, he stood straight and reached for his wallet.

'I should have you all kicked out, and you reported, Inspector,' Daniels growled. Then he saw the picture that Platt had pulled from his wallet and showed. It was the same picture but with different people. The two women in Morris' painting had dark hair, whereas Platt's family members were blonde ... nevertheless the same pose and the same location.

'My God, how is this even possible?' Daniels asked, looking back and forth between the two pictures. 'Inspector, when did you take this picture?' Daniels rushed to the painting to check the date at the bottom.

'It was taken around April, five years ago I think, can't be sure,' Platt said with a shrug.

'How can you *not* remember?' Summers asked him with a disappointed look.

'Because he wasn't there, he was in London on another murder case,' Elford answered, looking at Summers and Daniels, who stood there with open mouths.

'So, who took the picture?' Summers asked, feeling a chilling tingle run down her spine, her eyes transfixed on the picture as though it were all too familiar.

'My wife had said she had gotten someone in the park to do it,' Platt replied as he looked up at the painting. 'Just some random stranger, a passer-by,' he added with an awkward smile, his gaze fixed on the background rather than the people.

'So, where is this park?' Daniels asked, regarding him closely.

'In North Yorkshire somewhere. In truth, she had said they had been to see an old friend, so I just figured they had gone to a nearby park. I didn't really pay attention,' Platt admitted, feeling the pain of his words. If only he had given his family the time instead of burying himself in work. 'I was too busy ... I was always too busy,' he said in a soft but angry tone – angry at himself for discarding his family all those months ago, years even.

'So, how does this help us with Morris?' Elford asked, feeling as if the point of their visit had been distracted by the similarities of the painting and Platt's photo.

'In the painting, the family is depicted as loved, worshipped even. William was one of the gentlest men in here. He kept to himself mostly but made friends where he could. He helped out in the library, the kitchens; in fact, he helped get this art workshop up and running,' Daniels explained. 'To say that this man had done those things to his family is unthinkable. There wasn't an angry bone in his body. I mean, sure he had gotten into trouble for fighting a few times when he first got in, but that's prison life for you, unfortunately. He knew he had to stand up for himself or he'd be a marked man all his prison life. But later, as people got to know him, he began to make a good name for himself.' Daniels looked around at the artwork that seemed to be mostly from one artist: Morris.

'Model prisoner, huh?' Elford asked, still not buying into it all. He'd seen plenty of cool customers act like angels in prison, and then became monsters when they got out.

'So, Morris does his time, gets let out early for good behaviour, then what?' Summers asked, her gaze shooting towards Platt, who was walking around, taking everything in as he looked at the pictures.

'Actually he didn't leave, he stayed on to run the art work-shop,' Daniels said with a surprised look, almost as if the police should have known this.

'But his file said—'

'Yes, officially he was released,' Daniels cut Elford off. 'But he requested the Board to stay on and run the library and work-shop for a small fee and lodgings. He told them he had nothing to go out too; he knew his wife had gotten someone else and had made peace with it.' Daniels smiled gently.

'Lodgings, he had a room ... in prison?' Platt asked, turning around with a broad grin. If there were any secrets, they would be in that no-longer-missing man's room.

CHAPTER FIFTY-SIX

THE REALISATION SHE HAD BEEN INCARCERATED UNDER false pretences all those years ago made Melanie all that more desperate to find the truth. She still had no idea where she had heard the voice that still lingered in her head. For all she knew, she could have heard it on TV.

But why send her to Larksford House? It seemed a little absurd, sending your eight-year-old to a head doctor for something she was muttering. Of course, if she had stood there with a butcher's knife, it would make sense. No, there must have been something that had set off her parents, made them fear for their lives ... possibly something they had heard before?

By looking at their backgrounds on the internet, Melanie knew her parents were educated, rational people, so why had they brought her here? Also, why had she no memory of when she was eight? She had a photographic memory, but still, she had no recollection of that time of her life.

Leaving the warm spot on the armchair, Melanie walked to the door to look out into the corridor. She wondered where Toby had gone to. She found it odd that she had not found him on the internet, but then she didn't know his last name. That would be in personnel files which she couldn't get to.

Melanie placed her face against the glass, but the mask prevented her from feeling that tingle of cold against her warm skin. She often thought about taking off the mask and letting the world see her as she was. But it wasn't time, not yet. It was all part of the plan, a plan her mentor had created.

Melanie sighed and went back to her chair. Her mind wandered. Thinking back to the woman who had raised her, taught her how to be strong. Those five years since she had left seemed like an eternity. Melanie smiled to herself. Her other mother was probably married with five kids of her own. Let loose in the world. It was a happy thought that she held onto. The alternative was too depressing to contemplate.

She glanced at the door and smiled. Maybe there was something on the internet, a file put onto the public record – a clue to where her other mother was.

She had looked before, years ago, but to no avail. Melanie had no idea where to start back then, she didn't have a name. But maybe she did now. The papers – if she could find out information on the killings, perhaps she could find something on the woman who mentored her? But it would have to wait. For now, the only important thing was to get out of Larksford, find her parents, and find who had started this series of events that had taken her life away.

Melanie would have to wait until that evening after shift change. She'd have time to check the internet and the hospital records. She wanted to see if there was any information on the woman or the man living on either side of her.

She would have liked nothing more than to have broken into their rooms for a chat, but she would have to check them out. No point rushing in if they would start screaming the place down. First, the background check on the two, something to talk about. Something to break the ice.

Melanie picked up the articles she had printed off. These were about the hospital, Hicks, the killings, and the murder in Nottingham. Somehow it was all connected. Something tied *everything* together. Melanie's gazed wandered across to the grounds and the pond, the fountain. It all looked so peaceful, tranquil. But then she had learned that looks could be deceiving, and so could people. The only person Melanie ever trusted was gone; now she was alone. The vote on Toby still wasn't in yet. There was something about him that pulled her towards him, yet something in the back of her mind set off alarm bells.

Melanie shook her head to bring back her train of thought. Too many thoughts, too many questions. She believed once she saw her parents, they would be able to shed light on what was going on and what had happened all those years ago. She looked over the documents once more, this time starting at the house in Nottingham. For Melanie, this was where everything had started. If the police reports on the latest murders were anything to go by, this was when the killer first struck.

She read through the reports again and again, in case something jumped out at her. But nothing had changed from when she had read them an hour ago, a day ago, a week ago. In truth, Melanie started to feel the more she read over things, the more information she was losing.

Melanie groaned with frustration and placed the papers back inside the book and closed it. She needed new data, but she wasn't going to get that until after dark, and that was hours away.

She only had a day and a half before her plan was to come into effect. This would be her last chance for a while, and the way things were going, possibly ever. She didn't believe the attack in the bathroom was random; sure, the freak had been spying on her for a while now, which was weird. She thought he preferred short blonde hair, but hey – a perv was a perv, she guessed. The man had been working there for years, possibly as long as she had been there – Hicks Senior's pet, a pet that should have been put down years ago. It had been him that had got the fountain made years ago when he was younger. Strange how something so beautiful could come out of the mind of someone so evil.

Saturday marked her ninth year there but, more importantly, it was also the day she was getting out. Nobody, however, knew that just yet.

End of Part One.
Not a friend of the family:
** Coming soon. **

ABOUT THE AUTHOR

 Stuart Field is the author of the John Steel thriller series.

He's born in the West Midlands, Great Britain. Later, he joined the armed forces where after 22 years of fun and adventure, he left to start as a writer. Married with a daughter, he still hasn't grown up, which helps with the imagination. He loves to travel and experience other cultures. He loves to love life.

————

To learn more about Stuart Field and discover more Next Chapter authors, visit our website at www.nextchapter.pub.

A Friend Of The Family
ISBN: 978-4-82415-206-0

Published by
Next Chapter
2-5-6 SANNO
SANNO BRIDGE
143-0023 Ota-Ku, Tokyo
+818035793528

28th September 2022

Lightning Source UK Ltd.
Milton Keynes UK
UKHW010030070223
416578UK00002B/410